# Erin
# LAWLESS

# The
# One with
# all the
# Bridesmaids

A division of HarperCollins*Publishers*
www.harpercollins.co.uk

Harper*Impulse* an imprint of
HarperCollins*Publishers*
The News Building
1 London Bridge Street
London SE1 9GF

www.harpercollins.co.uk

This paperback edition 2017

First published in Great Britain in ebook format by
HarperCollins*Publishers* 2017

A catalogue record for this book
is available from the British Library

ISBN: 9780008181789

Set in Birka by Palimpsest Book Production Limited,
Falkirk, Stirlingshire

Printed and bound in Great Britain

## About the Author

Erin  awless lives a happy life full of wonderful friends, in
love  th a man who buys her books instead of flowers. To
mix  ngs up a little, she writes books where friends and
lov  it obstacles and (usually) overcome them. When she's
n  1g that she reads 'absolutely everything she can get
h  ls on, spends an inordinate amount of time in pyjamas
.  .s a fun-but-informative blog on British history.

🐦 @rinylou
f facebook.com/erinlawlessauthor
www.erinlawless.co.uk

## Also by Erin Lawless

*Somewhere Only We Know*
*The Best Thing I Never Had*

For Jacqui, Joanne, Ksenia and Nicola – my beautiful, brilliant bridesmaids, and for all of my Lawless Hens: I'll never forget the amazing weekend when we all met The Juan.

# Author Note

As I arrived in my mid-twenties, something very strange started to happen – my friends started to get engaged. Seriously? – I thought, staring at the fat, glossy invitations appearing through the post – I swear it was only this time last year you were snogging strangers in clubs, and now I'm Saving the Date? And I should put how much aside for your Hen Do!?

Ever since then, my weekends – particularly in the summer – have been a veritable nuptial string of engagement parties in pubs, dress fittings in boutiques, hen dos in spas and clubs and, of course, the weddings themselves (I gave as good as I got, of course, when I got married myself in 2014). The narrative of being a wedding guest (or knowing a bridezilla) has been so woven into the lives of my friends and I for so many years (and for so many more years to come, no doubt) that I really wanted to capture some of that in a story.

So here we have: one bride, and four bridesmaids, from proposal to altar.

Interspersed through the books, I've collated some real life anecdotes about perfect proposals, disastrous dance floors, suspicious strippers, bad bridesmaids and gorgeous groomsmen. Get in touch on social media and share your stories!

# *Character List*

Please Save the Date
for the wedding of
NORA EILEEN DERVAN
*and*
HENRY ROBERT CLARKE

*New Year's Eve*

**THE MAIDS**
Beatrice Milton
Cleo Adkins
Daisy Frankel
Sarah Norris

**THE MEN**
Cole Norris
Archie Clarke
Elliott Hale
Barlow Osbourne

# Chapter 1

*I was surprised to be asked to be a bridesmaid for someone I would have considered more a friend-of-a-friend. I realised really quickly that it wasn't the honour it had first seemed – she had twelve bridesmaids. Then the emails started. Until the wedding was over we were banned from dying or cutting our hair, getting any tattoos or piercings, putting on weight (losing it was apparently fine). The wedding at this time was two years away. We took it as just a bad joke . . . until one maid cut in a fringe and was promptly fired and replaced with someone from the 'bridesmaid bench'.*

Erika, Poole

Sarah was there first, as Nora had expected, armed with a half dozen glossy bridal magazines and good-natured excitement. Bea and Cleo arrived pretty much at the same time, each having to hug Nora five or six times before they could take their seats. Daisy completed the group, having stopped off at the bar en route to the table to order a bottle of something bubbly and expensive.

'So, go on,' Cleo urged, the second Daisy had taken her coat off. 'Give us the story.'

Nora laughed, holding both hands to her face to feign shyness; the solitaire diamond ring they were all there to celebrate winked at them from her left hand. 'I've already told you!'

'Then tell us again,' Daisy demanded. 'Get the practice in, you're going to be telling this story a lot.'

'For the rest of your life,' added Sarah, smiling. 'Trust me – I'm still asked to tell my proposal story all the time.'

'Okay, okay, fine!' Nora made a show of agreeing, still laughing. 'If you insist. So, you know, Harry was away with work for most of February, so we had a really belated Valentine's Day dinner booked.'

'Valentine's Day,' Bea repeated, rolling her eyes, but her smile was wide.

'He's such a cutie pie,' agreed Daisy, moving slightly to the side to allow the arriving waitress to place the ice bucket in the middle of their table.

'But, you know, there was a Tube strike. And it was going to be a complete pain in the arse to get across to London Bridge, where the restaurant was,' Nora continued, still idly fiddling with her new accessory. 'So I said, let's leave it, too much hassle, love, let's just get some takeaway curries and stay in and watch Netflix.'

The girls all started to giggle as they imagined Harry's panic at that moment. He was a great one for a plan, was Harry, and now there he was – on arguably one of the most important nights of his life – scuppered, stressed, cursing the railworkers' union for ruining his chance at eternal happiness.

'And Harry was . . . shall we say, uncharacteristically insistent,' Nora carried on, giggling too. 'He was banging on about how it was our first proper Valentine's Day as a couple. Then he told me we simply *had* to go, because he'd put a huge deposit down on the table and he wouldn't get his money back! And I was thinking, Christ, what kind of a restaurant *is this?*'

Nora paused to join the girls in a mini-cheer as the waitress deftly opened the champagne with a festive pop and began to fill the waiting flutes.

'So, he said he'd order us an Uber, and – of course – everyone in London wants to get in a taxi right then because the Tube is so up the spout, so we have to wait for ages. And he's pacing through the lounge, glaring at his phone, glaring out of the window, glaring at me – and I was wondering what was bloody wrong with the man!'

'And you didn't even have the slightest inkling what was coming?' Sarah asked, breathlessly, an eternal romantic.

Nora shook her head. 'Not a clue. I thought he'd just had a bad day at work, or something. So anyway, the car arrived and we got to the restaurant and, you know, it's mostly empty. They haven't given away our table or anything – I mean, come on, it's like a Tuesday night! – and once we get sat down, Harry calms down a bit. And you know how normally I have to decide right off when I go to a restaurant if I'm going to have a starter or a pudding? Well, Harry tells me immediately that we're going to have a pudding because they do this special called the 'Lover's Platter' for dessert, and hey, it's our fake Valentine's Day after all, so I'm like, sure, okay, fine.'

'How could you not have known what was coming?' howled Daisy. 'He was being so obvious!'

Nora shook her head again. 'Anyway, so we ordered mains—'

'What did you have?' Bea demanded, determined to wring as many little details out of this story as possible.

'Er, well, it was an Italian. I had this like, sweet chilli-prawn spaghetti thing. Harry had a calzone.'

'No!' groaned Bea. 'That's so unromantic!'

Nora raised an eyebrow. 'You'd rather we'd eaten oysters and strawberries or something?'

'Anything but pizza and pasta!' Daisy agreed. 'Too mundane for such an important anecdote, hun.'

'Sorry to disappoint! We even had garlic bread on the side,' Nora grinned, achieving a chorus of disapproving moans. 'So anyway, everything's pretty normal and we finish and they clear away the plates and then Harry orders this Lover's Platter thing and they bring it out super-quick, like, too quick. And to be honest, I was still pretty full and I didn't really fancy anything more. And it was this whole great big plate for two people, full of macaroons, and little truffles and pastries with cream and tiny brownies cut into heart shapes.' Nora paused, a small smile playing on her face. 'It was pretty sweet.'

'Anyway, then I stood up – because I wanted to take a picture of it from above, you know? And Harry jumped up too and was all, what's wrong, where are you going? I said, nowhere! I just want to take a shot of this for my Instagram, it's so nice . . . and we sat back down and I was busy trying different filters on for size and not really paying attention. So

I uploaded the picture and, you know, everything's still pretty normal . . .'

'Yes, and?' Bea prompted, impatiently.

'Go on!' Sarah insisted.

'Yeah, then what happened?' urged the excited waitress, champagne bottle still in hand.

'Well, Harry's just staring at me, properly staring. And then he asks me why I'm not eating, so I tell him I need a break because I'm still pretty full from all that spaghetti I just nailed. And he starts telling me to eat one of the profiteroles at least – you love profiteroles, he keeps saying – so, basically, just to shut him up, I forked a profiterole.'

'And?' Daisy grinned. 'And?'

'And the fork goes – clink! And I look at what's there, and it's, well . . .' Nora wiggled her left fingers and laughed. 'Under the profiteroles. And I don't even know when he did it, but I suddenly realise that Harry's on the floor next to me, on one knee and everything, and he said – oh, a bunch of stuff! I can't even remember, I was so shocked! But at the end of whatever he was saying he said – you know, the important bit – 'So, will you marry me?' – and I realised it was actually happening.

'And I, naturally, burst into horrendous ugly-crying. I couldn't speak. I just got down on the floor next to him and hugged him and bawled. I got mascara *all* over his shirt collar! We've had to take it into the dry-cleaners, it's a state. Anyway. I eventually managed to actually say the word 'yes' and all the waiting staff were cheering and clapping, and all the other people in the restaurant and randomers started sending over champagne. It was amazing.'

Nora admired her engagement ring again; she couldn't help it. She was just so very, very, wonderfully happy. She was getting to marry one of her best friends, after all.

'And so here we all are,' finished Bea, holding her glass of champagne aloft. 'So let's toast.'

The others obediently lifted their flutes, the pale liquid shining and glittering in the light from the candles, and even the waitress motioned cheerfully with the rest of the bottle. Nora glanced around at the faces ringed around her at the table and pushed aside her slight misgivings; she didn't want that weight on her heart, not tonight. They might not all get on between themselves, but she knew they all loved her like she loved them and she wouldn't – couldn't – be without a single one of them by her side for this. Her best friends. Her bridesmaids.

Bea blew Nora a kiss across the table. Cleo laughed and cheered. 'To the Dervan-Clarke wedding!'

# Chapter 2

Cleo jabbed the magic button the millisecond the mug was in place and ready and waiting to receive coffee; after three years at this place she'd perfected the timing.

Gray – Oakland Academy's favourite history teacher – was also ready and waiting, holding out the plastic carton of communal milk, slipping his own mug in to replace Cleo's on the machine's drip-tray as soon as he could. It was pretty indecent the way they fled their classrooms at the break-bell – faster than some of the kids – but twenty minutes was a very short time to get sufficiently caffeinated of a mid-morning.

Caffeine was required even more fiercely than normal this morning: firstly, it was a Monday, and secondly, Cleo still felt vaguely hung over from going out on Saturday night. She hadn't even been feeling it, but by merit of Cole being both a best friend and turning thirty, she hadn't exactly been able to take a rain check. She needed to have a word with herself about automatically going for the house wine; it was always the sulphates in cheap plonk that got her like this (she also needed to have a word with herself about going out for a nice, grown-up dinner and ending up barefoot on a sticky dance floor come two o' clock in the morning).

In companionable silence Gray and Cleo made their way over to their spot. It wasn't much to speak of: two old chairs that had long ago been removed from a classroom for being unstable, and next to the equally ancient staff room printer, which gave off an alarming amount of both heat and noise. But in the grand scheme of things they were both relatively new to Oakland Academy and you had to put in at least a good decade there to get one of the chairs that still had padding.

'Good weekend?' Cleo asked without preamble, taking a determined gulp of too-hot coffee, using her free hand to check her Facebook on her phone as she spoke.

'Can't complain. Few pints. Domino's takeaway. Liverpool won their game.' Gray checked his phone for notifications too; they had the speedy break routine down to a fine art. 'How was Saturday night?'

'I don't remember the last few hours of it,' Cleo admitted ruefully. 'Although there are some pictures on my friend's phone of me joining in with what I can only assume was the *Macarena* right towards the end.'

'A success, then,' Gray grinned. 'I wish I'd seen that. I *love* Drunk Cleo.'

Cleo buried her blushing face in her mug. This was Gray's first year teaching at Oakland and she'd managed to keep her cool for precisely one term before getting plastered, arguing loudly with her head of department about politics and up-chucking amuse-bouches all over the new guy 'Graham's' novelty Christmas jumper. It wasn't all bad, though – since then they'd been best work buddies. Everyone needed one.

'Well the birthday boy had a good time, so definitely a success.' She held out her phone to Gray, her gallery open, so he could scroll through some of the pictures she'd taken Saturday night.

'Nice dress.' Gray gave easy compliments; Cleo almost didn't notice them any more. 'Any tension with the Queen Bea?' he asked. Cleo winced; she sometimes wished she didn't tell him *quite* so much about her life. (At least not so much that he had nicknames for her friends.)

'The Queen was on her best behaviour,' Cleo retorted primly. 'She hasn't made a scene in years,' she admitted, grudgingly.

'Hmmm,' was all Gray offered, carefully non-committal (she obviously bitched about Bea a little too often).

Cleo sighed. Her coffee – much like her break – was half gone. 'What have you got now?'

'Cuban Missile Crisis with the Year Elevens,' Gray answered. 'I'm sure they're all already queuing at the door in fevered anticipation. You?'

'Factorising expressions with the Nines.'

Gray gulped down the remnants of his drink and grinned. 'I wonder which of our lessons these kids will actually need most in real life.' It was his usual tease. 'Cos, you know, most phones have a calculator on them now, love.'

'Yeah, and the Wikipedia app too,' Cleo shot back, downing her own coffee. 'Your turn to do the washing up, *love*.'

'Yeah, yeah.' Gray gathered up the mugs. 'Nag, nag, nag.'

'See you at lunch?' Cleo asked, as she swung her satchel up onto her shoulder and Gray moved across to the wonky kitchenette to swill their mugs out in the sink.

'I'll be here.' Gray grinned at her over his shoulder.

\* \* \*

Any working week that started with you pissing on your own hand and then coming in to a hundred and eighty-five 'urgent' unread emails should really be considered a write-off from the get-go, thought Sarah. She sat blankly at her desk, clicking about Outlook at random and assigning emails with varying flag colours in case anyone was watching her, but taking nothing in.

She'd been a lot better this year. She didn't test willy nilly any more. She'd been pretty sure this time. She'd had *an inkling*. When her period hadn't made its appearance on Friday, as expected, she'd remained quite placid – her cycle sometimes varied a few days each way – but still she'd made an extra special point of not having anything to drink on Saturday night when they'd all gone out, hadn't ordered pâté as a starter even though it was her favourite; better to be safe than sorry. She'd waited patiently throughout all of (a still period-free) Sunday, fancying she was already experiencing the mythical centred serenity of pregnancy. She'd waited until Monday morning, in fact – she'd read countless articles about how you've got more of the pregnancy hormone there in your urine in the mornings – before taking that little plastic stick into the bathroom with her.

So then. Another singular line of failure. No tiny little life to avoid wine and pâté for after all. Another *inkling* turned out to be so much delusion. And still no period. Maybe they'd just packed in altogether. After all, what was the point of an unfertile woman menstruating at all? Sarah was only glad she hadn't shared her stupid *inkling* with Cole this time, but – maybe – it was time to talk to her husband about the elephant that wasn't in the room.

Raina, the PA to the other CEO, sat opposite, impossibly hefty at the best of times, but currently seven cruel months' pregnant, moaning about something – probably her back, or her swollen feet, or the fact she'd been up six times in the night to have a wee. This was going to be Raina's third child under the age of five; she'd basically spent the entire time Sarah had known her either on maternity leave or largely pregnant. Sarah found it difficult to be solicitous to her at the best of times; today it was near-impossible. So she just sat and clicked and flagged.

A new calendar request slid into the corner of her screen and Sarah clicked to open it on reflex: Kim the office manager was kindly reminding one and all about Raina's baby-shower lunch on Friday via the use of a picture of cartoon baby sat atop a pyramid of building blocks spelling out MUMMY. How precious.

Instead of responding Sarah, clicked onto Google and determinedly searched for 'fertility enhancing superfoods'.

\* \* \*

It turned out putting her phone on vibrate wasn't good enough: Bea was slowly being driven insane by the irregular buzzing from her handbag. Something was going on, but what? She tortured herself with images of Nora waiting in the rain outside of Bea's empty flat, bedraggled and crying – the wedding off – sending text after text to her unresponsive best friend, wondering where she was . . . Okay, so that was all fairly unlikely, but still. If her date didn't need to go to the bathroom soon, Bea might just have to suck it up, apologise for the poor date-etiquette and check her damn messages.

'Oh, we're at that age, aren't we?' the man opposite was saying, rolling his eyes with good humour. 'For the past few years my entire summers have just been stags and weddings!'

'Totally,' Bea agreed. 'But at least this is two best friends in one swoop for me, so at least it's a more efficient use of my time.'

'Isn't it a bit weird for you?' her date asked. 'That your two best mates randomly shacked up?' Bea considered the question over a mouthful of wine (ignoring the new buzzing from the depths of her handbag).

'I guess it was weird at first,' she put it lightly. 'Me, them and our other friend have been joined at the hips since we were so tiny.' She dropped her voice conspiratorially. 'To be honest with you, it was a bit like being told my brother and sister were shagging,' Bea laughed. 'But it obviously wasn't so weird for them,' she conceded with a smile. It had been sixteen months, one pregnancy scare, two very temporary break-ups and a huge engagement ring since the night Nora had told her she was in love with Harry, and Bea and Cole had agreed that while it would never *not* be a bit weird it was lovely to see them so happy.

It might be a bit of a cliché, but Nora Dervan and Beatrice Milton had been destined to be best friends. Their young, first-time mothers had met at the local antenatal class and had immediately hit it off. A few months later their two baby girls were born just seventy-two hours apart. When Bea's mother returned to work after her maternity leave Nora's mother, Eileen, had taken on the role of Bea's childminder, and the two girls grew up as close as sisters – closer perhaps, as they'd never bickered, never fought. (Well, actually, there had been *that one time*. But they didn't ever talk about *that one time*, so Bea was happy that it didn't count, not really.)

And when the girls had gone to primary school there had been little Harry Clarke, who everyone in their class thought was super-cool because he knew all the best song lyrics and how to count to fourteen in Spanish (and ten in French). The two girls, Harry and his best friend Cole had made a blissful, uncomplicated foursome for the next two decades. Even when they were in their teens the notoriously strict Roman Catholic Eileen didn't insist Nora kept her bedroom door open when 'the boys' were in there.

No, for Nora and Harry, love had waited until the most convenient moment, their hearts not catching on one another until they were heading out of their twenties: the fumbling inexperience and the dramas, the cheating exes and the hassle all done and behind them. It seemed unfairly effortless to a more-than-slightly jaded Bea. For her, love was all tossed and tangled with screaming arguments on rainy street corners;

discovered flirty text messages; wilful misunderstandings; late nights spent Facebook-stalking exes with a bitterness in her throat that wine couldn't mask; men that either loved her too much or never enough.

Nora had tried to explain it to Bea once, that first night. Bea had been so completely floored by the sudden and severe change in circumstances between her nearest and dearest that her first question to Nora (once she'd become able to form words) was to ask if they'd been drunk. That was easier to understand, somehow, that they'd got so plastered they'd forgotten who the other was, who they were themselves.

'No. It was just like, one day, I saw Harry and I thought, oh, there you are,' Nora had answered, simply. 'Do you get it?'

Bea hadn't been able to get it. So she'd got drunk instead and when Nora left the bar (to go and see Harry, no doubt) Bea stayed to see off the bottle of wine, staring at the pock-marked table top, feeling happy and sad and excited and scared, all at once. And here she was, five hundred days later, with another bottle of Pinot Grigio in front of her, telling a stranger all about how crazy in love her best friends were. Her shoes hurt. She suddenly felt ancient, and so tired.

'I'm so sorry,' Bea said finally, grabbing her handbag. 'I just need to check my phone, it's going mental.'

'Yeah, I thought I could hear it,' her date smiled graciously. 'No problem. Do you want another drink? Or to share some bar snacks, maybe?'

Bea hesitated. She did want another drink. She did want bar snacks. She wanted to sit here with this nice man for the rest of the evening and find out some of his secrets. She

14

wanted to take him home and take him to bed and wake up with the sunshine, in his arms on Sunday mornings. She was beginning to think, however, that Nice Guy Rob was far too nice a guy for the likes of her. But, hell, surely the universe wouldn't begrudge her the one last drink.

'I could have another glass, if you could?'

'Coming right up,' he smiled, leaving her with her multiple new messages and heading over to take his place in the queue at the busy bar.

Bea had invitations to join no fewer than nine new WhatsApp group conversations. One was all the bridesmaids with Nora. One was all the bridesmaids without Nora. One was the entire wedding party. One was specifically for discussing the hen do, yet another was for the engagement party Nora and Harry were planning for next month. Bea couldn't even be bothered to work out what the other ones were for. They were already crammed full of overly emotive messages, pictures and links. Bea did a double-take; she'd assumed they were from Nora, but the invitations were from Sarah. Ugh. Attack of the bridesmaidzilla. This was going to get old, and fast.

Eli had messaged her too, an hour or so ago; Bea clutched at the normality that was a stupid meme image forwarded by an old friend. She was still scouring the Google Image search results for the perfect response to him when her smiling date returned from the bar with her glass of wine.

# Chapter 3

*We were on holiday in Thailand and, as you do, decided to go for a walk on the moonlit beach. Another couple were there releasing a lantern, and it really was the most romantic of settings. My boyfriend dropped to one knee and did the deed – not that I can remember a word of what he said – and of course, I said yes. Romanticism was cut short however – the crashing waves combined with all the beers I'd necked that evening meant I needed to get back to the hotel and use the facilities, sharpish. Of course then we had to call our parents and all our friends and tell them the good news, so by the time we were ready to go out and celebrate all the bars were closed (except for an Irish bar, which was blasting out 'Cotton Eye Joe'). Instead we went back to our room and shared a lukewarm can of lager from the minibar. The next day, I woke up with food poisoning.*

Katy, Chesterfield

'Okay so, here's the thing.' Nora's face was far too concerned considering the subject matter. 'So, Harry prefers documentary-style photography. You know, lifestyle approach. But I think I'm leaning more classic. And I really love the sort of depth that shooting on film gets, right? But Harry thinks digital is much more crisp. I honestly don't know what to do. Help!'

All four bridesmaids eyed each other in the hope that someone else would speak first.

Daisy bit. 'Okay, back up here a sec. What the eff is documentary-style photography? What, are they gonna serialise your wedding and stick it up on Netflix?'

'Do you have some examples?' Cleo agreed.

'Did you not see the stuff I pinned onto the Photography Board?' Nora asked impatiently, grabbing her iPad and navigating to the Pinterest app.

'I did,' Sarah assured her. 'It's the sort of reportage style, right? Candid rather than posed? It's nice. Really modern.'

Nora bit her lip. 'Is modern what I'm going for?'

Sarah laughed. 'You tell us, sweetie!'

Bea rolled her eyes. 'How can you go for modern? I mean, when the very concept of marriage is completely—'

'Traditional,' Cleo butted in (she wasn't sure where Bea had been going there, but her word choice was probably less tactful than 'traditional'). 'Bea's right, though, surely you need to think about whether or not you're going to have a traditional or modern venue, set-up, not to mention the dress . . .'

'All the wedding blogs and magazines say that the best photographers are booked up *years in advance,*' Nora argued. 'You need to get your deposit with one *as soon as possible.* So the whole wedding planning is *literally at a standstill.*' She shoved the iPad at Bea. 'So what do you think?'

Biting back the response that she thought Nora was veering into bridezilla territory, Bea cast her eye over the selection of wedding photos that Nora had pinned for reference. She couldn't see masses of difference: woman in white, man in suit, bright flowers in bouquets, bright teeth in smiles. She passed the iPad across to Sarah.

'What was the style you and Cole had for your wedding pics?' she asked her. 'I guess I liked that sort of effect.'

Sarah was visibly delighted with the praise; Bea-compliments were few and far between, even for the people she really liked, and Sarah was pretty certain, most of the time, that she was not of that number. 'Well we had quite a contemporary photographer. Unusual angles, strong light. But then we had an urban wedding. It probably wouldn't work as well for those sorts of rustic, burlap-and-lace-type weddings you pinned, Nor.' She passed the iPad to Daisy, who held it out so Cleo could see too. 'And I really wouldn't worry, you know. Cole and I put our entire wedding together in just a couple of months, after all. You have bags of time.'

'Yeah, but I think you need to think venue first, hun, I really do.' Daisy passed the iPad back to Nora. 'All things will flow from there.'

'Okay.' Nora deftly switched Pinterest board to the 'Venues' one. 'Well, here's the shortlist.'

Daisy arched an eyebrow as she saw the number of thumbnails pinned. 'More like a longlist. So, for starters, I think you need to strike some of these off.'

'Okay, so here's the thing . . .' And Nora gave her most winning smile, the one that all of the girls recognised as the precursor for asking some outrageous favour.

\* \* \*

'So should we, like, hold hands or something?' Eli might be massively out of his comfort zone, but it wasn't in his nature to do a half-arsed job.

Bea laughed. 'It's not like they're going to be watching out and will take us to one side if they think we're not touchy-feely enough with one another. There aren't going to be any Fake Fiancé Bouncers. Relax.'

'You know, when we made plans to do something together this weekend, this really wasn't what I had in mind.'

'Hey, I'd hardly been dreaming that when I visited my first wedding fair it would be with you, you know,' Bea shot back, slamming the car door for emphasis.

Eli grinned his disarming grin. 'Really? Don't you remember our beautiful wedding day?' He clutched dramatically at his supposedly broken heart.

Bea rolled her eyes but decided not to fight the smile. It was the day Elliott Hale had been formally inducted into their little group of friends. Nora had been to a family wedding the weekend before and was full of utter Catholic pomp about it, promising she'd show Bea how it was done by officiating a marriage between her and a willing boy on the playground that lunchtime.

When neither Harry nor Cole proved willing . . . 'You,

then,' seven-year-old Nora had decreed, waving impatiently at a nearby classmate. Young Eli was stretched and gangly (oddly, for someone who would grow up to be of an average height) and had knees that seemed way too large for the rest of his legs. He'd looked up from his Pogs in alarm.

'Me?'

'Yes, you.' Already an older sister several times over by then, Nora had little-to-no patience with slow uptake. 'Come over here and be the groom.'

Reasonably obedient by nature – back then and now – Eli had obliged, gathering up his snackbox and his Pogs and moving across to stand with the four of them; he'd never managed to completely extricate himself again.

'Of course I remember, snookums,' Bea teased, moving closer to fling a companionable arm around her friend's shoulders as they made their way down the crunching gravel walkway that lead from the car park to the venue. 'Shame that didn't work out. At least we'll always have the playground.'

'Welcome to Hucclecote Barn,' a smiling woman in a matching skirt-suit the colour of a new bruise greeted them, handing them each a goodie bag. 'When's the big day?'

Bea curled her ringless finger away behind the plastic handles of the bag. 'We haven't booked anything yet,' she lied smoothly. 'It's early days. In fact, we're not just here to see the suppliers at the fair, we're here to look at the Barn as a possible venue.'

'Oh, super-duper!' the lady beamed. 'Well, why don't you two have a good look around and later I can connect you with our events coordinator?'

'That would be . . . super,' Eli concurred, thankfully avoiding eye contact with Bea, who was quite sure she had never heard the term 'super-duper' used non-sarcastically before in her life.

'Super!' agreed the goodie-bag lady, waving them on. 'Enjoy!'

Bea and Eli chuckled quietly to themselves as they moved away. In front of them was the Barn-with-a-capital-B in question, liberally draped with charming cream and baby-blue bunting flags. They thought they'd be getting there early, but the fair was already in full swing, suppliers hawking out their services and wares from display tables erected in a wonky semi-circle around the main doors. Couples, arm in arm, twirled leisurely around the outside.

'I don't think this place suits us or our wedding plans, Bea my darling,' Eli decided, faux-regretful. He gestured at a stall selling bedazzled bridal wellington boots. 'It's a bit twee.'

Bea thwapped his chest with one of the glossy wedding magazines she'd found in her goodie bag. 'Oh, is that because you're more a castle-with-a-cream-tea sort of guy, dearest?'

Eli laughed. 'I do actually wonder what these allocations say about Harry and Nora's opinion of our personalities. Like, why do we get the hay bales and horseshit and Baz and Cleo get the stately home, huh?'

'Barlow begged off this morning, actually,' Bea told him, looking down at the messages about just that in the WhatsApp bridesmaids' group. Barlow was one of the other groomsmen, although with a busy pub to run Bea wasn't quite sure how much help he was going to get to be in the run-up to this wedding. 'He'd arranged for the assistant manager to come in and cover him but she called in sick. Cleo's had to call up this guy she knows from work and get him to drive her out there.'

Eli immediately looked interested. 'What guy from work? Is it Mr Fifty Shades?'

Bea sighed; Eli was always pretty interested in what Cleo was up to, naturally. 'Seriously, Eli. We've talked about this. This is how you start rumours.'

'I'm just saying! Who calls themselves Gray? He's just *asking* for the comparison.'

'Well, until he's *asking* you for planning permission help to build a red room of pain, it's probably an unfair comparison.'

'I'll keep that in mind. Because we architects get that all the time, by the way. Gotta be constantly on the lookout for all the sex perverts. Speaking of which, where've they sent Daisy?'

'Nowhere. Unsurprisingly, Daisy felt like it probably wasn't a wonderful idea for her to tell the guy she's been on five dates with and only shagged for the first time last week that they were going wedding venue window-shopping,' Bea pointed out.

Eli's fair eyebrows disappeared into his fringe. 'Fair enough!' Even though that year he was knocking on the door of thirty, Eli persisted on modelling his look on boybands-of-the-day; he'd had frosted spikes as a kid, greasy curtains as a teenager and now had some sort of floppy, asymmetrical 'do that meant it took him twenty minutes to style it so it looked like he'd just gotten out of bed. He tended to date equally irritatingly coiffured women; the last one had a severe undercut dyed in an elaborate leopard-spot pattern. Daisy had got so shit-faced once she'd tried to stroke her. 'Cole and Sarah?' he queried.

'Apparently Sarah has a doctor's appointment today, or something. Jesus. Look at this,' Bea tutted from the depths of the so-called goodie bag. 'Mixed messages much? I've got a box of gourmet truffles in here, and a leaflet that gives me my first month free at Slimming World.' She looked up. 'What have you got?'

Eli rummaged through his (helpfully colour-coded blue) bag. 'Ooh, truffles too; nice. Er, discount vouchers for wine at Majestic; *very* nice. Austin Reed catalogue. Erm.'

'So no subtle signals that you are a fat, hideous creature and that you should starve yourself until your wedding day, then?'

'Nope.' Eli grinned and popped one of the truffles into his mouth. 'Now come on, you fat, hideous creature, let's get on with it.' Bea allowed him to push a truffle through her lips, managing to stay atop of the urge to nip at his fingertips. Just. 'Have you got the checklist open?'

# Chapter 4

'I'm just saying, I think it's better that we go sooner rather than later.'

'I appreciate that, love, I do. It just seems a little bit drastic. We've only been trying for a couple of months, after all.'

Sarah stared at her handsome, stupid husband. 'I came off the pill when we got engaged, Cole. It's been seventeen months. Seventeen cycles.'

Cole winced away. 'Jeez, do you have to say 'cycles'? It's so clinical. What the hell happened to let's just have fun, have sex; let's just see what happens. You promised me you wouldn't turn into one of these nut-job women charting their temperatures and testing the consistency of their cervical mucus.' He pulled a face of utter disgust. Sarah, who had been doing exactly those things secretly by way of an app on her phone for almost a year now, struggled to regroup her thoughts.

'Cycles, months, whatever. Whatever wording you want me to use, I think it's obvious that we have a fertility problem. And we need to see a doctor about it.'

'How can we have a fertility problem?' Cole blustered. 'You

only went for that test you have to do this year, and you said it all came back fine?'

'Cole, a smear test is nothing to do with fertility,' Sarah snapped. 'And besides, why do you automatically assume any problem has to be with me?'

The set of her husband's jaw was mutinous. 'Hey, don't pile this on me. I'm doing my bit.'

'Your bit?' Sarah repeated, incredulous.

'You know what I mean,' Cole snapped, refusing to take the apology bait. 'Don't be like this. God, I don't remember you being half so over-the-top when we met.' He grabbed up the navy Superdry hoodie he'd thrown over the back of their armchair. 'And as you've taken it upon yourself to tell my friends that we're too busy to help them with their wedding planning, I'm going to give Harry a call and see if I can do anything. I'll see you later.'

And that was that. Cole pulled the front door closed a little harder than was strictly necessary. Sarah sank into the armchair, pulling her feet up underneath herself like a child. She'd known that he was going to be on the defensive like this – she'd practically scheduled in this fight after all, clearing their weekend for it – but the row still echoed through her all the same, for all it was the same old story: Cole could do no wrong; 'their' friends became 'his' friends; she was taken to task for not being the same person she'd been when they met, like he was thinking of going to Trading Standards and demanding a refund because his carefree, twenty-something girlfriend had become his thirty-something wife: a dress size or two larger, a hell of a lot more stressed and always ever-so-slightly behind with her waxing.

And perhaps with redundant ovaries to boot.

Sighing, Sarah reached for her phone. Although she didn't know who she was planning to call. Her mum and the rest of her family were all the way over in Wales and her old school and uni friends were now just people on Facebook with new surnames and fat-faced babies as their profile pictures. She could call Nora, or one of the other girls, she supposed, but – as Cole had been very quick to remind her – they were all foremost *his* and never just for her.

So instead she spoke to Siri.

'What's the ideal weight a woman should be to help with conception?' she asked, ruefully.

# Chapter 5

Gray gave a low whistle as he got out of the car. 'You sure now how to treat a guy, Miss Adkins.'

Cleo couldn't help but stare too, sliding her sunglasses down from where they were perched atop her pinned-back fringe; she had to – it felt like the crenelated turret of Withysteeple Hall was touching the sun. 'Christ. Nora would love this for sure. Ooh la la. Very Downton Abbey.'

'Completely,' Gray agreed. 'Why hasn't she come out to see it?'

Cleo made a face. 'She's had to go see a venue with her family. Don't ask. Long story. Involves God and her overbearing Irish-Catholic mother, who I believe has more power than the former. She said she'd come out here to meet with the wedding coordinator if I reported back it was worth the meeting.'

'Well, if she's looking to get married in the splendid manner of a Jane Austen heroine, then I already think, yeah, it's worth the meeting,' Gray laughed. 'This place couldn't be more stunning!'

Cleo hadn't had Gray pegged for a regency-romantic – she smiled, filing that piece of information away – but she couldn't help but agree with him. The manor house sat atop a gentle, natural mound – like it needed to look *more* impressive, Cleo thought, amused – beatifically crowning a thick carpet of surrounding meadow: fat columbines and forget-me-nots and creamy cow parsley, so dense you couldn't see the grass.

Okay, so it wouldn't be so gorgeous come the winter – perhaps it might even be a little gothic for some tastes – but Cleo could already imagine the tall windows of the house lit up with firelight from within, the swollen-globe lights that strung the path from the car park at the gates to the front door glowing comfortingly, perhaps even a few shining flakes of snow swirling gently down from a starry sky. The four bridesmaids, each with fat fur stoles across their shoulders. Nora, all in white, glowing in the half-light of a winter after-noon. Amazing. She hadn't even seen the inside yet and she was pretty sold.

'Ooh, the café is open,' Gray interrupted her reverie, having clocked the delightfully renovated stables selling cakes and concessions off to one side of the main building. 'I could murder a scone.'

Cleo laughed. 'I did basically insist you drive me out to the countryside with fifteen minutes' notice on a Saturday morning – a scone would be the least I could do! But really, thank you,' she insisted. 'You saved my arse. I really need to learn how to drive.'

Gray cocked a smile. 'But then how would I keep in scones?'

'Well, there is that,' Cleo nodded. 'I can't believe my luck that you had nothing better to do!'

'What could be better than driving out to the home counties of a weekend to play fake-fiancé with my best friend from work?'

'Plus getting to eat scones,' Cleo reminded him.

'Plus scones, of course,' Gray agreed solemnly. 'Shall we?' He made a move towards the stables' courtyard.

'Nora's given me a pretty long list of things I need to check out.' Cleo waved her phone. Nora had insisted that her bridesmaids all download a group scheduler app for just such a purpose. 'So maybe let's do the necessary inside, and then we can be a little bit more leisurely about our baked goods? After all, there's no rush.'

Gray hesitated. (Oh. Oh.) And Cleo felt supremely stupid.

'Except there is a rush,' she corrected herself, smiling through the pressure of the awkwardness. 'Sorry, that was . . . horrendously presumptive of me.'

'Not a rush, as such, not at all,' Gray rushed to assure her. 'I can always see her later, or another night. I mean, it's just a Tinder date. In fact, don't even think about it. She's not even the one I was most looking forward to going out with.'

Cleo goggled at him. 'You've got another date lined up?'

'God yeah! I've another one on Tuesday – just going to the cinema, casual, you know – and one on Wednesday – that's the real stunner, I can show you her photo – and I might have another one going in for Friday night, I'll see how I feel later in the week. Sometimes you just want a night in, you know?'

Cleo didn't know. Most of her nights seemed to be nights in. She usually took the piss out of Daisy for being on Tinder and Badoo constantly, but maybe she was missing a trick here.

She wondered if Daisy and Gray had ever 'matched' up on one of those things. It was a very disquieting image. Maybe *she* should be matching them up? Was she being a totally remiss friend here?

(Stop. That way madness lies.) 'Okay, so, scones first?' she managed, to Gray's enthusiastic nods.

'Mostly because I didn't have breakfast,' he admitted, falling into step with Cleo as she headed towards the swing doors into the café. 'I'll wolf it down, I promise.' A bright-haired barely-teen with too much red lipstick greeted them at the threshold.

'Welcome to Withysteeple Hall!' She pressed glossy brochures into their hands faster than they could grasp them. 'Fuel stop?' She carried full-steam on before anyone had a chance to answer. 'Unfortunately you've missed the first guided tour of the house, but there are ones on the hour, at one and at three. We have Marshall Pickworthy exhibiting in the main hall, of course; he's the chap that choreographs an interpretive dance based on the story of your relationship. On the South Field you can see Everlasting Love Equestrians – they train ponies and small horses to be ring-bearers: only the thoroughbreds, of course, grade horses don't really have the intelligence. And in the ballroom we have a selection of our recommended caterers exhibiting, so make sure you leave some room for the samplers!' She leaned in conspiratorially. 'The shots of chilled vichyssoise are the talk of the fair!'

Cleo blinked, clutching the shiny brochure to her chest.

'You . . . you don't say,' Gray managed.

'So, how long until the Big Day?' the girl asked, managing somehow to imbue the words with requisite capitalisation.

Despite having said earlier in the car that he wouldn't be fazed, Gray immediately blushed. 'Oh, we're not—'

'We're here for a friend,' Cleo interrupted bluntly.

'Yeah, we're not dating,' Gray clarified.

'Which apparently puts me in the minority,' Cleo couldn't help but mutter to herself.

\* \* \*

'Okay, so . . .' Bea flipped through the paperwork the bruise-lady had given her to read through, referring to the checklist on her phone in the other hand. 'Nora needs to know about capacity, availability, corkage, catering, parking, accommodation, references from recent brides – Christ, really? – and what the chairs are like. Apparently.' She blinked. 'Wow. Oddly specific. . .'

'What the chairs are like?' Eli echoed, puzzled. 'Well, they're hardly going to be armchairs, are they?'

'You'd hope.'

They were settled in a staging area – a billowy but surprisingly unromantic cream marquee – to the back of the main barn, awaiting the events coordinator. Eli paced the small distance, peering into all the stacked storage crates. Bea scanned through the papers again.

'It's a whole new world this,' she muttered. 'Who the fuck thought there'd ever be regulations concerning confetti?'

'It's a wedding venue!' Eli agreed, nodding. 'Why would they have any beef with confetti?'

'Not the foggiest. Okay, so, are we carrying on with pretending this is for us?' Bea asked; they'd agreed in the car that they were likely to get straighter answers if that was the case.

'Yeah, but you'd better do most of the talking. I'll give us away in a heartbeat. She'll ask us where we met and I'll panic and tell her we're second cousins, or something.'

Bea burst out laughing. 'No, don't you remember? We met at an AA meeting,' she suggested.

'On a nudist beach,' Eli countered, grinning.

'At the GUM clinic. We swapped tips on how best to manage our flare-ups of genital warts.'

'Wait . . .' Eli pretended to look thoughtful, 'wasn't it actually on the online message forum for that fetish club that we met?'

'Yeah. Because you've got that thing where you dress up like a sexy My Little Pony,' Bea shot back.

'Hey, whatever gets you off, babe,' Eli countered without missing a beat.

'Okay, okay!' Bea held her palms up in defeat. 'Point taken. I'll do all the talking. Do you think she'll actually bother asking us how we met? Look at her job! She must have stupid engaged couples and their stupid stories coming out of her ears.'

Eli shrugged. 'I don't know. It's acceptable small talk, isn't it? Maybe we can distract her by going straight in with the whole chair controversy?'

'Good plan. If she *does* ask, though, I'll just stay safe with "we met online".'

'No, wait.' Eli looked at her, his eyes soft. 'We met at school. And we were best friends for years until one day, when the time was right, we fell in love. And here we are.'

Bea tried to smile at the romanticism, but the taste of it caught at the back of her throat and she had to look away. He's not done it on purpose, she knows that, but moments from *him* and from *that night* began flashing all the same: how the taste of sweat on his skin was sharp; how he'd complained that her toenails were too long and had scratched him as she wrapped her legs up and around his hips; the horrendous trip to the pharmacy for the morning-after pill the next day, ignoring calls from Nora on her phone, sick with shame and the worst hangover of her life.

'Bea?' Eli prompted; she'd obviously hesitated too long. 'You know, like Harry and Nora? We might as well adopt their story in this instance, don't you think?'

Bea rallied herself and swallowed back the past. 'Okay. Whatever. She's really not going to need any intimate detail, though, surely?'

'Am I interrupting?' The promised events coordinator beamed at them, so entirely perky that she even put the Goodie Bag Lady of Super-Duper fame to shame.

'Elliott,' Eli thrust his hand out and returned the jaunty shake with enthusiasm. Bea got to her feet a little slowly – this day was starting to really take it out of her.

'Bea,' she introduced herself in turn, catching Eli's eye as she did so, wrinkling her nose at him. 'We met at school.'

# Chapter 6

*About a week before the wedding day, the bridezilla decided that all of the bridesmaids couldn't wear the shoes we'd purchased for the wedding and instead needed to wear shoes specifically dyed to match the dresses. Obviously the dye didn't have enough time to set . . . our feet were the colour of Ribena for weeks afterwards!*

Charlie, Oxford

'Oh, my God,' Nora sighed over the selfie Cleo and Gray had taken in front of Withysteeple Hall. 'You guys are just *the cutest*. Why haven't you jumped those bones yet, lady? Daise, take a look.' She tossed Cleo's phone across the table; Daisy – mouth full of burrito – made appreciative noises.

'He *is* cute,' Sarah agreed, peering at the photo over Daisy's shoulder. At that, Queen Bea deigned to take a glance at the screen.

'Yeah, he's cute,' Cleo conceded. (There was no point denying it. She *had* eyes.) 'But he's my colleague—'

'You're so funny about that, aren't you,' Bea frowned. 'I've slept with *loads* of people I've worked with.'

'Yeah, but, Bea, remember you had to leave that one job when that IT guy got all stalky?' Nora giggled. 'So you're not exactly being a role model for it there!'

'They do say "Don't shit where you eat",' Daisy added sagely.

'They do say that, yes.' Cleo rolled her eyes. 'Beautifully put.'

'Hey, as long as one person isn't the other person's manager or anything complicated like that,' Bea shrugged. 'I say play ball.'

Sarah took a very determined gulp from her Hibiscus Margarita; she'd been on a bit of a health kick lately and laying off the drink, but she seemed to be back on the cocktail horse with a vengeance this evening. Belatedly, Cleo remembered – of course – that Sarah's dickhead ex-boyfriend had left her for his PA, and clumsily rushed to change the subject.

'He also appears to be dating most of London,' she revealed dramatically.

'What? What do you mean?' Nora demanded; she had been very pro the idea of Cleo getting together with Gray ever since Christmas. Cleo could probably tell her Gray was flamingly homosexual and it probably wouldn't dampen her enthusiasm for the idea all that much; she was convinced that Gray was The One for Cleo (or, at least, A One).

'Well, the half that's on Tinder anyway,' she clarified.

'Oooh.' In a flash Daisy's phone was in her hand, the app in question already loading. 'I don't think I've ever seen him, though. I definitely wouldn't have swiped left for him!' A parade of men appeared immediately at her fingertips. 'So, if you're not going to jump those bones, hun, would you mind if I took a ride?' She waggled her eyebrows at Cleo mischievously.

Cleo glared back at her across the salt-dusted rim of her cocktail glass. 'What about The Photographer?' she asked. They didn't really bother learning the names of Daisy's gentlemen friends until Daisy herself bothered referring to them by name; the downside to being more or less happy to go on a date with anyone who asked her was that there were only so many men's names in the world – and it got confusing.

'Yes, what about him?' Nora echoed, in alarm. 'I was hoping for mates' rates for the wedding if I needed to use him.'

'Darren is great,' Daisy informed them calmly.

'Darren!' squealed Nora, clearly noting the use of actual name and off already imagining what her friend's future children would look like.

'But it's always good to have a strong bench waiting,' Daisy laughed, ignoring Nora's excitement. 'And as he's *just your colleague*, surely you don't mind . . . ?'

Refusing to rise to the tease, Cleo turned squarely to face Nora and changed the subject. 'So, what did you think after you read my email with all the information about the Hall?' she asked. 'Is it looking like a contender?'

'Oh, definitely,' Nora assured her. 'We'll have to make time this weekend or next to go there ourselves. It's not too expensive for what it is, and they're not all that prohibitive with outside suppliers, like some places can be, and, I mean – just look at it – it's the perfect princess fairy-tale wedding venue! The little girl in me is crying out for it!'

Of course (unlike Bea), Cleo had never known Little Girl Nora. She'd met Nora when they were both eighteen. Nora had had a fat, frizzy fringe back then, greasy dark roots and a helix cartilage piercing (long gone, now) and wore a lot of black pencil liner all around her eyes, like she felt she had to ring them or people wouldn't know where to look for her. She was that little bit lost, in the way that most eighteen-year-old girls are, especially during those first few nebulous years of the noughties (Cleo always thought of them all as being Generation Y point five).

They'd met in the strip-lit hallway of their shared student accommodation, mint-green paint badly faded and peeling away around the doorframes. Cleo, midway through unpacking, had been wearing a polka-dot-print headscarf – a little retro, but the hair she'd inherited from her father – his mother's dominant Caribbean genes coming to the fore – was an absolute nightmare to get dust out of.

Nora's heavily lined eyes had opened wide when she'd caught sight of her. 'Oh, I love your hair! Hi! I've tried that so many times but I just *can't* pull it off!' She spoke then – as she did now – in a musical tumble, the saturation in the Irish brogue during her formative years lending the slightest of softness to an otherwise strong London accent. 'I'm Nora.' She'd gestured to the door opposite Cleo's. '3C.'

At first she'd thought Nora was a little weird and needy (Cleo cringes to think of it now), but now of course she knows it was just that Nora was one of those girls who had always been used to being surrounded by a crowd of friends, a mob of siblings, and there at uni she was truly alone for the first time in her life. Her best friend from home had decided against going to university at all (although Cleo thinks now it might be that Bea never got the grades, more like) and Nora was all over the place with guilt, with nerves, with excitement. One day she was homesick, and the next she was having the time of her life, and everything in between.

She was the mummy of the corridor – making endless cups of tea and always studying with her door propped open just in case anybody fancied a chat. If you ever needed a painkiller, Nora'd be sure to have a foil of ibuprofen; if you broke up with your boyfriend, Nora'd sit quietly with you and watch *Friends* over a hot chocolate, or join you in a half spliff and dancing till dawn (whichever was your preference). Nora was the one that everyone wanted to live with when it came time to choose housemates for the next academic year, and Cleo had been first in line.

Not everyone was so lucky as to make a best friend for always within the first hour of their first day of university life. Cleo felt a huge swell of affection for Nora and Harry and everyone else – even Bea.

'But do you really want something so cliché?' Bea was saying, rolling those infamous eyes again. 'I think you can probably find somewhere better, Nor. I thought you wanted to go more rustic, anyway?'

Okay, maybe not Bea.

# Chapter 7

Darren was getting very familiar very quickly. Earlier he'd wandered into the bathroom as Daisy had been exfoliating in there and let forth a tremendous splashing piss without so much as a 'good morning'. Then he'd wandered out without washing his hands. And he'd left the toilet seat up. Horror piled on horror. Perhaps this was an English blokey thing? A quick text to Nora confirmed that, no, this was unacceptable behaviour either side of the Atlantic. Damn. Just when she'd started using the guy's name.

Feeling a little smug, Daisy finished packing her gym bag. Last pay day she'd gone out and equipped herself – sports bras of varying colours, leggings of various lengths, baggy tee-shirts with block-type slogans that announced things like SHUT UP AND SQUAT! and SWEAT IS FAT CRYING. She'd never been a gym bunny, but she was damned if she was going to be the 'fat bridesmaid' at this wedding. So now she joined Sarah for pre-work yoga sessions twice a week, did Zumba on a Thursday night and paid a veiny personal trainer fourteen pounds an hour to scream at her on as many of the other evenings as she could spare. Damn right her fat was going to cry.

Sarah was already dressed for the class when Daisy met her in the gym lobby (she wasn't quite ready to ride the Tube in the exercise leggings yet). Sarah was always quite quiet in the mornings, but was even more so than usual; she only raised the weakest of outrage at the uninvited-pissing story.

'Is everything okay?' Daisy questioned her as they queued outside the studio door. 'You seem distracted lately.'

Sarah gave a mirthless laugh. 'Funny, that choice of word. I've actually been in a bit of trouble at work for just that. Being distracted. Making stupid mistakes.' She sighed.

'Shit, hun, I'm sorry.'

'No, no. You're right. They're right. I have been distracted. I've been . . . arguing with Cole a bit recently. And I'm not sleeping well.'

'What are you guys arguing about?' Daisy pressed.

Sarah's gaze slid away. 'Oh, you know. Just domestic stuff. Boring. Nothing worth talking about.'

'Oh. Well, let me know if I can do anything, hun.' Daisy was genuinely very fond of Sarah. They were both Johnny-come-latelies, in a way, and Sarah had a sweet, unassuming way about her. They'd all written her off, back when she started dating Cole – pegged her as one of the fangirl types he normally went for that would never see more than one of your birthdays, or more than one Christmas drinks. She'd surprised them all; Cole probably most of all.

'Anyway,' Daisy continued, as they made their way into the flood-lit studio and began unfurling their yoga mats. Their instructor waved at them from the corner, where she was plugging her iPod into the speaker system. Daisy clocked her gym tee – NAMASTE . . . IN BED! it proclaimed – love it! She had to get that one . . . 'I'm sure you couldn't have managed to do something terribly disruptive at work.' Sarah's job as an executive's PA at a stiff, corporate FTSE company was infamously tedious.

A smile finally twitched at Sarah's lips. 'Well. No. But the straw that finally broke HR's back was the other day when I accidentally ordered 200,000 jiffy bags from the stationery supplier instead of two hundred.'

Daisy cracked up laughing. 'You monster.'

Sarah gave in and laughed too. 'I think they might still decide to take it out of my pay.'

'In which case I guess you'll be setting up a side-business selling padded envelopes, then!'

'It's nice to have a Plan B,' Sarah giggled, sliding into a warm-up stretch. 'I can call it Sarah's Stationery Staples.'

'So long as the stationery staple you're after is a jiffy bag.'

Sarah laughed again, before she dropped into Flowering Lotus. 'That can be in the small print.'

# Chapter 8

'I think this is beyond the call of duty,' Cleo hissed under her breath so the masses around them didn't hear. 'BENEDICT. STOP THAT. I mean, you got a nice day out and a cream tea. This is – AIMEE, BACK IN LINE – this is hardly proportionate. DAVID, GET YOUR FINGERS OUT OF THERE.'

'Hey, you agreed, any favour,' Gray countered. 'BENEDICT. MISS ADKINS SAID TO STOP THAT. And if you're good, I'll see if I can find you a teacake.'

Cleo was near certain that teaching was going to put her off having kids of her own. Okay, fair enough, seventy hyped-up thirteen-year-olds three hours from home were not going to be the best example, but still. She was exhausted and the whole weekend event had barely started. She hated doing field trips. As a maths teacher they weren't something she had had all that much to do with since her teacher training. But, she conceded grudgingly, she had told Gray 'anything' . . . (and she'd never been to the Black Country Museum before so, well, there was that.)

Gray momentarily dipped back to herd some wayward tweens back into their crocodile. The parent 'helper' who was meant to be watching the rear of the line was instead watching YouTube on her phone (earphones in and everything). The two older, cannier teachers seemed to have split the group just so that Gray and Cleo got the trouble-makers (the dicks).

'What time do thirteen-year-olds go to bed these days?' Cleo asked Gray as he returned to her side, looking as decidedly frazzled as she felt, his hair sticking up around his normally impeccable parting. 'BENEDICT. SERIOUSLY. LESS HORSEPLAY, MORE WALKING.' Cleo just about stopped herself from clapping her hands crossly (she'd sworn to herself she'd never be the sort of teacher that claps at children, but she hadn't known then what she knows now).

He shot her a conciliatory smile. 'Chin up. Only five hours of scintillating Industrial Revolution fun to get through before dinner.' He just about managed to avoid tripping over Aimee, who had once again stepped out of line in order to take a selfie with some interesting graffiti.

Cleo bit back a laugh as she watched Aimee simper and smirk as Gray put out his hands to steady her. There had been a marked increase in girls wanting to take history as a GCSE next year since the dashing Mr Sommers had joined the staff at Oakland. He was the very cliché of hunky professor, tall and well put together, just enough stubble to be interesting, Harry Potter-style glasses that Cleo wasn't entirely sure he actually needed to wear, and with an astounding array of V-necked sweater vests that he wore well, over crisp shirts with the sleeves rolled up to his elbow. Hell, thirteen-year-old Cleo would have completely bought into it (even twenty-nine-year-old Cleo wasn't entirely unaffected).

Cleo did another head count as they reached the glass-fronted entrance to the museum, just to be sure. She watched Gray's lips moving as he counted too, under his breath. Helpful Helper Mum of Helpfulness finally tugged her earphones out and wound them around her iPhone, looking about herself expectantly.

'OKAY GUYS, HAVE YOUR PRINT OUTS READY TO SHOW AT THE COUNTER, AND REMEMBER TO STAY IN YOUR BUDDY PAIR AT ALL TIMES.' Gray steered the first clutch of students through to the ticket area and nodded companionably at Cleo. 'See you on the other side of 1850, Miss Adkins.'

\* \* \*

Eight hours, one near-miss, where the class clown nearly had a face-to-face meeting with the canal and a train of heaped plates of vinegary fish and chips later Cleo finally got to sit down. She flicked off her pinching Primark pumps and pulled the toe of her tights straight. 'That wasn't too bad, actually,' she allowed. 'I loved that story about the chain-makers going on strike. Got me all riled up: "shoulder to shoulder into the fray" and all that. Did you know that women still earn on average twenty per cent less than men in this country? In this day and age!' Cleo shook her head in disgust. 'Those women back then were so brave . . . You know, I should go to a protest or something. I couldn't be bothered to march when they put up tuition fees because I'd already graduated, and I've always felt shit about it. What do you think?'

Gray sank his head into his hands. 'Please, no. No. Turn your teacher switch off. Can we just have a drink and a chat rather than analyse the socio-political landscape? Please?'

Cleo laughed. 'Okay.' They were off the clock, after all, with the senior teachers charged with roaming the corridors and keeping teenaged peace; the night was their own.

The hotel was almost entirely booked out with the kids, so the lounge area was empty. It had been quite a mild day out in the fresh air but the building was old and heavy-walled so there was a fire lit in the grate; the old, cracked leather of the wingback chairs in front of it was pleasantly warm against Cleo's skin. She closed her eyes and let the heat kiss her face (maybe field trips weren't that bad after all).

After only a few moments Gray was back cradling two crystal tumblers of ice in one large hand and carrying the matching decanter by its neck in the other. Cleo recognised the smell as he pulled the stopper out and groaned.

'Yup,' Gray grinned. 'Your favourite.' Cleo had gone through a big amaretto-and-cranberry stage at the end of last year, and it was precisely that delightful mixture she'd vomited all over Gray at the staff Christmas party (he'd joked that he'd smelt like a Bakewell tart for the rest of the holidays). Gray poured them both healthy measures over crackling ice cubes and sat back down in the other armchair. The chairs were only slightly angled, so they both watched the fire in silence for a few moments, enjoying their first few sips of the almond liqueur and the feeling of peace settling over them after the manic day. Gray's profile was painted orange; holding the delicate etched tumbler in his big hand, he looked like the lord of the manor. Cleo thought back to the cheesy selfie they'd snapped in front of the porch of Withysteeple Hall last month and sighed.

'So, how is trying to complete Tinder going?' she asked. 'Any future Mrs Sommers there in the mix?'

Gray looked at her, curiously. 'I'm not sure many people find their wives on Tinder,' he pointed out. 'It's more for fun.'

'Not everyone sees it that way,' Cleo immediately argued, thinking of Daisy, who loves to be in love and all the hopeful swipe-rights her fingers have given.

'I can guarantee you that most of the men do at least,' Gray assured her. Cleo fell silent at the thought of all those missed connections: one person looking for a forever, the other just looking for a shag. She refilled her drink, feeling vindicated.

'And that's exactly why I don't go on these things,' she confided. 'I'd feel like some sort of cheap impulse buy, left out at the tills.'

'Yeah, I, er, noticed that you'd never come up on Tinder for me,' Gray poked his finger into the button indent on the arm of the chair.

'I have technically been on a Tinder date, though,' Cleo said. 'I went out with this guy for about two months after my friend Daisy decided they didn't have any chemistry together, and she'd met him on Tinder initially; does that count?'

'If you want it to,' Gray laughed.

'Seriously, though, what is the appeal? If you're not actually looking for a girlfriend, I mean. If you just want someone to go to the cinema or to have a drink with, well, there's always me.' (Ack.) Cleo regretted it the moment she'd said it; not the sort of thing you say to your colleague, however flirty (or dishy) he was. Gray regarded her thoughtfully.

'I don't know. I guess it was because one day I realised that I was thirty-two and had wasted my entire twenties in a really toxic relationship. All my mates had done their wild-oat sowing back then and were starting to settle down, but it was like I was coming at life backwards. Making up for lost time.' He smiled ruefully and topped up their glasses a little bit more. 'Anyway. You don't feel like sowing any oats, then?'

Cleo grimaced. 'Well, you have to remember, of course, that I am the *field* in this lovely analogy.'

Gray burst out laughing. 'You are *so* not the field. You are the sort of girl that makes men want to settle down.'

'You make me sound like some sort of mousy housewife,' Cleo complained (but secretly she was filing that away as a compliment).

'I don't mean to,' Gray assured her, still looking thoughtful. Cleo pulled her skirt a little further down her thighs. The combination of the heat from the fire and the gravity caused by Gray's attention was leaving her a little breathless. 'So, then how *do* you meet your dates?' he queried.

'The old-fashioned way, I guess,' Cleo shrugged. 'Through friends. At bars. I don't know. Once I met someone waiting for a bus. I don't really go on all that many dates, to be honest.'

'That's such a waste,' Gray shook his head regretfully and Cleo lost hold of her breath again.

Gray seemed to sense something in her silence and sat back in his chair; Cleo hadn't even realised how much he'd been leaning in towards her. 'Sorry.' He smiled sheepishly. 'I'm being unprofessional, aren't I, Miss Adkins.'

Cleo took a drink to lubricate her senses. 'Not at all, Mr Sommers, not at all,' she managed to tease back, just about pulling back to an even keel.

Gray studied the remnants of his drink. 'Good. Because – trust me – I could get quite unprofessional this evening, if I was allowed.'

The popping of the fire seemed over-loud, and over-important.

Would it be so terrible if she slept with him, tonight, just this once? Because, God, in that moment she really wanted to. Grownups did it all the time (as Bea was always quick to scathingly point out). It wasn't like Cleo had never had a one-night stand before, or slept with someone a little too close to home (must smile graciously at Harry and Archie's cousin if I see him at the wedding, Cleo reminded herself, to lessen embarrassment at having been up close and personal with his knob last year). And (if she was being honest), there had been many, many unguarded moments over the last few months where Cleo had caught herself wondering how Gray felt beneath her fingertips.

But then she thought of the staff-room chats that would never happen, and of how Bea had once felt forced to leave her job, and of the disappointed awkwardness that might fall between them when Gray realised she was just another field to him, after all. And life was too ugly a place to be without a friend that you could call up at 8.30am on a Saturday and ask for a two-hour lift. And so rather than top up her drink, Cleo pushed it aside.

'I'm really wiped,' she announced, and Gray smiled sadly at her like she'd said something else.

'Okay. Sleep well.'

'You too. I'm sorry,' Cleo gestured to the still mostly full decanter.

'Hey, you've got to save yourself for the big party next week, after all,' Gray said mildly.

*Invite him*, the Nora that Cleo had long-since internalised howled in her head: *invite him!*

Cleo's fingertips tingled. He was her friend. Where was the harm?

'Actually, speaking of the engagement party. If you're not busy . . . ?'

# Chapter 9

Cleo's face really, really hurt.

It was a combination of all the smiling and, of course, the balloons. How she had ended up responsible for the balloons, she didn't know.

Daisy was literally of no help, chatting away brightly. 'Right?' she asked Cleo, waving a limp balloon around expressively as she did so as opposed to blowing it up.

Across the function room Sarah was opening the French doors through to the beer garden, sending the balloons that Cleo had already managed to get inflated and tied off rolling around in every direction. Immediately Harry and Eli abandoned their efforts to get the folding tables up and started enthusiastically kicking the balloons into the corner. Cleo – mouth otherwise occupied – eyed them furiously over the swell of the balloon she was currently seeing to, to no avail.

Bea was – as usual – nowhere to be found, and Cleo could only assume that the three missing groomsmen were causing more trouble than those in the room. This was Day One, nuptial Ground Zero; if a generously large wedding party of eight couldn't efficiently set up an engagement party in the local pub, how the hell were they meant to assist pulling off a spectacular wedding for a hundred and twenty guests in just under a year's time? Nora was going to flap, definitely. Cleo sighed, redoubling her balloon-related efforts.

'Hey,' Bea groaned, finally making an appearance from the back room, balancing three Marks and Spencer sandwich platters somewhat precariously and realising she had no tables to place them down on. 'A little help here, guys?' she snapped. A sheepish Harry and Eli returned to their task.

'Bea, is Cole in the kitchen?' Sarah called across from where she was rummaging in one of the bags near the doors.

Bea just about managed to keep her eye-roll internal; she wasn't above referring to Sarah as 'Cole's late-arriving Siamese twin,' when she was feeling her cattiest. 'Not a minute ago anyway,' she answered before dumping the platters on the hastily erected tables and beginning to rip away the plastic coverings, batting away Harry's hand as it snuck in for a hoisin duck mini-wrap.

'Hey,' Harry protested, swiping one anyway. 'I paid for them.'

'I thought Dad did,' Harry's younger brother corrected, characteristically appearing from nowhere the minute the food was revealed and grabbing the biggest sausage roll bite before Bea could react. Harry retaliated by snatching up his own sausage roll and following Archie out into the sunshine of the beer garden to argue the point. Eli approached the table hopefully.

'Don't even think about it,' Bea told him flatly, putting herself bodily between the man and the platter. 'Go and be useful, help Sarah untangle those fairy lights or something,' she instructed as she physically shooed him away.

Daisy paused in her recounting of general life, love and work since she saw Cleo last to check her phone for the time. 'When is Nora getting here? It's late.'

'She's had to go and pick up her mum,' Cleo explained, slightly breathlessly between balloons. 'Eileen didn't trust herself driving with a cake in the passenger seat, apparently, so Nora's got to go up to Kilburn to get them both. Her mum and the cake, that is.'

Daisy laughed, clicking onto Tinder while her phone was in her hand, so Cleo could only assume that poor Darren was indeed on his way out the door. 'I wonder which one gets shotgun.'

Cole finally appeared, waving something above his head like it was the Holy Grail. 'Blu-Tac,' he announced, dramatically. 'Can't believe we forgot about Blu-Tac.'

Sarah abandoned Eli to the snarl of wires that purported to be fairy lights and swept to her husband's side. 'Have you not got the photo wall up yet?' she asked, a bit redundantly, being as she could certainly see that the designated wall was still bare.

'How could I without any Blu-Tac?' Cole pointed out reasonably. 'I'm on it now.'

'It's gone six,' Sarah continued to fret, glancing at the pool of balloons filling the floor, also waiting for some Blu-Tac attention. 'We've got to get a move on.'

'Chill out, love, its fine.' There was no getting around it; Sarah was all too aware that she was a bit of a political bridesmaid – the wife of the best man – and she was determined to overcome this by ensuring said bridesmaiding was completely beyond reproach, resulting in her being, quite possibly, more emotionally invested in this wedding-planning even than Nora.

Sarah had been surprised when Nora had asked her to be a bridesmaid. Nora was one of those girls who had always had friends coming out of her ears, and while she'd been lovely to Sarah since day one, Sarah had never felt like Nora would have considered her one of her *best* friends. Nora hadn't even been one of Sarah's bridesmaids – she and Cole had got married so quickly in the end, and kept it so small, she hadn't had any.

'Here, why don't you help if you're so worried?' Cole continued, distracting Sarah from her chain of thought, handing her a ripped-off chunk of Blu-Tac. With a glance back over at Eli to check he was still working away at the bird's nest of lights, Sarah grabbed up a handful of photographs, sticking precise little dots of the tack in each of the corners.

'Oh, God, this holiday,' her husband laughed after a minute, still holding the first picture he'd picked up. He passed it across to Sarah, who gave it a polite glance. The fresh faces of young Harry, Cole, Nora and Bea grinned out at her, eighteen or nineteen, something like that, but still with the rounded cheeks of their childhood, their complexions reddened by the sun, or perhaps by the cheap alcohol in the cocktail fishbowl they were drinking liberally from. 'This was the one where Bea got that tattoo she had to have covered up last year. We started drinking when we came in off the beach for lunch, and . . .'

Sarah tuned out; she'd heard this story plenty of times before. She wondered if she would appear at all in this wall of memories she was oh so carefully sticking into place.

Daisy paused in her generous swiping-rights to reply to a message from Nora, now finally en route with her two precious passengers and wanting an update on how things were going from her bridesmaids' group WhatsApp chat. Daisy glanced over to where Bea was ferrying rubbish back through to the staging area rooms, Sarah and Cole were industriously sticking photographs to the far wall, and in front of her, where Cleo was looking alarmingly red in the face. All dandy, she replied on behalf of the four of them, adding a smiley face and a be-veiled bride emoticon for good measure.

\* \* \*

Nora and her mother swept in just as the last trio of balloons were being mercilessly Blu-Tac'd into a corner, the multiple strands of fairy lights were being switched on and Daisy finished syncing her phone to the Bluetooth speakers and started up the Spotify playlist she'd created especially for the event. Nora clapped her hands, her eyes shining, the hemline on her contextually appropriate lacy white dress flipping.

'Oh, you guys! It looks great.'

Harry made an appearance, surreptitiously brushing sausage-roll flakes from his hands onto his chinos. '*You* look great,' he corrected his fiancée, kissing her cheek. 'Eileen, do you want me to take that?'

Nora's mother was delicately clutching a large cake box like it was a new-born baby.

'That's okay, Henry,' she assured him. 'If you'll just show me where the kitchen is.' Harry dutifully led the way. Eileen was the only person who actually called Harry, Henry; even his own mother didn't call him Henry.

Nora sidled up to Bea, sat at one of the round tables, exchanging her Toms for a party-perfect pair of pink stilettos. 'How's it going, Mel?' she asked, leaning on the back of Bea's chair.

Bea straightened and grinned up at her. 'Going okay, Mel.' They were always asked, but, no, they couldn't remember when or why they'd started calling one another Mel. Like most things from their childhood, it was more than likely related to the Spice Girls. 'Don't you look pure?'

Nora winked. 'As the driven snow. It's virginal Catholic bride chic. I need to keep away from guests wielding red wine.'

'And penises,' Bea added solemnly.

'Yes, those too.' Nora agreed, laughing, giddy with celebratory spirit already, kissing her old friend's head. 'Come on, I'm getting a drink.'

Harry was permitted to carry the cake, now on its stand, out of the kitchen, to place it as the centrepiece of the food table, the diminutive Eileen hovering anxiously at his elbow.

'You've outdone yourself, Eileen,' Bea told the older woman, standing and moving across to take her by the elbow and kiss her on the cheek, deftly removing the possibility she might trip poor Harry and send both him and her confectionary masterpiece flying.

'Beatrice, for the love of,' Eileen flapped at her godchild good-naturedly. Ever fearful of blaspheming, Eileen Dervan never took the Lord's name in vain, but that didn't stop her saying the rest of the sentence. 'Will you ever put some clothes on you? Sure, do you not feel the cold in here?' Eileen bustled away to find something to pick at, wrapping her arms around herself against the apparent 'cold'.

From the other side of the nearby table, Daisy raised an eyebrow at Bea. 'To be sure, to be sure, will you ever put some clothes on, Be-a-trice?' she whispered, in an exaggerated caricature of Eileen's strong Cork accent.

Bea laughed, gesturing at her relatively modest black skinny jeans and beaded camisole top combination. 'I can't win, trust me Daise. She said it to me when I was wearing a Christmas jumper and jogging bottoms once, I swear.'

Fashionably late, carrying a small ale barrel under each arm, Barlow finally made an appearance, the final groomsman, completing the wedding party contingent.

'I know, I know,' he got in there before anyone else could point out his poor punctuality. 'It's mad up there. There's a match on.' He immediately busied himself plumbing in the barrels to the taps of the small bar area in the corner.

'Meanwhile, we've been dying of thirst,' Cole complained, impatiently moving across to claim the first of the clean pint glasses Cleo had already arrayed.

'Hold on, big guy,' Barlow said, as unruffled as usual. 'This stuff is worth the wait. It's from a brewery in South Wales, it's the business.'

There were many benefits to having Barlow as a mate, not

least of which were the free drinks and free function space. Harry's best mate from university, he had dropped out a term into his final year, despite everyone thinking him an absolute idiot for doing so, and became assistant manager in the village pub where he'd spent his summers pot-washing since he was thirteen. Fast-forward ten years and he was the owner, proprietor and general manager of The Hand in Hand, one of the best gastro-pubs in Wimbledon.

Definitely one the *busiest* pubs in Wimbledon, Sarah thought to herself, still immensely grateful for The Hand in Hand and the impact it had had on her life. Five years ago a younger, stupider Sarah had followed a man following a job, all the way to London. That man had promptly started 'following' his blonde, size-zero PA (gah!) leaving Sarah heartbroken, with the entire rent on their 'dream' central-SW19 flat for good measure. Three months later, with her carefully arranged payment plan about to fall down around her ears, Sarah had ducked into the newly opened pub on her walk home from the office, ostensibly to get out of the rain, but she knew from the off that she was about to spend her carefully budgeted few quid for that night's dinner on a large glass of something more emotionally substantial.

It had been relatively early and the place had been pretty quiet, so the nice guy behind the bar had chatted with her a bit, insisting that he didn't want to leave a dribble in the already-open bottle, thus pouring her the largest glass of wine she'd ever seen. But it was more the offered ear that had got her talking – all her friends were back on the Welsh coast and she was embarrassingly lonely in those days – and way before the glass was even empty the poor guy had had to suffer through hearing in great detail all about the collapse of her relationship and the wince-worthy state of her finances.

'I'm sorry,' Sarah had sighed, as she drained the glass and fumbled awkwardly for her handbag. 'I don't mean to bang on and take up your entire night. You must be busy.'

The guy behind the bar had just grinned at her and scratched his chin through his beard – the neater side of hipster – and said the words that would change Sarah's life.

'It will start getting busy in here round about now, yeah. You know, I've been thinking. Sorry, what's your name?'

'Sarah.'

'Sarah. I'm Barlow. Sarah, I don't suppose you know how to pour a fair pint, do you?'

And that was that. Sarah started at The Hand in Hand straight away; she stayed to have her training that very evening: four nights a week after she had finished at the office, plus as many hours as she could physically hack each weekend. With the decent hourly wage, plus tips, she managed to clear the bulk of the rental arrears within a few months and Barlow even helped her source a flatmate. In the end she kept on the Saturday shift at The Hand in Hand just because she loved it, and because Barlow had become a friend. And then, one night, about eighteen months after she'd started working at the pub, Barlow had decided that the break in her heart had healed enough, and arranged that fateful double date.

Sarah studied her husband of about a year now. Cole was built like a swimmer – unfairly, as he did no swimming – cultivated a devil-may-care sort of artful stubble, and although his hairline had started to recede as he approached thirty, the dramatic widow's peak actually quite worked for him. He'd been dark where her ex had been fair, generous where her ex had been stingy and so flirtatious Sarah worried the blush would be burned onto her face by the end of that first date. And like a woman who didn't learn her lesson, Sarah had fallen in love, all at once and all too quickly.

'Cole!' The next party guest through the doors made an immediate beeline for him; Cole stooped to wrap the petite blonde in a bear hug. Sarah swallowed a sigh. Hers was a face in far too many of the pictures on the photo wall.

'Hello, Clairey. You look gorgeous. What are you drinking?' Cole gestured behind him to where the drinks were lined up waiting. It was a serve-yourself bottle bar – Barlow didn't want to be stuck behind the taps all night at one of his best friend's engagement party.

Claire dramatically nudged Cole with her shoulder and rolled her eyes. 'White wine, obviously!'

'Obviously,' Cole grinned back, moving to open the first bottle of wine of the evening. 'Sarah, come say hi to Claire,' he called as he worked the corkscrew. Sarah smiled on cue, but even she felt how thin it was on her face. Claire didn't even bother with that; her lips just pressed together like she was trying to stop herself from saying something she shouldn't. Sarah wearily filled in the blanks herself: Randomer; Chav from the Valleys; Interloper. Blah, blah.

'Of course,' Sarah managed. 'Hi, Claire, how have you been?'

Cleo read Claire from across the room and knew she should probably head over and rescue poor Sarah, but she was trapped

– quite literally, cornered – by Eileen and one of the twins (even after over a decade of knowing the Dervan family, she still couldn't quite tell the identical girls apart).

'But she must have an idea,' wailed the twin. 'A shortlist?'

'Well, I don't know, I don't know, but there are only a very few acceptable colours for a winter wedding,' sniffed Eileen. 'And she could never pick red. It would be ghastly. Just *ghastly*.'

'Do you have the Pinterest app on your phone?' The twin asked suddenly, setting a beady eye on Cleo's clutch bag. 'Can I just have a look at the sort of things she's pinning?'

Cleo clutched said clutch bag a little tighter. 'Sorry, it's a secret board. You should ask your sister. She's really not done much, er, pinning yet anyway. Honestly. We'll all try on some bridesmaids' dresses when we go into the shops for her wedding dress, apparently, and we'll go from there.'

'A nice sage green,' Eileen continued, mostly to herself. 'Or champagne. And definitely sleeves. Or those nice fringed pashminas, Alanna, you know the ones. They sell them down that market on the Kilburn High Road, I've seen them.'

Cleo, paling at the thought of wearing fringed-anything, desperately tried to change the subject. 'Are your other children coming tonight?'

Eileen looked at her calmly, but a bit like she was simple. 'Cillian will be along later, with that fancy piece he had at Christmas.' Cleo could only make the assumption that Eileen was referring to her son's new girlfriend, who she'd actually met and thought was thoroughly nice and acceptably un-fancy. 'But no young child of mine will be setting foot in a public house. Finola has the babysitter in.'

Cleo supressed a sigh on behalf of the no-doubt frustrated fifteen-going-on-twenty-five-year-old Fin. It had been hard enough for the others, but Fin was Eileen's baby – an identity she would probably never be able to shed.

'Mrs Dervan,' Barlow arrived to save the day. 'Can I get you a drink? I've got that sherry in that you like.'

Eileen flushed prettily and even patted at her hairspray-armoured bob; she adored Barlow, mostly because he insisted on calling her Mrs Dervan, no matter how many times she insisted in turn that he call her Eileen. And because he always remembered to get that sherry in.

'Oh, well, I think I will. It's a celebration, isn't it? But a small one, now, a small one,' she smiled, knowing as well as Barlow did that this was their code that he should pour the sherries large and often until she went home. Cleo took the opportunity to slip away, feigning the need for an urgent conversation with Daisy.

Daisy, as usual, was being DJ. Although she was secretly horrified she was such a cliché – an American named after Gatsby's Daisy Buchanan (well, either that or Daisy Duke, and she'd never had the thighs for hot pants) – she felt she might as well live up to the trope and always throw the best parties. She had a bewildering number of Spotify playlists, each one completely appropriate for its designated mood, venue or context. She'd been working on Nora's engagement party playlist since approximately six seconds after being told Harry had popped the question – and it was a cheesy masterpiece. Currently Geri Halliwell was wailing about not being able to find her Chico Latino, and the designated dance area had already filled to capacity with gamely salsa-ing women of a certain age (a bit like a Zumba class in heels, Daisy thought, with great amusement).

Nora adored the sort of nineties and noughties crap that everyone secretly loves, but would never admit to and, for Daisy, it was all inextricably tied up with so many good memories, a sort of soundtrack to their friendship.

The group that Daisy had travelled out with that year after college had one by one gotten homesick or run out of money (not to mention the one who'd gotten pregnant – talk about your souvenir to take home) and so Daisy had been alone arriving in Croatia that spring. Embarking on the coach that was to be her home for the next ten hours as they travelled overnight from Zagreb to Dubrovnik, Daisy had made the snap decision that she'd rather sit next to the already-dozing brunette who looked around her age than the human sweat-patch that was sat next to the only other empty seat.

Ninety minutes into the journey, that brunette awoke with a start, 'completely mortified' that she'd been drooling on a stranger's shoulder.

'I'm completely mortified,' the girl had apologised to Daisy.

'Don't worry about it!' Daisy had laughed. 'You gotta catch your Zs when you can, am I right?' And that was all it had taken to strike up conversation. They covered the usual ground ('You're English, right?'/'Are you American or Canadian, or . . . ?') and as the night wore on and the coach fell hushed around them, Daisy's new friend, Nora, had pulled out a battered iPod Classic and a pair of candy-pink earbuds and offered one to her. In the seven hours that remained, Daisy had had a whistle-stop tour through the delights of the chees-iest of Britpop: 5ive and the Sugababes and Busted and much, much more. And by the time the coach arrived at the coast Nora and Daisy were inseparable. They'd spent the next six months jaunting around Europe together, working for cash-in-hand pouring drinks in their bikinis or convincing fellow English-speaking tourists that they really want to go into this one particular nightclub in order to save up to pay their coach fares and their two-euros-a-night hostel bed bills.

Returning to real life had been a horrible wrench for Daisy, and part of that was having to say goodbye to Nora, who returned to London after a thoroughly gapped gap year to pack away her tiny bikinis and take up a graduate scheme position in finance, date a succession of tie-wearing, red-wine-drinking men and generally grow up.

When the opportunity had arrived three years later for Daisy to move across the pond to her own firm's London branch, she had quite literally jumped at it (she blamed the fact that her great-grandparents on her father's side were Scottish for the serious Europhile feelings she'd always had) and immediately sent Nora Dervan an excited Facebook message.

Nora had just broken up with one of the tie/wine city men and instantly invited Daisy to stay with her in her little flat in Hoxton while she got herself sorted. The 'sorting' had taken a long time. Daisy had actually ended up living with Nora for years, until Harry happened. And, whenever one of them had had a shit day at work, they'd come home and put on the playlist Daisy had lovingly entitled 'Overnight to

Dubrovnik', whack up the volume and spin and scream along with Atomic Kitten, Blue or Steps. It had never failed them.

'I just love the music,' one of Harry's colleagues called out to Daisy as she danced past, waving a glass of rosé wine around alarmingly in time with the pumping pop beats. 'Sooooooo ironic.'

Daisy just laughed wryly. 'If you like this, just wait for the wedding reception playlist.'

Darren, who had made his appearance about twenty minutes ago, grinned at her over the head of his cider and black. 'It's gonna be your magnum opus, babe.'

'Hey.' Cleo appeared, greeting Darren politely before turning to Daisy. 'Where's Nora? Everything okay?'

Daisy nodded over to where Nora and Bea were dancing in the centre of a small clutch of friends; Bea was already barefoot (Daisy didn't even know why she bothered with the pretence of the heels when she went out). Nora had her tell-tale white-wine flush pinking her face and her collarbones. Daisy could hear her laughing even over the music.

'All quiet on the Western Front, sir,' she assured Cleo sarcastically. 'Chill out. Have a drink. You're really stressing me out.'

Cleo shook her head. 'I need to stay on the ball in case I'm needed for something.'

'Look, the only thing you're going to be needed for is to do the Locomotion,' Daisy informed her archly, lining the song up on the playlist as she said it.

Cleo groaned. 'Maybe I will need that drink . . .'

'It's going to be a very long engagement if you and Sarah insist on being such bridesmaidzillas the entire time. Now

69

fuck off and get yourself some wine. You've got about forty-five seconds.'

'God, Daise, I hate it when you mince your words,' Cleo stuck her tongue out even as she went to obey the order. 'Why don't you say what you really think?'

'Thirty-seven seconds . . .'

Cleo made a swift exit (via the bar).

# Chapter 10

*My boyfriend sent me to have a mani and a spray tan and I thought I was being spoiled – then he told me to pack a bag, we were headed for the airport! He'd already arranged with my work that I could have annual leave and whisked me away to Prague, remembering that years ago I'd told him that I thought the Charles Bridge was the most romantic place in the world. Standing on the bridge in the snow, he proposed with a ring he'd had specially made to look like one from my favourite film, and below the bridge 500 swans took flight! He said he arranged the swans specially, but I'm not sure about that . . . I was thankful for the manicure though – he'd thoughtfully realised that I'd be taking a lot of photographs of my hand!*

Amber, Gloucestershire

Bea really couldn't be arsed to have this conversation. It was not the time, and it was definitely not the place and she was ever-so-slightly too inebriated to think fast enough to avoid accidental agreement (although, secretly she completely agreed with Claire, so it wouldn't really be truly accidental agreement, merely accidental disclosure of that fact . . . or something like that . . . maybe she *was* drunk . . . ).

'I mean, I mean, she'd have been one of mine,' Claire wailed on; it was quite hard to be heard even at close range over Enrique Iglesias' heartfelt crooning.

Nora had known this was coming and luckily had fed Bea the 'party line' response should Claire start bitching to her about it. Well, here we go: Claire had started bitching about it. Bea sighed and dived in, opening with: 'she could only have four bridesmaids, Claire, it's nothing personal, honest.'

'I know, I know. It just seems SO WRONG that she HAS to have Sarah as a bridesmaid just because she's married to Cole. Do you think Harry FORCED Nora to have her?'

Bea, biting back a laugh at the thought of Harry forcing Nora to do anything, shook her head. 'You know how it is. Wedding politics.'

'Yeah, but, Sarah would ALREADY have been involved just from being the wife of the best man!' Claire was clearly not going to let this drop. 'I just thought we'd ALL be bridesmaids, all together, you know?' Melodramatic sniff. 'And now the first one of us to actually get engaged, and I'm out in the COLD.'

'Oh Claire, you are not!' Bea wanted to tell Claire to stop being dramatic, but she knew from the experience of their long-standing friendship that Claire always reacted horrendously dramatically to being told she was being dramatic, so it was quicker not to go there. 'Listen, Nora was actually saying the other day . . . she asked me, did I think you'd mind being in charge of the games at the hen do?'

Claire's lower lip ceased to be quite so tremulous. 'Really? She was saying that?'

Bea nodded enthusiastically. 'Yeah. She said she couldn't think of anyone better to get the fun started.'

'Well, that's so funny, because I actually just happened to read a load of articles about hen-party games the other day . . . you know, I was so bored at work . . .'

Yeah, I'll just bet that was the reason . . . thought Bea. 'Yeah, so she'll probably ask you about it closer to the time.'

'Oh, no, I'll have to start thinking about it straight away!' Claire tutted. 'A truly great hen-do scavenger hunt can't be put together in just a few weeks!'

I am instantly regretting this, thought Bea, making a mental note to warn Nora about her unexpected and overexcited new party planner.

Claire had taken on the orbit of their group not long after they'd moved up to secondary school. She'd probably fancied one of the boys initially – Bea can't really remember now – but despite the fact that nothing had happened there she'd stayed around. She had been – and still was – hard work sometimes, but Bea still loved her to death. And she'd been an absolute godsend to her when Nora upped and left to go to university. . .

'Come on, Nora wants a bride-and-bridesmaids picture before the speeches,' Daisy summoned Bea, thoughtfully already having diverted around the far table to collect the latter's discarded heels. Bea winced as she saw Claire's face fall again. It was going to be a really long year. She could only hope that Claire's friendship with Nora would survive it intact.

Nora, merry and bright, held out her hands for Bea's as she neared, pulling her neatly into her appointed slot next to her; Bea on the right, Cleo on the left, as usual. Sarah chose to complete Cleo's side – Bea couldn't help but wonder if it could be on purpose? – and Daisy moved into place next to Bea. Assorted guests gathered around them in a loose circle began snapping away on their own phones but the girls angled their faces and focused their smiles at Eli, the official photographer of the evening.

'Cleo,' he called suddenly, gesturing awkwardly at his own forehead. 'Your hair-thing's gone a little bit . . .' Cleo immediately turned to Nora for assistance, who pushed the thin jewelled headband back into place and smoothed her friend's hair around it. 'Perfect,' Eli announced, as Cleo shot him a grateful smile. '1, 2, 3 . . .'

Bea barely managed to swallow down that particular throat-full of annoyance, just in the nick of time before it would have shown on her face: immortalised on Eli's phone, immediately on Facebook. And – despite the firm agreement that she'd made with herself – she was back wondering: about Cleo, and about Nora, and about which of the two of them she was going to pick as her maid of honour.

'Everybody say WEDDING!' Eli cheered as he captured the moment.

'WEDDING!' the bridal quintet grinned, even though they knew it would put their mouths and their faces into a stupid shape.

'WEDDING!' Barlow echoed as he appeared from the back room, several fat green bottles of Cava held to his chest.

'Speech, speech!' Everyone howled their agreement. Bea accepted a healthy helping of the bubbles, even though she was probably already slightly too tipsy for good sense. Those who had initially based themselves in the beer garden had pressed into the room, driven as much by the chilly evening as the toast, and the room felt suddenly far smaller. Everyone pressed close, closer. Harry reached for Nora's hand, pulled her fully to his side, held their joined fingers for a moment at his heart. They were framed by the loops of fairy lights Sarah and Eli had carefully pinned into place. The twins and Cillian crowded in, beaming at their sister and even Eileen's famously iron expression was soft. Nora, already in white, face flushed; Harry, looking smart in crisp chinos and a slim-fit shirt, eyes shining. They were so perfect and so happy, Bea almost had to look away.

Cole threw a heavy arm over her shoulders. 'Ah, Beebee.' She hadn't heard that old nickname for a while. 'Look at them. Who would have thought it?'

'I'd like to thank everyone for coming,' Harry had started, unimaginative to the last. 'It means a lot to me and to N— my future wife!' Cue requisite cheering, whooping. 'I don't want to spoil the main event, of course, so I won't go on for too long, ('Good!' some joker heckled from the crowd of guests). So, as you guys know, Nora and I met when we were four, in Miss Proctor's reception class. Needless to say, it wasn't love at first sight!' Harry joined his audience with a laugh. 'I thought she was the bossiest little madam going. Okay so, some things never change.' Nora playfully slapped at her fiancé's chest in protest. 'But regardless, we became best mates. And we stayed close even when we went to secondary school, through that time when we were fourteen and I thought she was secretly in love with Cole!' Nora threw Cole a kiss and he returned a wink. 'And then she went away to university, and to be a gap-year wanker, and moved to the arsehole of East London – and still we were friends.

'And I was nice to all her boyfriends. And I was always a go-to cinema date when she didn't have one.' Harry was speaking softer now, rubbing Nora's fingers with his thumb. 'And one day we were at the cinema – two for one, you know – *The Amazing Spider-Man 2*, of all bloody films!' He laughed sheepishly. 'I wish it had been something a little cooler, but how was I to know I'd ever be telling this story? Because it was just a normal Wednesday evening. And then, it suddenly wasn't, because I realised I was in love with my best friend. Right there. In the Wimbledon Odeon. Over the salted popcorn and Andrew Garfield's weird mug gurning at me on-screen.

'And so here we are! Celebrating the fact that my best mate not only fell in love with me back, but that I haven't put her off in the last year and a half, and she's mental enough to want to marry me!' Harry laughed, delighted, fizzing, brimming with joy, raising his glass of Cava. 'Quick turnaround, I know, I know, but I couldn't wait any longer to ask. I'd waited long enough to be with the love of my life, after all.

'So, everyone. Eat. Drink. Be merry. Dance. Thanks Daisy for the tunes, and Barlow for the booze and Eileen for the cake, which we'll be cutting now, so get in line. And thanks so much, again, for coming.' Harry was laughing now, distracted, Nora hanging off of him like her very body was light with happiness. 'And see you all at the wedding!'

# Chapter 11

Her feet, bare as they were, couldn't take the required bouncing for Kriss Kross's *Jump*, so Bea made a swift exit, dance-floor right, claiming a seat at a table, empty but for general party detritus: paper plates with sandwich crusts and unwanted samosa triangles; discarded cardigans and handbags; the jagged skins of burst balloons. She tried to dust off the soles of her feet but they were smudged so grey she gave that up as a bad lot and sat back in the chair.

'Are you alright there, child?' A red-faced Eileen was there almost immediately, hovering at Bea's elbow. She'd always mothered her far more than her real mum; Bea only pretended to mind. 'Sure, you should go on home, if you're tired. I'll be off myself before too long now.' The sherry must be finished, thought Bea with a smile.

'I'm fine,' Bea assured her godmother. 'I'm just resting.' She gestured at her well-danced-upon feet.

'Ah, yes now, I'm the same. The dogs are barking.' And with that Eileen lowered her stiff frame into the chair next to Bea's and placed her cool hand over hers. 'It's a shame Hannah couldn't make it tonight.' Bea sighed in agreement. Her mother was currently living the ex-pat lifestyle in Portugal and seemed to have washed her hands of all motherly – and godmotherly – responsibilities as a result. Bea had only seen her twice in the last five years. With no dad ever in the picture, and no siblings, it had definitely left her a little adrift. And Eileen knew it. 'Now, Nora tells me nothing these days, my girl. Has your special someone made an appearance, now? There's nobody you thought to bring tonight?'

Bea's mind flitted to Nice Guy Rob and to the three text messages he'd sent her before taking the hint. 'Nobody special, no, not yet.' Eileen had drummed the idea that there was one perfect someone in the world for each of the girls. Granted, it was to get them to consider no sex before marriage, but still, the concept had stuck.

'Ah, he'll be along. He's a man, my girl, and they are all inconvenience, so it will be when you least expect it,' Eileen informed her authoritatively, settling back in the chair. Bea braced herself for an indeterminable onslaught of unwarranted love-life advice from her widowed godmother.

'Mammy, I'm going outside for a fag, do you want one?' Nora's brother Cillian called out as he made his way past the table, beautiful new girlfriend in tow. He winked at Bea; she shot him a grateful look.

'Cillian, that's a filthy habit,' Eileen intoned mildly, as she got up to follow her son out into the darkened beer garden and indulge in said habit. Bea exhaled, left in peace as both her head and her feet pounded in time with the bass of the music.

'Here.' Eli thunked a dripping pint glass of tap water down on the table in front of her. Bea squeezed his forearm in thanks and drank deeply. Eli, holding his own glass, joined her at the little round table. 'I don't think Baz got enough drink in. Everyone's been very much enjoying the open bar.'

'That's because an open bar is a thing of beauty,' Bea pointed out.

'It's going to be one drunken wedding if the engagement party is anything to go by. It's nice, isn't it, how there's no big bride/groom split, really? Harry and Nora have shared friends for so long, everybody knows everybody. It's nice. It's—'

'Incestuous?' Bea supplied, sullenly.

Eli just laughed, used to her occasional darkness. 'Come on. I know you of old, Beatrice Milton, and you are no way near as prickly as you pretend to be.' He glanced over wistfully to where Nora was chatting and dancing with Cleo, both holding over-full glasses of wine aloft, shining in the lights. 'You wouldn't like what they have? To fall in love with your best friend? You can't tell me that Harry's speech didn't touch you deep in that hedgehog heart of yours.'

'You're drunk,' Bea laughed.

'Well, you're a hedgehog,' Eli repeated, matter-of-fact. 'Let's dance.'

\* \* \*

There was a soft touch to the small of her back, a voice in her ear, pitched low to sound under the music. 'There you are.'

Cleo immediately sloshed wine over the hand that had been holding her wine glass steady. 'Gray, hi! Oh I forgot you might be coming,' she lied. She'd religiously checked her phone from seven, until she'd given him up as a no-show sometime around nine.

'That friend I was helping move house wanted to take me out for a few beers to thank me afterwards,' Gray explained, still leaning into her to be heard. His breath was warm on her ear; she could smell the hops. 'I couldn't get rid of him! I'm so sorry, did you see my text?'

Cleo shook her head, gesturing over to where she'd discarded her handbag in a pile of belongings. 'I couldn't be bothered to keep my things on me when I was dancing,' she explained.

Gray's smile spread wider. 'Oh, I know. I've been here for about half an hour, you know. I, er, didn't want to interrupt.' Cleo's eyes fluttered closed momentarily as her brain supplied her with the memory of her dance-floor debauchery over the last thirty minutes or so. She'd split her tights trying to 'get low, low, low' to Flo Rida, but the next song had been too good to miss too, so she'd stripped them off right there on the dance floor, one hand on Claire's shoulder to keep her balance, before throwing them onto the nearest table top and carrying on.

(Fuck.)

'Looks like I've been missing one hell of a party,' Gray continued, eyes full of amusement. 'But I'm here now. So what are we drinking?'

Cleo belatedly remembered that one hand was dripping with wine and quickly wiped it against her dress before thinking it through. (Fuck!) Oh well, it was a dark dress and a dark room – hopefully nobody would be able to see the smear. And it was 10pm on a Saturday night and she was at her best friend's engagement party, who cared if she was pissed? Gray had seen worse at the Christmas party, after all. Of course, back then, Cleo had not yet spent so much time studying the tilt of his nose and the curve of his mouth and overthinking them both.

(She'd used to think she had *such great* self-control . . . )

'How many beers have you had?'

Gray grinned. 'Three or four.'

Cleo shook her head. 'You need to catch up.' She moved to the other side of the bar and reached up on her bare tip toes to reach the padlock key before bending down to unlock the one secured store cupboard. Gray raised an eyebrow questioningly. Cleo shrugged her shoulders. 'Call it a wedding-party perk.' She pulled out the bottle of Disaronno Barlow had told her was there for her if she fancied it, and snapped the lock back in place before returning the key. 'No ice left, I'm afraid,' she admitted, waving the bottle at Gray. 'But then, you *are* four hours late.'

'Fair,' Gray acknowledged as she poured for him. 'But better late than never.' He met her eyes over the rim of the glass as he took a deep drink and suddenly Cleo felt like they could be talking about something else. Over Gray's shoulder she could see Nora, Claire and even Bea goggling at her from the centre of the dance floor. Daisy too paused in her drunken dance-floor make-out session with Darren to shoot her a grin and a thumbs-up.

She studied him for a moment. He was dressed too nicely,

in expensive-looking dark jeans and a well-fitting shirt – he must have gone home to change after helping his friend lug boxes all day. She wished for a moment that he'd been able to see her as she'd been at the start of the evening: hair carefully in place, heels on and eyeliner expertly applied. She hadn't looked in the mirror for a while but she knew, without needing to, that her bare feet were sticky and dirty, and that her skin was damp with sweat under her hair and where her dress cinched in at the waist.

Almost on cue, Gray spoke again. 'You look amazing. Why don't you dress like that for work?' he teased.

Cleo couldn't help but laugh. 'Please, I have enough trouble with some of the older boys being creeps-in-training. You know those Year 11s are still all doing that thing where they drop their pens to try to get me to bend down and pick it up for them?' She rolled her eyes. 'That's the future of our country, right there.'

'Cheeky sods,' Gray agreed, topping up his drink. (Cleo noticed just how hard he was having to concentrate at doing it smoothly and realised that it must have been much more than three or four beers . . . )

'I bet you were a lot worse at their age,' she managed, after a moment's pause.

Gray shot her a look of disbelief. 'Me? No way. I wouldn't have known what to do if I'd had a teacher as hot as you. I would have failed maths because I wouldn't have been able to concentrate, that's for sure.' He seemed to realise as he reached the end of his sentence what he'd said and gave an embarrassed smile, busying himself with taking a sip of his drink. 'And then I wouldn't have been able to qualify as a teacher and then where would we be?' he joked weakly.

The mood in the room had changed. The pumping of The Killers had been followed by Ed Sheeran's *Kiss Me* and the room seemed suddenly impossibly full of couples. Harry and Nora swayed together in the centre, he holding her head, his fingertips showing through her hair, her arms looped around his waist, as they looked into each other's eyes and didn't speak. Nearby Sarah had the side of her face pressed against Cole's chest and her eyes closed as they moved easily together, one of his big hands on one of her hips, an uncharacteristic softness on his face. Even Daisy and Darren were dancing together over by the patio doors, mouths open in private laughter.

Cleo looked back to Gray, to the tilt of his nose, to the way his lips parted slightly as he sighed.

'Sorry, Miss Adkins,' he said lightly. 'I'm being unprofessional again.'

Cleo nodded slowly. 'It must be what Disaronno does to you,' she said lightly.

'Must be.'

'Well, if we've already veered into unprofessional territory . . .' Gray pushed his drink back, away from the edge of the bar; Cleo noticed how he was swallowing deeply, his Adam's apple bouncing at his throat, and realised that he *could* in fact be nervous. 'How about a dance?'

(And maybe it was down to the fact that in that moment she genuinely wanted nothing more, that Cleo paused, clinging by her fingernails to the very edge of her famed self-control.) She shook her head ruefully. 'I would just show you up. My rhythm is appalling at the best of times, and I'm pretty damn drunk . . .'

Gray swallowed again. Undeterred he held out his hand to her and smiled. 'But I *love* Drunk Cleo,' he reminded her.

# Chapter 12

'Cheers, guys,' Cleo thanked them sarcastically, as she waved them in.

The balloons were oversized: huge and a glossy pink. The 3 twirled lazily in the air, refusing to stay straight, meaning the effect was rather more 'SO' than '30'.

Cleo *wasn't* thirty – not quite yet – her actual birthday was on Tuesday (4.21 pm on Tuesday, to be precise) so she was still a twenty-something for almost three full days yet. (She didn't know why that felt so important, but it did.)

It was still early, and only the usual nearest and dearest were in attendance, but already her average-sized Acton flat was feeling pretty cramped. Daisy and Cole jockeyed for space at the hall mirror; for reasons Cleo hoped would soon become clear Daisy was daubing her considerable cleavage with green face paint, whilst Cole was fixated with straightening his bow tie. Cleo grinned; she was probably a little old for fancy dress parties, but still, she felt a little frisson of excitement.

Trailing the balloons, she followed a chatting Nora through to the kitchen where Nora immediately set about pulling glasses down from the cupboards and calling out for drinks orders. Sarah sidestepped the rogue floating 3 to give Cleo a hug.

'Happy Birthday,' she wished her, handing her a perfectly gift-wrapped box. 'I know it's boring, but you said you wanted smellies. And here's the veil,' she added as an afterthought, passing across another bag.

'Thank you so much, Sar. You look great!' And she did: foxy in a figure-hugging black evening dress split almost to the hip (although Bea would no doubt have something cutting to say about Sarah having no identity of her own by way of the fact her costume was merely in compliment to her husband's . . . ).

'My knockout wife,' Cole agreed, throwing an arm heavily over Sarah's shoulders, making her turn almost as pink as the balloons with pleasure.

'The name's Bond, I presume?' Cleo laughed, looking the be-tuxedoed Cole up and down.

'James Bond,' Cole agreed. 'And this is my lovely date, Hootie McBoobs.'

'Hootie,' Cleo nodded at Sarah, 'it's a pleasure. What can I get you guys to drink?' She carefully freed Sarah's pretty bird-cage-style wedding veil from its wrapping and clipped it on, thus completing her own outfit.

'I can't be bothered to make you martinis,' Nora warned them as she continued clattering about over at the breakfast bar. 'Mostly because I can't be arsed. But also because your costumes are pretty theme-tenuous.'

'Oh, come on!' Cole protested. 'Have you *seen* Baz's piss-poor attempt?'

The man in question, digging around at the back of the fridge for the coldest possible beer, gave them a grin; he was wearing an Arsenal football shirt and jeans. 'So, who's coming this evening?' he asked as he opened his lager using the bottle opener magnet with practiced ease. (This was recognised Barlow-code for 'will there be any talent'?)

'Pretty much just the usual crowd,' Cleo answered. 'Although a couple of people from work are coming. Mostly guys,' she clarified, before Barlow could get his hopes up. Poor Baz's working hours were so antisocial he never got to meet anyone. (Cleo was pretty chuffed that her thirtieth birthday had been deemed important enough to generate one of his very rare Saturday nights off.) Cleo ducked as Nora passed a luridly coloured something-and-mixer over her head for Bea to take to Daisy, who was still glued to the mirror by the front door.

Daisy was already almost totally be-greened, and was just smoothing the creases around her nose and eyes with her fingertips.

'I know there's a joke in here somewhere,' Bea said wistfully, leaning back against the opposite wall and folding her arms across her chest. 'Something about you being green with jealously that I look so hot, or something. But I feel like such a massive twat tonight, I just can't bring myself to make it.'

Daisy laughed, reaching to take her drink. 'Hun, you look great. As you well know.' With her other hand she swept up her pointy hat (with built in black, straggly wig, naturally) and popped it atop her head. 'And don't go moaning to the one with green tits that *you* feel like a twat.'

'I assumed this was yours,' Eli interrupted, holding out a gently fizzing gin and tonic to Bea who accepted it eagerly.

'Now this, I don't get,' Daisy complained, gesturing at Eli. 'Am I being the dumb American again?'

'Yes,' Eli told her, with affection, before turning to Bea expectantly.

'Don't look at me!' she said after a minute. 'I haven't the foggiest what you're meant to be.'

'Seriously?' Eli waved the hand he had a packet of Sainsbury's wafer thin ham liberally sellotaped to. 'Come on!'

'Nope.'

He slapped his hands together like he was making a sandwich. 'You see?'

'I so don't see,' Bea assured him archly. Eli futilely clapped his hands together again. 'You know, that really isn't helping any,' she snapped.

'Let me put you out of your misery,' Harry interjected, crowding the small entrance hall even further. He rolled his eyes. 'He's Clapham.'

Eli cheerfully clapped his ham again. 'Geddit?'

'Yes, but I wish I didn't,' was Bea's blunt feedback.

'What's with the hat then?' Daisy asked, confused; Eli was mystifyingly wearing a Burberry baseball cap.

He grinned. 'I'm Clapham *Common*.'

Groaning, Daisy side-stepped past and followed Harry back through to the kitchen to see to the music situation.

'You are *so lame*,' Bea informed Eli, shaking her head fondly.

'Come on, deep down you think I'm really funny and you know it.'

'*Really* deep down.'

Eli stretched a tentative hand out and stroked Bea's feathers. 'I like these,' he told her quietly.

'Yeah, well, they're going to be a right pain in the arse once this tiny place starts filling up,' Bea moaned.

'They suit you.'

Bea arched an eyebrow. 'Angel wings suit me?' Eli nodded, smiling widely. 'They were meant to be ironic,' she laughed. Eli opened his mouth to respond, then clamped it shut as the flat buzzer shredded the silence.

'DOOR, PLEASE,' Cleo bellowed from the depths of the kitchen and Bea, by merit of being closest, turned to welcome the next party guest. It was Claire, fittingly with what appeared to be half of Claire's Accessories clipped to her long mane of fair hair ('I'm *Bow Road*!' she informed everyone with delight). Dumping a token bottle of room temperature, corner-shop wine on the breakfast bar, Claire helped herself to a gin and tonic and disappeared off to gossip with Bea and Nora.

'So, when you say people from work are coming,' Eli asked Cleo, leaning against the breakfast bar next to her and Daisy. 'Are you including Mr Fifty Shades?'

Cleo groaned. 'Seriously, Eli, do not get drunk tonight and call him that. I'm not kidding. I'm embarrassed enough around him as it is at the moment.'

'I can't believe you didn't tap that,' Daisy shook her head (this had been her and Nora's favourite theme for the past several weeks).

'I don't even know if I fancy him,' Cleo lied.

Daisy made a pffft noise. 'Girl, please. I haven't even actually met him and I fancy him.'

'It might just be, you know, that he's really good-looking. And I like spending time with him.'

'At the risk of getting bogged down into this swamp of oestrogen, I think you've basically just summed up what fancying someone is there, Cleo,' Eli ventured with a grin.

'Elliott, darling, I love you, I do – but you should really get your own house in order before you try and give out love advice,' Cleo scolded, only half-joking, with a pointed look across at Bea. Eli took the hint and he and his beer made a swift exit.

'Speaking of men who are being tapped, Darren is going to make an appearance later. When he's done festering in that pub,' Daisy rolled her eyes, her fingers restless on her phone's touchscreen. Tonight's playlist-of-choice was a magnum opus in 90s R&B, although Cleo did feel faintly ridiculous to be standing in her kitchen dressed in a French Maid's outfit from Ann Summers complete with friend's wedding accessory (she was 'Maida Vale', of course) while Ginuwine's *Pony* blasted from the Bluetooth speakers.

'Why are you so down on this poor guy? You're either going to have to dump him or start being nice to him, Daise, seriously.'

'I know, I know. I'm getting round to it, honest. I'll dump him soon.'

'The poor guy. Why don't you just tell him you don't appreciate him pissing in front of you?'

'It's not just that. God, if only. You see, his toenails are weird. They're really sorta square. And he talks over the TV when I'm trying to watch *Special Victims Unit*. He wears those weird baggy-style of boxers – seriously, why do they even make them like that? His sister is a Scientologist; super creepy. And his thighs are completely hairless, it's bizarre.'

'His thighs? But what about the shins?' Cleo managed to ask through her giggles. 'Surely it all hangs on the shin situation?'

'Perfectly normal. I don't know *what* is going on above the knees. He's *smooth* until you get to the nuts. Which, if anything, are *overly* hairy. Very selective hairiness, with that man; it's creepy.' Daisy shuddered theatrically.

'Okay, okay, Daise, you're hardly bigging him up here, but I've gotta tell you – this isn't the sort of stuff you notice when you really like someone.'

'It's true,' Daisy sighed. 'Basically, the thing is, Darren is just not the guy I'm going to marry, is he?'

'They don't all have to be, you know,' Cleo pointed out. 'Some of them are just for fun.'

Daisy raised one green eyebrow. 'I know that hun. Do you?' And with that she wandered away, holding her witch's hat in place with one hand, presumably in search of a conversational companion who would be more gratifyingly affronted by her boyfriend's bald shins/hirsute nuts combination.

Cleo glanced at her kitchen wall clock for what was definitely the eighth or ninth time in fifteen minutes. Maybe if she'd pinned Gray down to a specific ETA she wouldn't be feeling so jittery? (Ack, no – someone saying 'sure, around eight o'clock?' was a perfectly acceptable party RSVP and she had to stop being vaguely psycho.)

She'd been right, of course (she was always bloody right). Dancing with him during Nora and Harry's engagement party had caused . . . issues. The party had been naturally approaching its conclusion, the tube ended for the night, the songs becoming all too slow and soft. Gray's palms had skimmed over the fabric of her dress while he'd breathed the almonds of his drink into her hair, and even after the gentler songs were done, and the pop tunes returned, he'd stayed too-close, too-slow. She'd shot desperate looks across the room at Nora, who was doggedly facing the other way, like she thought she was giving them privacy at the centre of a crowded function room. She'd been even surer then that Gray was drunker than he'd let on; his eyes were too careless as they'd met hers, his movements just that little bit graceless. She'd pictured him getting lathered with his mate in the pub earlier that evening, and wondered how many beers it had taken before Gray decided he was going to turn up at this party after all, decided that in the absence of any other bedwarmer, his mate from work would do for the night.

And just as Cleo's head had successfully managed to temper her heart (and genitals) Bea had appeared, bare-foot, jaw set, pint glass of water in hand.

'Hey, sorry to butt in,' she'd announced, not sounding very sorry at all. 'Just need her for some photos real quick. Here, do you want this?' Before Gray had a chance to answer either way, like a magic trick – presto chango – the pint glass was in his hand and Cleo's arm was in Bea's as she'd marched her across the room in the direction of the Ladies.

'Sorry if I misread you and that was a total cockblock

move,' Bea had murmured as they moved out of Gray's earshot. 'But you've been making RESCUE ME eyes for at least the last two songs.'

Cleo had been startled into a laugh. 'Yeah, thanks. I think we were getting to the point where I was either going to have to let him kiss me, or be very rude.'

'Kiss you?' Bea had echoed, with a bark of a laugh. 'He looked more like he wanted to eat you.'

Cleo had felt a little lust shiver down her back, but fought it to silence. 'He's really drunk.'

'No kidding. Look,' Bea had said, suddenly, in a way that was characteristically frank, with eyes that were uncharacter-istically soft. 'I know a bit about sleeping with people you shouldn't have, and having to see them afterwards and how when they just get on with their lives it makes you feel like complete crap.' Cleo had nodded slowly, remembering the stories about Bea's awkward affairs with colleagues in the past. 'And it sucks. So, be sure, okay?' Cleo had just nodded again and Bea had walked away. (Thinking back, that was probably the nicest moment Cleo had ever had with Bea after over a decade of supposed friendship . . . )

By the time she returned to find Gray (two sickly-sweet shots of Archers with Daisy and Darren later, for courage), he'd been found and adopted by Harry's brother Archie and the two were locked in an animated conversation about some-thing to do with cars. Cleo had more or less left them to it for what little remained of the evening. Gray had wished her goodbye with a kiss to her cheek so soft she wasn't even sure if there'd been physical contact there at all. Come Monday morning, he'd been waiting expectantly at the coffee machine as usual – waving his stained mug about as he complained about a bratty child in his first class of the week – and, in that stark moment, the thought that Gray had ever been angling for a shag seemed faintly ridiculous, so Cleo had decided to let it lie (whatever 'it' was).

Another month, another party. The birthday girl sighed, and checked the clock again before taking a healthy gulp from her drink: a strong, dark rum with tropical juice; Cleo was off the Disaronno for the moment.

Bea wriggled herself into the small gap between her best friend and the end of the sofa, swinging her body so that her feet were underneath her bum and her knees across Nora's lap. The – already irritating – angel wings hung neatly over the arm to the floor providing her with, she hoped, a modicum of grace. On Nora's other side sat Harry, scratching unthinkingly under his bright green wig, knocking it askew; said wig, plus the black shirt and clerical collar combination, served to make him Parsons Green. Trust Cleo to choose a theme as obnoxious as 'Tube Station fancy dress', Bea thought, knocking back more of her G&T. The angel-wings grated softly against the carpet, as if chastising her for her bad mood, and she felt herself smile.

Nora abandoned her conversation to turn to her old friend, resting the point of her elbows on Bea's thighs. 'Ah, Mel!' she moaned theatrically, although her eyes were amused. 'I'm going to regret this.'

'Regret what?'

'This, this!' Nora waved her drink around precariously. 'I

was super good the rest of the week because I knew it would all go to pot tonight, but still. Just this ONE drink is two point five syns!'

'Is there even such a thing as half a sin?' Bea mused.

'I'm not going to get a sticker at the next weigh in,' Nora continued, drinking away nonetheless.

'Didn't we used to take the piss out of women who said things like that?'

'Yes. But those women were thirty and probably desperate to fit into a size ten wedding dress in a few months' time. And we were, like, twenty two, and bitches.'

'Ah. True. Rein it in though, Mel,' Bea advised, gently. 'You don't want to lose your boobs.'

'That would make the dress hang weirdly,' Nora agreed with a smile. 'And, not to mention, give poor Harry a bit of a honeymoon shock.'

'You're doing great though,' Claire interjected from where she'd been perched leaning against the back of the sofa. 'Your face is looking SO much thinner lately.'

'Thank you!' Nora beamed, apparently unbothered at the suggestion her face had been somewhat flabby prior to her starting her pre-wedding diet. 'I think it's because I've swapped all carbs for quinoa.'

'Oh, really?' Claire brightened. 'I tried the bulgur wheat diet once, but I actually ended up more bloated than I was before I started! And, god, you wouldn't believe the—'

'I'm going to get another drink,' Bea announced hurriedly, levering herself from the sofa, before the conversation turned any more digestive.

The birthday party was in full swing and it was becoming much harder to navigate around the compact living space, for all that Cleo was in to modern, Scandinavian minimalist design (aka, the Ikea catalogue). Bea body-swerved two strangers talking to a long-haired guy she was reasonably sure Nora (or maybe Cleo?) had dated whilst at university and slipped into the kitchen.

'Yeah, she was at the engagement party,' Cleo was saying, over by the sink. Her hot colleague Gray had arrived. Apparently he hadn't quite grasped the concept of a Tube station fancy dress theme – inexplicably, he was dressed as Elvis. He was listening attentively to Cleo as she babbled on, although Bea couldn't quite read his expression thanks to the false sideburns and oversized aviator sunglasses. She took one look at Cleo's flushed face and decided to change direction, picking her way through the crowd to where Sarah and Cole were in conversation by the front door.

Bea realised too late she was walking in on something private. Cole's arms were rigid, like a cage around Sarah as he leaned against the wall behind her. His square jaw was even squarer than usual, her eyes more moist.

'You know what they say,' she was hissing. 'Drink until it's pink.' As if to illustrate her point, she took a hearty swallow from her something-and-coke. 'Besides, why should I be the one to make all the sacrifices? You're telling me I can't even have a bloody drink while you're refusing to basically just have a wank. Yeah, that's fair.' Sarah took another too-deep drink.

'I'm just saying that it wouldn't hurt to look after yourself a little more,' Cole snapped back, eyeing his wife's almost-empty glass like he was minded to snatch it from her. 'A bottle of wine can't be good for your, you know, eggs. And things like the amount of salt you eat. And all that butter you put on your roast potatoes on Sunday? Things like that.'

Sarah physically drew herself back, and for a split second Bea was certain Cole was about to get decked. But, in her sudden movement, Sarah had spotted Bea in the shadows of the corridor. All at once she deflated; Cole turned to see himself what had stopped his wife's rage in its tracks.

'Bea, hey,' he managed, after a moment, producing a reasonable impression of normality. 'What's up?'

'Er, nothing.' Bea groped after the same level of ordinariness. Sarah was finding the array of coats on hooks near the front door extremely fascinating, but her tell-tale fingers trembled against her glass. 'I was just seeing if anyone needed a top up?' Bea announced, thankful for the bolt of inspiration.

'Me,' Sarah announced, extricating herself from her husband without a second look. She linked arms with Bea and marched them both into the kitchen. Stopping at a just-opened bottle of red, she proceeded to neck what remained of her spirit and mixer and fill up her half-pint tumbler with the dark wine.

\* \* \*

'Cleo will wring your neck if you spill that,' Barlow said gently, taking the over-full glass from Sarah's still shaky hands. 'Here, let's pour a bit out into a glass for me,' he advised, walking her over towards the sink to do just that.

99

Cleo had half-turned at the sound of her name, hopeful for distraction; she was tits-deep in a conversation she had *not* anticipated (the fact that it was entirely of her own making notwithstanding).

It wasn't Gray's fault. He probably didn't even realise when he was flirting. Cleo felt sorry for him really – he was just too lovely (and too gorgeous), the barista he ordered his morning coffee from probably thought they were in a relationship; was it any wonder that Cleo had found herself a little muddled? It was a close proximity thing – like looking too directly at the sun. Thank god, thank god, thank *god* the metaphorical little solar spots of lust hadn't blinded her too badly – but still, spooling through her head on repeat, an unwanted cinematic experience of how it so easily could have gone down at the engagement party: drunk Cleo, lurching at Gray, lips smacking obscenely, like a cartoon character; Gray – too much of a gentleman to let his disgust show too much – calmly holding her at arm's length and apologising, explaining that she'd completely misread the situation.

Imagined embarrassment gnawed at Cleo's stomach. She fed it some alcohol. Still, her insides cringed at the thought that Gray might guess at the run of her thoughts when she looked at him.

Hence: Claire.

Claire was a wonder – petite and cute, with skin as smooth and tanned as a Werther's Original, set off perfectly by her Disney Princess blondeness. Standing next to Gray's broadness and darkness just set her off all the better; these were the aesthetics that made sense.

'History was my, like, third favourite subject at school,' Claire was saying. 'I mean, I didn't take it for GCSE or anything, because I took Geography instead, but still, History's *great*. We can learn so much from it, you know?'

'Er, yeah. I guess I always thought so.' Gray shot a quick sideways glance at Cleo, as if to double-check she was still present. 'And I always say that it's more like the study of the condition of being human. I always tell the kids that it's the closest we'll ever get to being able to guess at the future, when we know where we came from. We can't escape the past,' Gray continued, really warming to his theme. 'And nor should we try, because I really hope that the amazing tales and truths of all the great men and women who have gone before us really inspire the kids to take that sort of action in their own lives. And remember: history is one giant story that leads straight to you.'

Gray lapsed into a thoughtful silence. Claire was completely spellbound, gripping her drink like it might fall straight out of her hands, pink-glossed bottom lip hanging slack. Cleo sighed. She'd been right – they *did* fancy each other (she was always bloody right).

'Yeah, yeah, enough of that, Mr Somers,' Cleo teased weakly, before he went the whole hog and had Claire planning their wedding by the end of the night. 'Save it for weekdays. No impressionable teenaged girls here.'

'I dunno!' Claire laughed, 'I may not be a teenager, but I'm certainly impressed. You make me wish I'd studied more History . . .' She looked at Gray meaningfully through her eyelashes. 'Mr Somers . . .'

'Oh, it's never too late,' Gray informed her earnestly. 'There are a ton of evening classes, even free courses online. I could send you some links. Add me on Facebook and I'll message them over to you.'

'Er. Sure, okay!' Claire wiggled her mobile phone loose from the tight pocket of her skinny jeans and tapped the blue F icon. Gray might not have realised that she was just flirting with him, but she'd gotten some contact information all the same, so Cleo guessed it didn't really matter.

'I'm just gonna, er, yeah,' she announced, mostly to herself, gesturing with her almost-empty glass and moved away from the new happy couple, both currently engrossed in admiring Claire's Facebook profile picture.

Nora was on her in an instant, bonking her on the forehead with her inflatable novelty microphone.

'What are you doing?' she hissed. Their drunk friend Rebecca barrelled past them, blowing wetly into the neon pink plastic whistle she had hanging from her neck ('Tooting Bec' – one of the more clever costumes of the evening).

'Getting a drink?' Cleo answered, trying to make her face as wide-eyed and innocent as possible; Nora was having none of it – Bea even less so.

'Do you enjoy being alone?' Bea asked. 'Is that what it is? Shall we start buying you cats?'

'You're a sabotager!' Nora accused. ('Saboteur,' Cleo corrected quietly, and was completely ignored.) 'A big, huge sabotager! *Oooh, this sexy, clever guy who I fancy the pants off is flirting with me. BETTER SET HIM UP WITH MY MAN-EATER FRIEND, QUICK, QUICK!*'

Cleo blinked. 'Was that voice supposed to be me . . . ?' Nora had lost most of her authoritative oomph due to the fact she was currently dressed as Agnetha from ABBA, in a shiny rayon flare-legged jumpsuit (she'd spent a fair bit of the party so far trying to bully Daisy into playing *Waterloo*; apparently she had a whole routine worked out).

'If you didn't want him, you could have at least of set him up with Daisy,' Bea pointed out.

'Bea, Darren is *right there*,' Cleo shushed.

Bea shrugged. 'For now.'

'This guy could be your lobster,' Nora wailed (never one to miss making a *Friends* reference). 'And you're packing him off to sleep with Claire! For god's sakes woman, WHY?'

'I'm not packing him off anywhere – and who says he's going to sleep with Claire anyway?'

Nora wordlessly spun Cleo around so she was facing back across the kitchen to where Gray and Claire – replenished drinks in hand – were still deep in conversation, a little patch of intimate quiet in the drunken hurly burly of the party.

Cleo felt her face heat again. 'Well. Well. Good for Claire. He's a really nice guy, she's a really nice girl; why shouldn't they go out?'

'So you're not madly in love with him?' Bea asked, in a doubtful tone.

'I don't even *fancy him*,' Cleo lied, for the second time that night.

'Bollocks you don't fancy him,' Bea snorted. 'He's fit as. I bloody fancy him – even dressed in that stupid Elvis costume. Why *is* he dressed like Elvis, by the way . . . ?'

Cleo couldn't stop a smile from tugging at her lips. 'Oh, he's got this whole routine where he pretends to be angry with you when he gets introduced to you . . . He's King's Cross,' she finally clarified, after a moment's confused silence.

Nora giggled appreciatively. Bea groaned and rolled her eyes. 'This theme was a poor choice.' She gestured behind them across the open-plan living room where Eli was offering guests slices of ham from the packet taped to his left hand, perfectly illustrating her point.

'I think this is the best theme we've ever done!' Nora cheered, throwing an arm around each of her friends (accidentally thwacking Bea with the inflatable microphone this time).

'Seriously, guys, don't make a big deal about the 'me and Gray' thing,' Cleo urged. 'I think I've bigged it up in my head, or something. He's not a lobster,' she informed Nora, firmly. 'He's not even a prawn. I swear.'

'Hmmm,' was Nora's careful, non-committal response. 'If you're sure . . . Sounds like he's a bit of a man-whore anyway . . .'

'*Looks* like he's a bit of a man-whore,' Bea muttered, eyeing the way Gray's expert hand was skimming the curve of Claire's hip as they spoke, as if it had forgotten how it had done just the same to Cleo when they'd danced at the engagement party.

'Best to steer clear of man-whores,' Nora told Cleo knowingly. 'You think you're going to be the one to change them, but in the end they're all always just a complete waste of eggs.'

Bea made a strange noise, half-choking on the mouthful

104

of cocktail she'd just taken. Nora helpfully whacked her on the back with the microphone. 'You okay there, Mel?'

'Potatoes. Eggs,' Bea echoed inanely, craning her neck first to Sarah, still standing over by the sink with Barlow, and then to Cole, all the way across the living space with Eli and Daisy. She dropped her voice. 'You guys, I think Cole and Sarah . . .'

# Chapter 13

*Combine a breakfast that consisted of Bucks Fizz that was more champers than OJ, with a corset-style bridesmaid's dress that I hadn't completely successfully slimmed down into. I just about made it to the top of the aisle – where I burped gutturally into the vicar's face.*

Gemma, Windsor

'So, we're not saying anything?' Cleo asked again, like she just had to make sure of the party line. 'I'm not sure I can manage that!'

'Manage it,' was Bea's helpful response.

'But, imagine it: we've all had a couple of glasses of wine – okay, well, maybe Sarah hasn't had any wine, of course – and it just slips out . . . how can I keep it in?'

'Keep it in.' Bea rolled her eyes and stabbed at her Mille-Feuille with her fork. There was still over an hour until their train, so the three intrepid bridesmaids who had arrived at Paddington Station early had decided to duck into Patisserie Valerie and treat themselves to a cake-based breakfast.

'I can't believe Cole and Sarah are trying for a baby,' Daisy sighed. 'How mad is that. And meanwhile, here *I* am, wishing my contraceptive pills came in extra strength!'

'Yup. I am so on the same page,' Bea agreed. She wasn't exactly the most sexually adventurous of women, but there was still always that moment of cold relief each month when old Aunt Flo came to visit. She'd had a pregnancy scare back in Sixth Form – she and the guy had been kids, really, and neither of them really knew how to put on a condom all that well; and, of course, there was no forgetting that time she'd had to slink to the pharmacy, humiliated and heartsick, and ask for a morning after pill; they'd been too drunk, too frantic for each other, to think of anything as practical as birth control.

After she'd taken the pill she'd sat in silence most of the afternoon, on her bedroom floor, unable to use her bed and put herself back in the place where it had happened, for all she'd stripped the sheets and thrown open the windows. She'd pictured the tiny tablet coursing through her, burning away any evidence that he'd ever touched her, that she'd ever touched him. Her flatmate Kirsty had been goggle-eyed and desperate for the gossip after she'd seen who Bea had had in bed doing the walk of shame out of the flat in the early hours. 'Isn't he your mate?' she'd shrieked at Bea. 'Well, what happens now!?'

'Well, do you remember though, a couple of years ago, how we thought they *were* pregnant,' Cleo was saying as she brought her wide-cupped caffè latte to her lips. 'With how quickly they got married!'

'Yeah,' Daisy nodded. 'Talk about zero to sixty.'

'They'd only been together about, what, six months when

they got engaged. Do you remember? It was right after Nora and Harry got together. Typical Cole, always got to be trying to out-do everyone else!' Cleo laughed.

'Yeah. We thought *for sure* Sarah was knocked up,' Daisy recalled.

'And now, apparently, she can't *get* pregnant,' Bea mused. 'It's ironic. And sad.'

'I can't believe she didn't feel like she could talk to us about it.' Cleo had obviously decided her milky coffee wasn't sweet enough and was slowly stirring in a sachet of Demerara sugar. She gave Bea a sideways glance through her eyelashes. 'At least one of us.'

Bea was distracted from a tetchy retaliation by her phone chirping at her. It was a picture message of a grossly obese woman swathed in miles of peach satin and taffeta. Eli had been sending over photos of the worst bridesmaid monstrosities the internet could provide him for the past few days. Bea knew it was just a tease, of course, but still, she shuddered. She'd already extricated a firm promise from Nora that their bridesmaids' dresses would not come in any sort of pastel shade, and most certainly would not involve any kind of ruching; anything else she thought she could live with for one day. Still, she wasn't looking forward to trying on dresses this weekend, under hot lights, in front of unforgiving mirrors, with terrifically-toned Cleo, brilliantly-busty Daisy and long-legged Sarah either side of her. She'd double-checked that morning before leaving her flat that she'd packed her Spanx.

*Looks good on you . . . have you lost weight?* she childishly typed back to the equally-immature Eli.

'Well, stuff to do with babies and fertility is very personal and we really shouldn't be gossiping about it,' Daisy allowed with a sigh. 'It's hard because I want her to know that we're there for her . . . without having to admit that we know, you know?'

'She must know I heard something,' Bea argued. 'It wasn't exactly a subtle conversation.'

'They probably didn't expect any eavesdroppers,' Cleo pointed out, still stirring her hot drink.

Bea glared at her. 'It was the middle of a party. I walked right up to them. It's not like I was hiding in the coats.'

'You guys,' Daisy warned suddenly, and Bea followed her eyes to where Sarah was clattering down the concourse in white strappy sandals and a peach sundress – typical, peach! – dragging a small wheelie suitcase behind her with one hand and waving at them with the other.

'Oh, good, I'm not the last one here,' she greeted them as she came to a stop by their table. 'And I even have time for a coffee!'

'I wanted to quickly go through the itinerary before Nor gets here,' Cleo added, rummaging in her oversized patent leather handbag and retrieving a clutch of coloured plastic wallets. She passed them out: yellow for Bea, pink for Sarah, blue for Daisy and red for herself, with the green one held back for Nora.

'Is this really necessary?' Bea left the folder on the table next to her plate of half-eaten cake. 'We're just going to a few wedding dress shops. It's hardly a military operation.'

Cleo sighed. 'I just know that Nora is a bit stressed about her mum coming along, and I just want to take all the hassle out of the weekend for her, that's all.'

Nora had done the done thing and invited her mother to

attend the dress fittings with her, thinking that there was *absolutely no way* that Eileen would come. Nora's youngest sister Finola was fifteen, but Eileen treated her like she was still five, and would never have left her alone overnight, let alone over two nights. Nora's plan had backfired spectacularly when Eileen had arranged for Fin to stay with her brother for the weekend and promptly booked a room in the boutique Cotswolds B&B the girls had already arranged to stay in.

'Just please, promise me,' Nora had begged, clutching Bea's arm, 'keep her away from the hen weekend!'

Sarah had returned from ordering her coffee and was leafing through the contents of her own plastic folder. 'That's . . . that's a lot of maps there, Cleo,' she eventually managed.

'Some of these little villages are a right arse to find,' Cleo pointed out. 'And I don't know if the hire car will have a sat-nav, or what. Best to be prepared.'

'Alright, alright, Girl Scouts of America,' Daisy teased, swilling her lemon slice around in her now-tepid green tea with her index finger.

'Damn you, I was about to go Scar from *The Lion King*,' Bea whined; Cleo shot them both pained looks.

'Anyway,' she said, pointedly. 'Nora wanted to do a cream tea, so when we get settled at the B&B we're going out for a late lunch at this place in the village—'

'The *Thanks A Latte Café*?' Sarah read aloud from her pack, sounding dubious.

Bea let her fork fall with a dramatic clatter to her plate. 'And you didn't feel like telling me we were going for a cream tea before I ordered this bloody huge pastry?'

Cleo shrugged and arched an eyebrow. 'You can have two loads of cake in one day. No judgment.'

'As long as this isn't like the last time where you guys got massively on my case because I put the jam on before the cream,' Daisy rolled her eyes. 'Like it even matters.'

'Daise, we got on your case mainly because you tried to then eat your scones with a knife and fork,' Bea countered.

'Yeah, yeah, let's all bully the Yank,' Daisy grumbled, a favourite refrain of hers, for all she was born and raised in Louisiana.

'Yes, so, the *Thanks A Latte Café*,' Cleo continued, 'and then the first three dress shops before we break for dinner. The appointments are at two, three-thirty and five-fifteen. See, there's a schedule in the back.'

'What's this?' Daisy asked, pulling a sheet of photographs of models wearing impossible dresses from towards the back of her folder.

'It's a mood board I made out of the sort of dresses that Nora's been putting on her Pinterest board,' Cleo explained, in a tone of voice that made it sound like she thought that was obvious. 'So, you know, keep your eye out for anything similar on the dress rails.' Bea pushed back the word 'bridesmaidzilla' by shovelling the last of her Mille-Feuille into her mouth.

'Anyway, tomorrow we have the bridesmaid dress boutique, first thing, in fact, so, just FYI . . . I'm going to keep my breakfast sort of carb light!' Cleo continued with a self-depreciating laugh; Bea wished she had some pastry left. 'And then shops four and five, then lunch, then a couple more shops . . .'

'She's looking for a wedding dress, not the Ark of the bloody Covenant. Does she really need to do like ten shops in one weekend?'

'It's just a question of logistics; the Cotswolds has a really good concentration of wedding dress boutiques, and she managed to find a weekend where we were all available, and-'

Sarah half-tuned out Bea and Cleo's squabbling and concentrated on pouring milk into the coffee the waiter had just delivered to the table. In the middle of a flash of guilt at the counter she'd ordered a decaff, but now she was back berating herself for pandering to fear and for internalising her controlling husband, who even as she sat at that table was snapping relentlessly at her as she added two sachets of sugar to her drink.

'You obviously don't want a baby that much,' Cole had murmured to her last night at dinner, barely audible over the sound of the wine pouring heavily into her empty glass.

This weekend, her body was a temple. No alcohol, no caffeine, no crap. She had a book confidently entitled 'Taking Charge of Your Fertility' loaded to her Kindle. By the time this wedding rolled around she'd be a dress size smaller, a whole lot healthier, and – hopefully, hopefully – growing a little secret inside her.

'Hello, bridesmaids!' trilled Nora, appearing at pace. Much like a wizard, she was never early, but never that late, either. Her mother Eileen followed at a more sedate speed, wearing a mauve skirt suit and wielding an alarming hat box. 'How are we doing for time?'

'Probably about ten minutes. The train's not in the platform yet,' Cleo answered, gesturing a little way across the station concourse to where a set of large departure boards were scrolling and flashing.

'Okay.' Instead of rushing to grab her own coffee, Nora helped herself to a few swallows of Cleo's latte. 'So, news! We're all booked in. So we have a date, and a venue, so we sure as hell better find me a dress this weekend!' The four bridesmaids responded with appropriate noises of excitement and one armed hugs.

'Where? When!' Sarah asked as she sat back down.

'The Hall. New Year's Eve. Go big, or go home, right?'

Cleo clapped her hands together in delight. 'Withysteeple? Oh Nor, I just knew you'd love it. I *saw you* getting married there. And New Year's Eve! So gorgeous. How perfect!'

'I still think your father is turning in his grave,' Eileen said tightly. 'What, may I ask, is wrong with the idea of getting married in church? The church where you and your brother and sisters were all baptised and confirmed? Where Father Michaels has known you every day of your life? I don't know what I'm going to say to everyone.' Eileen sniffed dramatically and returned to staring grimly out across the station concourse, hat box balanced on her knees.

Nora's lapsed Catholicism had always been a thorn in her mother's side. Nora and Harry had been geared up for her inevitable anger and disappointment, but they would not be moved by it.

'I CANNOT get married at Our Lady With Consumption!' Nora had hissed at Bea (actually, the church was called Our Lady of the Assumption, but they'd come up with the immature nickname when they were about ten years old, and it had stuck).

Fair enough, Nora didn't want to get hitched in the old church – but it was *so typical* she'd pick the venue Cleo had been pushing. Bea tapped her nails sharply against the table top, fighting against the turn of her thoughts. Nora hadn't even bothered to go and see the Barn that Bea and Eli had scouted for her.

'Mammy,' Nora was saying now, sounding bored but firm. 'We've talked about this. Harry isn't even baptised so I don't think we'd be able to get married at Our Lady even if we wanted to. Father Michaels can come to the reception, if you want. All your Prayer Club too,' she added, magnanimously. Eileen only answer to this generosity was to sniff loudly again.

'Oh look, that's us,' Sarah chirped against the tension, rising to her feet. 'Platform Seven.'

'Let's go!' cheered Nora, flinging a companionable arm around Sarah, who teetered a little in her white heels but laughed, and wrapped her arms around Nora in turn. 'Off to the country!' Nora cried, putting on an over-the-top West Country burr, with shades of the Ambrosia custard advert. 'I've got a surprise for over lunch.'

# Chapter 14

The Badger's Den was everything TripAdvisor had promised it to be: twee from head to toe. Against the darkness of the thatch and the dense green tangle of English ivy climbing the Cotswold stone walls, the front garden of cornflowers and zinnias was a riot of colour. Frothy curtains the deep colour of buttercream framed heavy piped windows, through one of which the proprietor, Mr Badgeworth ('Call me Badger'), was enthusiastically waving.

Nora finally gave up trying to get the rented 7-seater car straight in the B&B's one parking space and pulled the handbrake up. The bridesmaids tumbled from the car, Daisy making exaggerated oofs and cries as she climbed over the seats to get out from the very rear (where she'd been shoved by everyone else by merit of having the shortest legs). The drive from the centre of Gloucester hadn't been very far, not really, but the day had already been a long one, and everyone was feeling a little disorientated, a little restless.

Cleo left her sunglasses perched atop her head, even though the summer sun was strong and she was squinting madly; her mother had always taught her that it was rude to talk to somebody with part of your face concealed. She had been the one to liaise with Mr. Badgeworth/Badger on their booking, so she made sure to greet the wizened old man first as he emerged from the heather-purple front door, blinking in the light.

'Don't worry about the bags, don't worry, I'll get 'em,' he insisted, through a deep Gloucestershire drawl, picking his way down the alarmingly irregular cobblestone path towards the car where Bea was already hefting overnight bags from the boot.

'Thank you, but its fine,' Bea assured him, holding her bag defiantly to her torso as the old man approached her. Badger could have been anywhere from 60 to 100 years old, wiry and brown limbed, with more hair growing from his ears than on his head. He quite literally shooed Bea to one side before collecting up all the remaining bags and starting back towards the house without missing a beat. A little nonplussed, Bea slowly pulled the boot closed.

Badger (or perhaps a behind-the-scenes Mrs. Badger) had laid out tea and biscuits in the lounge area; no would not be taken for an answer, even when the girls pleaded that they were just about to go out for a full cream tea. Sarah nursed a small cup of Earl Grey and nibbled unhappily on a Custard Cream biscuit while Cleo busied herself with the check in formalities; so much for being good this weekend.

Daisy circled the small room peering politely at all of the picture frames: a scattering of unfathomable family shots in amongst standard postcard-pretty watercolours of chocolate-box villages – the whole 'English country garden' thing still hadn't gotten old with her.

Nora consulted the tatty map of the village that was liberally sellotaped to the front desk, the laminated corners peeling and rolling back. 'The tea-rooms aren't far,' she announced. 'We should probably just dump our stuff and go though. We'll have time to come back and pick up the car for the first appointment. She turned to Eileen. 'Mammy, are you coming for the cream tea?'

Eileen patted her stomach delicately. 'Sure, that's a bit too much for me. I'll let you girls get on, and I'll have a bit of a rest up here, now.' Nora shot Bea a look of relief that was so stark that Bea had to bite back a giggle. Eileen would be more than fine – she had whichever novel belonging to that year's Richard and Judy book club she had gotten up to – plus the rest of the tea and biscuits.

'There's a fair nice ramble up through to the shops,' Badger said, as he leisurely passed Cleo three room keys and one heavy metal one, which was for the front door to the cottage. 'Forty, forty-five minutes. It's been dry recently, so it won't be all muddy.'

'Oh.' Nora blinked in alarm and looked back at the map. 'I thought we'd just be able to walk along the main bit, here.' She indicated with her finger. 'Maybe ten minutes?'

'Aye.' Badger looked at Nora like she was a little crazy. 'You won't have much of a view though. Nettles and hedgerows.' Realisation dawned on his face. 'Will you be wanting to do much walking, this weekend?'

Nora bit her bottom lip, awkward, and tried very hard not to make any eye-contact with a quietly giggling Daisy, or to think about Sarah's beautiful white sling-back heels. 'I don't think we'll have all that much time,' she said apologetically.

'We're a bit on a mission,' Cleo added, tapping her palm against the red itinerary folder she still held to her chest.

'I reckon we'll manage a walk to the pub later, though!' Bea laughed. 'Don't tell me we'll have to crawl through nettles to get there, please.'

\* \* \*

Bea felt pleasantly like she might be sick. After her French patisserie experience at breakfast she hadn't felt able to face a full round of scones, jams and cream, but the toasted teacake – bursting with candied peel, plastered with a layer of melting butter, and roughly the size of a car hubcap – had certainly hit the spot. She glanced over at Nora, who had nailed an impressive amount of finger sandwiches and at least three scones, apparently completely unfazed that she was going to spend the rest of the day being wrestled into 'sample size ten' bridal gowns. Daisy was licking clotted cream off the fingers of one hand while she used her other to cycle through filters on the Instagram shot she'd taken of her perfectly crafted scone before she'd demolished it. Sarah was running her fingertip along her plate, picking up the fat crumbs that had fallen from her half-eaten treat, looking like she was barely managing to listen to Cleo's cheerful bridesmaid-tirade, and Bea felt a little pang of affection for the quiet girl she never usually had the patience for. Her eyes dropped to Sarah's midriff, and imagined a cluster of cells catching there, somewhere behind the peach cotton – something like a sea monkey, but genetically half of one of her oldest friends. . .

'Okay, okay!' Nora clapped her hands, half for attention, and half in excitement. 'So, I've got a little game. And I just wanted to say again, thank you, thank you guys for agreeing to be my bridesmaids and for being so much help – already! – and for taking a long weekend.'

'I know, it's such a hardship!' Daisy scoffed.

Nora laughed. 'But seriously. It means the world to me, and to Harry, that we've got such amazing friends. We're so happy to get to share all the wedding stuff with you guys. Because even when we're stressing about money, or my mother is driving me bloody mad banging on about the church, or I feel all the calorie guilt on a cheat day . . .' Nora eyed the multitude of empty plates and cake stands on the table ruefully. 'You guys make it all right again.' She smiled a Nora smile, open and honest. 'And we love you to absolute bits.'

'Awww, Nor!' Cleo leaned around the table to give Nora a one-armed hug. 'And we love you too.'

'And we're *honoured* to be in your wedding party,' Sarah added, face flushed with pleasure.

'Okay, everybody loves everybody!' Bea laughed, throwing her own arm around her best friend once Cleo had relinquished her. 'So what's in the bloody box already?' Nora had walked all the way here carefully balancing Eileen's hat box.

After clearing as much space as she could on the table top, Nora retrieved the box from where it had been safely stowed at her feet. 'Ta da,' she crowed, removing the lid with a flourish, to a moment's stunned silence.

'You're kidding me,' Bea managed after a minute. 'Are you

Erin Lawless

trying to tell us something, Nor? Do you think I've got some sort of a problem?'

'Yeah,' Daisy agreed. 'I mean, I'm not saying your mom's cupcakes aren't amazing, but . . .' She trailed off, laughing.

'Humour me! I didn't know we were going to have a cream tea for lunch until after I arranged this,' Nora explained, rotating the box around so her bridesmaids could see the content all the better. Four fat-frosted cupcakes sat neatly, wedged safely thanks to copious amounts of crepe paper, each a different colour, a different flavour. 'You don't have to eat them now,' Nora allowed, rolling her eyes. 'But you have to pick one. It's a fortune telling game, a modern twist on this old Victorian tradition; there's a different good luck charm inside each cake.'

'So, the charm tells the future?' Sarah asked, gazing at the cupcakes with something approaching reverence.

'Cool.' Daisy immediately dove to swipe the prettiest cupcake: vanilla, liberally peppered with Hundreds-and-Thousands sprinkles of every colour. 'Dibs!'

'Bea?' Nora nudged the box in Bea's direction; Bea eyed the only chocolate cupcake: a cocoa frosting so dark it was almost black, the dusting of large granules of sea salt hinting at the caramel within.

'Well, it's got to be chocolate, as long as nobody else wants it?' Bea looked around as she reached for the treat.

'Go for it,' Cleo shrugged. 'I've got my eye on the Red Velvet anyway!'

'Ooh, good.' Sarah sounded genuinely relieved, leaning to pluck the last of the options from the box: a fruit sponge and

122

buttercream number, decorated with a whole strawberry. 'Sorted!'

'Okay.' Nora was smiling widely. 'If you pull down the casing, you'll see a little ring.'

Bea peeled the paper back to reveal a little silver ring, hooked in on itself; whatever it was attached to was lost inside the sponge of the cupcake. The other girls followed suit, looking expectantly at Nora.

'Okay, let's see what you've got,' instructed Nora, still smiling.

Bea hooked her index finger inside the ring and pulled gently; Eileen's cupcakes were a moist marvel, and the tiny charm slipped out with barely any crumbling. Bea held her finger up to her eye line and watched the little silver anchor spin slowly on its short chain. Beside her, Sarah was doing the same to a small, shiny star. Daisy cooed at the cuteness of hers, a hot air balloon, while Cleo inspected a miniature silver penny.

'Okay, so: *clearly* I'm going to be shortly swept off my feet by a billionaire who travels by hot air balloon,' Daisy laughed. 'But what does everyone else's mean?'

'You're close, actually!' Nora insisted. 'The balloon is a great one. It means that a new adventure is about to start.'

'I'll take that!' Daisy grinned. 'What about the coin? Is Cleo about to win the lottery?'

'The penny means you'll become rich in whatever makes you happy,' Nora explained. 'The star means that your greatest wish will come true.'

'Result!' Sarah said. 'Can't argue with that!'

'That's the best one,' Daisy complained.

'The anchor—'

'Wait, don't tell me,' Bea interrupted Nora. 'I'm going to fall in love with a sailor. No, no, wait – I'm going to join the navy?'

'The anchor stands for a love that is steady and constant.' Nora gave Bea a look that Bea decided to ignore.

'Lucky me,' Bea managed after a minute. 'That'll be you then, Mel; the most constant relationship of my entire life!' She was only half joking; Nora knew it, and gave her a wordless hug.

'Well, I think we're all making out rather well then, aren't we?' Sarah smiled, looking down again at the twirling star.

'They're wine-glass charms,' Nora pointed out, taking Daisy's little balloon from her to demonstrate to everyone how the circle slipped apart and back together to fit around a glass stem.

'Brilliant! You won't have any excuse to "accidentally" drink from other people's wine now, Nora,' Bea teased; Nora stuck her tongue out.

'We'd better get a move on,' Cleo warned. 'If we're going to get back to the B&B for your mum and the car.'

'Oh, crap.' Nora began gathering up her things. 'Here, stick the cakes back in the box if you don't want to eat them now – we can have them for refuelling between appointments later, maybe!' She threw the two unmanaged scones into the hat box for good measure. Cleo, Daisy and Sarah moved up towards the counter with the archaic-looking till – and even older proprietor – to settle the bill.

Bea hung back, watching Nora slide the lid back onto the box of cakes. 'You totally rigged that,' she accused, linking arms with her oldest friend as they turned to walk towards the others.

'Hey, hey,' Nora protested, albeit weakly, 'how could I possibly have rigged it? You all had a completely free choice of which cake you wanted!'

'Yeah, yeah,' Bea smirked. 'And you just had absolutely *no idea* which of the four extremely different flavoured cupcakes each of your four extremely different friends would want.'

Nora laughed, pulling Bea closer, the hat box of fortune-telling cupcakes wobbling precariously as she did. Nora smelt like sugar. Bea remembered how Eileen used to call them Sugar and Spice when they were little, inseparable as they were, chanting the rest of the rhyme: *and all things nice – that's what little girls are made of!*

'Where are we off to first?' Nora asked as they reached the tills; Cleo referred to her ubiquitous schedule.

'We're going to a village called Middleslaughter – for the *Lady In White*, bridal boutique,' she read out.

Bea groaned. 'Is everything in this godforsaken part of the country named with a pun?'

# Chapter 15

*I was so excited the day I went shopping for my wedding dress. I'd been dreaming about it since the first day I'd put a hand-towel over my head as a kid and pretended it was a veil. I knew I was going to be a little curvier than the standard sample size dresses may cater for, but hey – I thought – the real thing will be made-to-measure and I'll look fabulous – so what if a few zips don't go all the way up to the top? I quickly found what looked on the hanger to be my Dream Dress – I couldn't wait to try it on! The reality, sadly, was an uncomfortable experience – emotionally and physically – where the woman from the shop had to stand on a stool behind me tugging the dress up while my poor mother crouched underneath the voluminous skirt and pulled my boobs down from below. We couldn't get it all the way up – or all the way down. I was trapped in it for fifteen minutes. It was meant to be one of the best days of my life, and instead I was left feeling obese and sad.*

Helena, London

The owner, general manager and head of sales of the *Lady in White* bridal boutique was one Pandora Pritchard-Bailey (although Cleo had obvious doubts about that being her real name). Either way, Pandora Pritchard-Bailey was a woman of a certain age, with a forehead stiff from Botox and a creamy pink lipstick that bled slightly into the fine lines around her mouth. She held a shiny Mont Blanc pen over-elegantly between two fingers, like she thought she was Audrey Hepburn and it was a cigarette holder. She did, however, insist her assistant fetch her customers a bottle from the 'champagne fridge', so Cleo decided she quite liked her.

'So ladies,' Pandora drawled, rolling that pen over her knuckles while she surveyed her audience. 'We have bride, and mummy, I presume. Now, where's my Chief?'

'These are all four of my bridesmaids.' Nora had spoken up quickly, and over-loud, and it took Cleo a moment more to realise that Pandora had been asking which one of them was Nora's Maid of Honour, and that Nora had spectacularly obviously dodged the question. 'This is Sarah, Bea, Cleo and Daisy,' Nora introduced. 'And yes, my mother: Eileen.' Pandora's eyes flicked to each of them in turn; then, alarmingly, she started to jot down some notes in a moleskin notebook.

'So, Nora, tell me about yourself and about your wedding,' Pandora instructed.

'Um. What do you want to know?' Nora clutched at her champagne flute awkwardly.

'Anything important,' Pandora answered, impatiently. 'It allows me to get a feel for the wedding so I know what sort of dress you'll be requiring.'

'Oh. I just thought we'd sort of just, look at what's on the rails and pick a couple to try on,' Nora mumbled.

Pandora clicked her pen in irritation. 'We don't do *rails* here,' she announced, imperiously. 'All of our sample dresses are stored downstairs in perfectly pH-neutral conditions, away from light, dust, pollution, and with the temperature set so that the relative humidity remains *under* 30%.' She sniffed. 'After the consultation I will use my experience to select six gowns and my assistants will bring them upstairs. That's how we work here at *Lady In White*.'

'Oh.' Nora looked around at her maids, eyes pleading for help.

'Er, well, Nora is getting married on New Year's Eve,' Sarah piped up, uneasily.

'Yes, in a 19th century country manor house,' Cleo supplied.

Eileen made a noise that would have made more sense coming out of a petulant teenager than a middle-aged mother of five; Nora shot her a look, half begging, half threatening.

'How many guests will be attending the wedding?'

'Well, we haven't finalised the list yet, but probably about 100 in the day, maybe 200 in the evening?' Nora answered meekly.

'I see. And the groom?' Pandora asked. 'Tell me about him.'

'Harry.' Nora's entire demeanour changed when she spoke about Harry; she relaxed in her chair and smiled up at the (frankly frightening) Pandora. 'We met at school when we were little, but we didn't get together until about two years ago, when—'

'What does he look like?' Pandora interrupted, still scribbling away.

'Oh. Mid-brown hair, brown eyes. About six foot tall. Er.'
Once again Nora scoured the room for help.

'I'm trying to get Facebook up for his profile picture, but
there's no 3G whatsoever,' Bea complained.

'Here.' Nora pulled her phone out from her handbag at
her feet and handed it over to Pandora; she had a photo of
her and Harry taken at their engagement party as her wall-
paper. Pandora gave the picture a cursory look before returning
the phone and making yet more notations in her book.

'And you, Nora – is that your natural hair colour?'

Nora put a guilty hand to the back of her head. 'Pretty
much.' And it was pretty much back to basics in recent years
– only perhaps ever so slightly more auburn than nature
intended – miles away from the years at university and in her
early twenties where Nora had almost ruined her hair
completely by ping-ponging between raven black and bleached
blonde.

'And you're how old?'

'Thirty.'

'And how old is,' Pandora referred to her notes in obvious
fashion, 'Harry?'

'Also thirty.'

'Hmm. Career girl, are you?' Pandora said the term like it
left a sour aftertaste.

'Excuse me?'

'Waiting to get married. I see it more and more often
nowadays.' Pandora shook her head sadly. 'You know, they
say that if you don't know you're going to marry the man
within a year of knowing him, it's not truly meant to be.'

'Well.' Nora was a little taken aback, but rallied valiantly. 'As that would have involved Harry and I getting engaged at age six, that probably isn't really relevant in our situation.'

Pandora swiftly changed the subject. 'And what sort of dress was it that you had in mind?'

Nora looked relieved; clearly she'd thought that Pandora wasn't actually going to ask this. 'Well, I've only really been looking online,' she disclaimered, 'but I think I'm leaning towards quite traditional, and as it's a winter wedding I was thinking Duchesse satin?'

'You're too old for Duchesse satin,' Pandora interrupted, with a dismissive wave of the pen. 'Maybe Charmeuse satin, with the right make-up.' She scrutinised Nora's complexion closely and jotted down another note. 'And what were you thinking about style?'

Nora took a moment to gather herself. 'Um. Well, I quite like fit-and-flare, mermaid-style.'

'Stand up,' Pandora barked, and Nora shot to her feet. 'No, you're too short for fit-and-flare,' was Pandora's damning conclusion. 'But maybe a sheath style with a bit of a trumpet.' She scribbled one last time into the moleskin. 'Okay.' Her two assistants appeared immediately, one at each elbow. 'These six.' Pandora passed them her notebook and they disappeared behind the scenes. 'Nora, if you'd like to come into the dressing area and get prepared. We'll need to wash your hands with our special soap.' Without waiting for a response, Pandora disappeared behind the curtains. Nora followed, with the gait more of someone headed for their execution than a bride about to try on her very first wedding dress.

It was ten minutes before Nora emerged, with a face like thunder and a dress that was somewhere between Grecian myth and porn. The material hung heavy, thick and shapeless; Nora's average-sized chest was just about held in place by the one bejewelled strap. It showed more than Nora's most risqué bikini ever had. Pandora was holding one of Nora's hands, and paraded her around the small sitting area like a trotting show pony in a ring before manoeuvring her onto a small box step in the very centre and fussing and faffing with the material of the gown.

'So ladies.' Pandora gestured towards Nora with one delicately French-manicured hand, as if there was a need to remind them all why they were there. 'First impressions.'

Cleo's entire consciousness was of Nora's unexpected cleavage. She was pretty certain that if she opened her mouth and tried to speak, she'd probably say boobs, tits and/or knockers. She glanced over at Bea and caught her mid-grimace and of little-to-no help.

'Oh, it makes an impression, alright,' Daisy said bluntly. 'Two big ones.'

Eileen's hand was fluttering at her collarbone like she was having some sort of an episode. 'I think we're looking for something a little more modest, now,' she said in a tight voice. (Cleo wondered what dear old Father Michaels would make of this dress.)

'Modest.' Pandora echoed the word like it was in a different language to hers. 'What are we thinking? An illusion neckline? Kate Middleton sleeves?'

'A front . . .?' Daisy suggested under her breath.

'Maybe something a little more traditional,' Nora clarified apologetically. 'And with a bit more oomph?' She gestured to the heavy fall of the sheath-style gown. Cleo may not be the owner, general manager and head of sales of a bridal gown salon, but even she could see that this dress was doing absolutely nothing for her friend.

Pandora surveyed Nora. 'Hmmm.' She resumed writing in her notebook before thrusting it in the vague general direction of one of her assistants. 'Replace three and six with these two gowns,' she ordered; the girl scurried off to do her bidding. 'Come on then.' Nora was shooed back into the changing area with a great deal less dignity than she'd been led in with.

Nora was on gown number five before they reached anything approximating what they'd been expecting to see. Pandora had finally been persuaded to put Nora into a mermaid-cut dress (even though they were apparently reserved for women five foot eight and over). The heavy beading on the flare of the skirt whispered against the floor as Nora performed her circuit of the room before stepping up on the box.

'Now we're getting somewhere,' Bea cheered. 'You look amazing, Mel.' Nora shot her a scrunched face smile.

'Now, this dress comes in ivory, alabaster, oyster, bone and winter white,' Pandora advised them, tugging at Nora's neckline in a surprisingly intimate fashion as she did.

'Which colour is this?' Sarah enquired.

Pandora turned her heavy stare on her. 'This is the oyster.'

'Oh.' Sarah blinked. 'Well, it's lovely on you, Nora.'

'Well, I think that the whole off-white colour palette washes you out, personally,' Pandora frowned. 'It must be the pale Irishness of you.'

Eileen, who up until that point had sat in a largely disapproving silence, drew herself up. 'I wore ivory on my wedding day,' she announced grandly. 'And I was very like our Nora. Granted I was a fair bit younger when I got married,' she acknowledged after a moment; Nora stared up at the ceiling lights as if praying for strength.

'I think you'd be much better off looking for a dress in champagne. Or perhaps blush,' Pandora insisted.

Eileen looked as horrified as if the woman had just suggested her daughter get wed in a Nazi Storm Trooper uniform. 'Oh no,' she fumed. 'It's bad enough she won't be getting married in the family church. She *will* be wearing white.'

'Mammy!' Nora's patience had reached its end. '*She* will be wearing whatever *she* wants to wear, because it's *her* wedding, remember?'

Eileen waved one impatient hand. 'Of course, of course; but there *are* limits, child.'

'Nora,' Cleo interjected quietly. 'You'd better hurry if you've got another dress to try on – the next appointment is in a village about fifteen minutes' drive from here.'

'You know what, I think I've seen enough here.' Nora unceremoniously hiked up the skirt of the dress as best she could and stepped down from the box step without waiting for Pandora's steadying hand and marched off to the changing area; Pandora trailed her, aghast and finally silent.

It was only when they got back to the hire car that they realised Nora had nailed three glasses of champagne whilst at the *Lady In White*, and was completely incapable of driving.

# Chapter 16

Nora was uncharacteristically quiet and subdued for the rest of the day. Sarah hadn't driven for over half a decade – not since she moved out of Wales – but she just about managed to chauffeur the seven-seater hire car from village to village down the winding country lanes, her knuckles white against the steering wheel at times. The staff at shops number two – *Something Blue Bridal* in Cobbledick – and number three – *UnRuffled* of Tatbury-on-the-Water – were far more polite – a veritable dream in the bruised-feelings wake of Pandora Pritchard-Bailey – but the spark seemed to have gone out of the day for Nora. She looked lifeless in the bridal finery the other boutiques draped her in – more like some sort of dress-up doll than an excited wife-to-be.

Conversely, Eileen got more and more vocal and tetchy, never missing an opportunity to harangue Nora about choosing a secular wedding, or for not having her three sisters as her bridesmaids. As they returned to the B&B to change for dinner Cleo felt exhausted; she hoped a good meal, a great bottle of wine and an even better sleep would see Nora to rights, and tomorrow would be another day. (And if Eileen happened to oversleep and somehow get left behind for the day, well, so much the better.)

You could tell the second that the car came within range of the B&B's WiFi – every phone in the vehicle suddenly became alive with Facebook notifications, Tweet alerts and WhatsApp messages.

'I'm starving,' Daisy announced, staring at her phone, thumb moving over the screen as they walked up through the front garden. It was well past seven in the evening, but the little row of stone cottages were south facing, and they were still bathed in warmth and light.

'Please don't tell me you're on Tinder right now,' Bea laughed, nodding her head at Daisy's phone.

Daisy laughed. 'No, I was just replying to Darren, but let's have a look shall we? It can't all be crotchety old men and cows out here, can it? Where are the sexy farm boys?'

'Do let me know if a cow actually comes up on there.' Bea was yawning too as she waited for Cleo to unlock the front door to the cottage. 'I'm wiped,' she confessed. 'Don't suppose there's any chance of a Deliveroo sort of set up out here? Or room service?'

Cleo overheard her and her face dropped. 'No, come on!' she urged. 'We have to go to the pub for dinner. Apparently it's all local produce and everything. And don't even try to pretend to me that you don't absolutely love sausage-and-mash.'

Bea rolled her eyes. 'Honestly, I'm so tired right now I can't even make an innuendo out of that.'

'Come on!' Cleo insisted. 'Half an hour. A strong coffee and a hot shower and you'll be set to go, I promise.'

'These better be excellent sausages,' Bea replied mildly as she took the stairs up to the bedrooms.

Cleo had known Beatrice Milton for over ten years now, and she was still no closer to understanding her than she had been a decade ago. It was like she lived to be a walking contradiction; she was the friendliest unfriendly person Cleo had ever met. One thing had been made unerringly clear from the off – Bea loved Nora more than anyone else in the world and Cleo often wondered, that if it wasn't for the raging jealously that sprang from that, if she and Bea would get on a lot better. At least, she consoled herself, it wasn't just directed at her; Bea had barely been able to speak normally to Harry for about three months after he and Nora had come out as being together, and he'd been one of her best friends for pretty much her entire life. Cleo remembered how anxious about it Nora had been at the time, pictured how she'd sat at the breakfast bar in Cleo's flat, worrying the wine in her glass.

'She's not taking it well,' she'd confided to Cleo, the concern written all over her face.

'I don't know why you pander to her,' Cleo had complained as she liberally topped up Nora's wine. 'She should just be happy that you guys are happy, like the rest of us are. She shouldn't be making it about her, as per usual.'

'You know it's not that,' Nora had rebuked gently. 'With Bea it's just this huge fear of rejection and abandonment. Her dad, her mum – a whole bunch of shitty boyfriends, one after the other. I'm basically the one constant she's had in her life and so the change has . . . shaken her up a little bit. You remember what she was like when I went to university . . .'

Erin Lawless

'Hell yeah I do.'

'It's the same thing.' Nora had shaken her head sadly. 'She thinks Harry will take me away from her, the way me going to uni did.' The words *and making friends with you* had hung in the air, unsaid.

'Well. I wouldn't worry too much. She always shakes herself out of it,' had been Cleo's matter-of-fact advice. And Bea did indeed always shake herself out of it; but never quite far enough that life lost its bite, or love lost its fear.

Badger's Den Bed and Breakfast may be old, but at least the en-suites were wonderfully modern. Cleo stood under the hot water breathing in steam and using generous amounts of the complimentary Molton Brown toiletries for far longer than she should have. She was still patting her curls dry with her micro-fibre hair towel when Nora came knocking.

'Just give me a second, I just need to put on my shoes,' Cleo apologised as she let Nora in.

'You're ready?' Nora asked, sounding dubious of that. Cleo turned back around to look at her friend properly for the first time and realised that in the last thirty minutes Nora had changed into a navy strappy sundress, blown out her hair and applied a slick of bright, summery lipstick. Nora was looking at Cleo's combo of boyfriend jeans and loose-fit raglan tee with the same amount of confusion.

'Oh, I didn't realise we were going "out" out,' Cleo groaned in dismay. 'I thought it was only a village pub?'

Nora shrugged. 'Still a girls' night though, isn't it? But it doesn't matter.'

'Are the others in dresses too? I haven't brought anything!'

'It doesn't matter!' Nora repeated. 'You look beautiful, as usual. Let's just get going. Sausages and wine will be just the ticket for me tonight.'

'Give me five minutes,' Cleo begged. 'I'll just have to put on what I had on earlier.' It was just a denim mini and a floral smock halter top, but it was a bit dressier than what she was currently wearing.

'Okay, if you want – see you downstairs in five.'

When Cleo arrived downstairs in the lounge area, approximately six minutes and twenty seconds later, she knew she'd been right to change. Even Eileen had her glad rags on, although her face was still a little sour. The six women set off, picking their way along the pavementless country road, mostly focused on making sure their exposed toes in flip-flopped or sandaled feet didn't meet with any nettles. Nora's mood had already improved some; she laughed and bounced a little as she walked up ahead, chatting with Sarah and Bea. Cleo forgot how beautiful her best friend was sometimes; Nora's job was a little full-on, and as a result she had of late become much more familiar in the skirt suits of her office, her naturally wavy hair GHDed into submission and pinned back into artificial sleekness. Now it hung loose and natural, and the last of that day's summer sun tumbled in it, pulling out the auburn lowlights.

The village pub was just that – called The Village Pub. The organisation demon inside of Cleo started to fret the minute they came close enough that she could see that most of the outside tables were occupied by clumps of casually dressed people drinking richly coloured ales from thick, squat glasses as they kept a weather eye on their dogs and kids, running free; should she have called ahead and made them a reservation?

The reason the beer garden was so busy became immediately apparent as the girls entered the oppressively dark pub. A few lone folks – stereotypical 'regulars' – sat in their shadowy corners, but otherwise the patrons seemed to all be outside making the most of the mild evening.

The lone bartender was looking at them expectantly; Cleo realised belatedly that they'd all just been stood gormlessly in the door for a shade too long.

'Hi.' She strode up to the bar, smiling. 'Would we be able to get a table for six, please? For dinner,' she added, after a moment, when the man behind the bar seemed amused.

'Are you girls staying up at Badger's Den?' he asked.

'Er, yes, that's us.'

'Badger said you'd be in for some food.' The bartender reached down into one of the waist-high refrigerators and pulled out a bottle of something artificially pink. 'Compliments of your host, ladies. Which one is the bride?'

Nora waved her hand stupidly from where she still loitered near the door.

'Congratulations, love. Will that be six glasses? Whereabouts d'you want to be sitting?'

'Can we sit outside?' asked Daisy.

The man shrugged. 'As you like. There's the menu.' He pointed to a chalk board on the far wall, covered with coloured letters. 'Come back and let me know what you want and where you're sitting when you're ready.' And with that he handed the wine bucketless bottle to Cleo and began to line up glasses for them on the bar.

Nora nudged Cleo playfully as the group made their way out into the bright gardens. 'Did you tell the old dear at the B&B that I like rosé wine?'

Cleo laughed. 'No, it's just a coincidence! What a nice guy.'

'Yeah, lucky for you,' moaned Bea. 'Can't bear rosé; it's so sickly. Cleo, want a gin?'

Cleo shot her frenemy a grateful nod. 'Yes please.'

'Would you take a look and see what sherries he has in, dear?' Eileen called after Bea as the latter doubled back towards the gloomy bar.

# Chapter 17

*Where on earth are you?* was Eli's almost-immediate response to Bea sending him a picture message of a dart board on the wall that was so ancient that it was more pin-holes than solid matter.

*Out for dinner. The village pub. It's actually called The Village Pub FFS. It's very Hot Fuzz here...*

*What?* Eli answered. *Are you going to fuck off up the model village tomorrow?* he quoted, with a winking face. *Any luck on the dress-front?*

'Two double gin and tonics, please,' Bea ordered, once the barman made eye contact with her.

'You're not having the wine, then?' he asked her mildly as he forewent tongs to grab wedges of rather dry looking lime and ice cubes with his bare hands and dropped them into the hi-ball tumbler glasses.

'Oh, don't worry, the bride will see to that,' Bea assured him, returning to Eli on her phone when the man turned his back on her to use the optics and pour out the double measures of gin.

*No luck*, she typed. *Every time N puts on something she*

*halfway likes, her mum tells her it's too modern, or the shop staff tell her it's the wrong cut for her. N fit to spit and I don't blame her. Can't believe there's a whole other day of this tomorrow!!*

*And tomorrow you'll be trying on the dresses too,* Eli pointed out. *If some old bat tells you something doesn't suit you but you like it, I hope you tell her to sod right off.*

Smiling to herself, Bea slipped her phone back into her handbag as she retrieved her purse to pay the (agreeably low compared to London prices) cost of the two G&Ts before carrying them back through to the garden.

'Ta.' Cleo immediately removed the straw the bartender had slipped into the drink and dropped it to the table top without missing a beat. Bea had known she'd do that – if she'd been paying attention at the bar rather than texting Eli she would have told the guy to not bother putting a straw in one of the gins; it was a Cleo-idiosyncrasy that she never used straws.

Bea remembered the first time she'd ever set eyes on Cleo Adkins. She'd given Nora loads of time to adjust to her new life before she'd taken the train to Sheffield to visit her at university, about six weeks or so; it was the longest time they'd been apart since they were born.

University had been this thing looming in the distance ever since the summer after their GCSEs. All of a sudden Harry was moaning about the fact that he hadn't managed to finish his Silver grade Duke of Edinburgh by the end of Year Eleven, and he needed to make sure he had the Gold Award for his UCAS personal statement. Eli started to subtly sound them all out about what universities they were thinking of applying to, not really ready to strike out on his own just yet. Claire and Cole swapped tips on where they'd been told were the best party university towns. Nora went on and on *ad nauseum* about which would be a better degree in terms of key transferable skills – Sociology or Media Studies? Or Communications? Or . . .?

Eventually even Bea had started to feel that frisson of excitement, of something big coming, of long-overdue change. Her form tutor supplied her with a pile of glossy prospectuses; her Maths teacher had gently encouraged her to consider a degree in Applied Mathematics. She'd been pouring over one of the brochures at the kitchen table one evening, staring with an almost guilty pleasure at the attainable entry requirements for Maths at one of her top target institutions.

Hannah had breezed in – Bea's mother never simply *entered* or *walked*: she sauntered or marched or slinked. She'd plucked the university prospectus out of Bea's unresisting grasp. And she'd laughed and laughed.

'Where do you think you're getting the money for this, then?' she'd scorned.

Bea had scowled, automatically showing a hard face to her hard-faced mother. She'd never in a million years thought there'd be any funding forthcoming from her childish, self-obsessed sole parent. 'I can get a student loan.'

'You'd be better off getting a job and standing on your own two feet,' Hannah had shot back. She'd made no secret of the fact that she was counting down the days until Bea finished school so that she could head off and seek the adventure that her unexpected teen-pregnancy had curtailed years earlier. She'd tossed the prospectus to the table top with derision. 'All that money just so you can feel superior to everyone else? You'll still end up working in a shop you know. You'll just have debt round your neck for the rest of your life as well.'

'Mum,' Bea had whined, and hated herself for it. 'Everyone's going to uni—'

'Wanting to stay sat on Nora Dervan's bloody coat-tails for three more years isn't a good reason to spend ten thousand pounds,' Hannah had snapped. 'It's alright for her. Eileen's still living off all that life insurance. Lucky bitch.' Bea turned away, a curl of disgust licking in her belly at the thought of Eileen being 'lucky' that out of the blue one day her young husband had been killed in an accident at work, leaving her with four children under the age of ten.

'I'm trying to help you,' Hannah had insisted, after a moment's reflection, dropping her hand heavily onto her daughter's shoulder; Bea turned to the fleeting show of warmth like a flower to the sun. 'To give you advice.' She took back her hand and busied herself making tea for them both – her usual silent apology when she realised she'd gone too far. 'Just think about it,' she pleaded. Bea nodded slowly – that was reasonable, of course – but her fingers still teased the curling edges of the prospectus' pages.

'Besides,' Hannah had continued airily, as she'd flicked the switch on the kettle. 'I don't know who you think you're fooling, love. Remember who's had to go to all your Parents' Evenings for the last ten bloody years. You're not exactly the brains of the operation!'

And so, Bea never went to university; she never even applied. The deadline came and went. The others all asked her tactfully why she'd chosen not to go into higher education and Bea had just parroted her mother, hating the taste of her words in her mouth: she didn't see the point, she just wanted to get a job and get on, and plus – she was a bit thick, and would probably barely pass her A Levels, she'd confided, with a self-depreciating laugh – so it was all a moot point.

She'd gone with her friends to collect their exam results, of course, on a golden August morning. They'd all stood around, all mingled with their classmates of seven years – best friends and good friends and ex friends and almost strangers – clutching those strange little brown envelopes emblazoned with their names, enclosing their futures. There had been shrieks and there had been tears and a multitude of hugs. And then they'd all swooped on the pub closest to the school, where the lady behind the bar congratulated them, but made their drinks pretty weak all night – because they were still such kids, after all – but they got wasted all the same. Everyone talked excitedly about the bars that were on their future campus, the halls they hoped to be living in, the student societies they hoped to join. And that was it: the beginning of the end of life as they knew it – but not in the way Bea had once dared to hope.

Her results sheets, screwed up in the bottom of her handbag, the grades glanced at and gone: she'd have gotten in to that university by miles.

That October had gone slowly for Bea. She'd gotten a temp job – data entry for a telesales company, it didn't set her world on fire, but it was decent money and experience – but all of her friends were just that little bit slower to reply to text messages, less frequently on MSN Messenger and available to chat. She signed in and out and in again, trying to catch their attentions. She felt Nora's absence like a phantom limb. She had never had to be without her, so how would she ever have realised that she didn't know how to do it?

Bea had bought a new dress to wear out at Nora's university, and a daringly red lipstick to match it. She felt gratifyingly grown up. She fully expected to be introduced to a host of folks; Nora had always had no problems attracting people and everyone knows that you spend your first term at university making as many new friends as possible (and the rest of the three years trying to shake off the ones you wish you hadn't made).

Nora had met her at the train station; she'd looked amazing: she'd somehow suddenly learned how to even out her eye make-up better, and looked effortlessly cool in cropped tights in a statement purple colour under a button-fronted denim mini-skirt and an oversized mannish coat to ward off the late-autumn chill. Nora had nattered the entire way to her halls of residence as they stood together, swaying lightly, holding onto the rails of the tram, full of anecdotes and little jokes about all the people she'd met and all the things she'd learned about herself.

When they'd arrived, Nora had opened the door to her room and held the door open so that Bea could shuffle through with her bag.

Bea had thought that Nora looked terribly cool, but she

had nothing on the girl that rose from where she'd been lounging on the narrow single bed, tugging her earphones out with one hand and unfolding slender legging-clad legs, smiling at Bea eagerly.

'Welcome to Sheffield,' she'd beamed, moving to take Bea's weekend luggage from her and usher her into the room. Bea had been momentarily confused – had Nora stopped off at someone else's room first? – but everything from the bedding to the pictures tacked to the wall above the desk were familiarly Nora's.

'I've heard so much about you,' the girl had continued. 'I'm Cleo.' And Bea had wondered why she hadn't heard a word about this Cleo, this girl who was quite clearly very good friends with her best friend already.

Cleo had tailed them all weekend, and the catching-up over drinks that Bea had envisaged ended up being the Nora-and-Cleo show, as the girls giggled through story after story, like some sort of comedy double act. Bea had boarded the London-bound train on Sunday evening feeling bruised and confused.

So in the end it was just bad timing; that was all. The week that followed Bea's disappointing trip to Sheffield was the week that an entire generation of British university students discovered something called Facebook. Way back then you needed to have a university institution email address to even set up a profile, and so Bea was locked out of all the friending fun. Eli came home to visit his parents that weekend and he'd let her have a look at the site on his laptop, ostensibly to show her the pictures he'd taken that term so far, but Bea had honed in on Nora's profile page.

Nora was with Cleo in the profile picture, in a club bathroom somewhere – Bea didn't recognise it, it wasn't one of the places she'd been taken the previous week. The two girls were of a height, and back then Cleo wore her hair as long as Nora did, the tight curls tumbling forever down her back. Their bodies were turned into one another's, perfect bookends, an effortless mirroring of pointed toes and curved hips and black dresses. And – again, that timing at work – Nora's most recent status: *Cleo just brought me in a mug of tea and a sandwich while I tackle some coursework . . . thanks wifey . . . best friend ever :)*

And Bea had swallowed back the surge of anxiety, put on her hard face and called Nora. After that conversation they didn't speak again for over two months.

Bea's gin and tonic is more than half gone and the conversation around the table miles away by the time she brings herself back from the noughties, blinks away the thoughtless eighteen year old Nora in her bright footless tights. Thirty year old Nora, in a navy Bardot-style sundress and round retro sunglasses, looked at her quizzically, second glass of wine in hand.

She regrets it now, of course. She's an adult and she knows that Nora loves her, that Nora always loved her, and that eighteen year old Cleo was just trying to be friendly and welcoming, excited to meet her new friend's best friend. And she knows that if she'd not made a massive awkward issue over it, and had made an effort to visit Nora at university more, she'd probably have made good friends with Cleo in her own right. But, as her godmother Eileen would say, if 'ifs' and 'ands' were pots and pans, there'd be no work for the tinker – or whatever the stupid phrase was.

'My round,' Cleo announced cheerily. 'Same again?' she asked Bea.

\* \* \*

Ostensibly Sarah was sharing the bottle of wine with Nora. Nora poured the last of the dregs of the bottle into Sarah's glass, filling it back to the top; Sarah had only been nursing her first drink really, so Nora had to have had the other three glasses-worth, and was looking accordingly merry. Sarah didn't begrudge her – it made it less obvious that she herself wasn't really drinking, plus it was nice to see Nora relax after being so stressy towards the end of the afternoon.

Eileen – always suspicious of food she hadn't prepared herself, as a rule – had picked at her plate of Hunter's Chicken, apparently oblivious to the way her presence was somewhat censoring the conversation around the table. Sarah had assumed Eileen would be heading back to the B&B when she'd finished her dinner, but Nora's mother didn't show any signs of moving any time soon. All attempts to involve her in the chatter had met with resistance, and even her beloved godchild Bea couldn't raise a smile from her. She sure had a stick up her arse about this wedding, and she wasn't afraid to show it.

Sarah's own mother had been thrown yet supportive when Sarah announced she was getting married. She couldn't blame her – at that point the woman had never even met Cole.

They'd been dating for less than six months, and they were usually far too busy at the weekends to trek back to the far coast of Wales. Two years earlier her mother had hugged her goodbye, tearful, holding her longer than was necessary, full of regurgitated paranoid advice about a life in London: don't get on a night bus alone; always double check the sell by dates on milk from corner shops; make sure the taxi you're getting into is a licensed black cab. Unfortunately, her mother hadn't known to warn her about her then-boyfriend, the then-love of her life – specifically about his proclivities towards women other than Sarah.

Sarah had always been a serial monogamist: high school boyfriend followed by university boyfriend, followed by the man she'd tailed to London, the man she'd thought she was going to marry. She'd never seen Cole coming, nor the surprisingly fierce, grown-up love she'd fallen straight into. Sarah sighed; Cole wasn't perfect, but being away from it all was helping to put things in perspective. She mustn't let her baby-craziness cloud her marriage. Cole Norris was the best thing that had ever happened to her. Sarah reached for her phone in response to the sudden need to be in contact with her husband, even if it was just via a quick text.

Nora returned from a trip to the bathroom with a new bottle of wine and fresh glasses, glancing at her mother as if daring her to pass comment. And when Sarah slightly shook her head, Nora said nothing – she just sloshed wine into her own empty glass.

# Chapter 18

*My mother-in-law wore black to my wedding. She did it because she was mourning the loss of her son's future, as he was marrying so below him. I know this because she told me – it was the first thing she said to me after the ceremony.*

Mia, New York

Nora was wasted. Not, like, *funny* wasted – like barely-sitting-up-straight wasted. She'd been seeing off the wine like it was some sort of personal mission to. Maybe it was. Nora had noticed a smear of dried ketchup across her wrist and she picked at it leisurely, sending flakes spinning down to the top of the picnic bench. Bea and Sarah were both preoccupied with text conversations. Eileen looked fit to spit. Cleo was gamely doing her best to keep the evening on an even keel. Ahh, weddings. Daisy forced herself to take another drink of the local ale she had ordered. It wasn't particularly agreeing with her; she was tired and looking forward to climbing into the single bed in the twin room she was sharing with Sarah that night.

'Are you going to have a look around the shop for yourself tomorrow?' Cleo asked Eileen politely. 'I bet they have beautiful stuff for the mothers of the brides – at least accessories. You could get a big hat!' she said brightly, teacher-voice in full strength.

'Now, I don't really want to be over-doing it,' Eileen answered with a sigh. 'After all, it's basically just like getting married in a big living room, isn't it?'

'Mammy.' Nora was drunk, sure, but she wasn't drunk enough to let that one slide. 'Harry and I are spending over six thousand pounds on this venue; could you please not refer to it as someone's living room?'

'Well, I'm sorry,' countered Eileen, in a tone that suggested she was anything but, 'but all the money in the world wouldn't make it a suitable place to get married. My own mother, God rest her, wouldn't even consider it official!'

'Eileen,' Cleo intervened carefully. 'They'll have a special license for marriages to be carried out, it's fine – it will be just as legally binding as any ceremony in a church, you know.'

'My mother told me not to go over to England,' Eileen continued, as if Cleo hadn't spoken. 'She told me, she did: she said, Eileen, your children will be godless. And she was right. Sure, my poor mother was always right.'

'Oh, you are so full of crap sometimes,' Nora burst out, sitting straighter on the bench. Bea and Sarah's texting fingers fell still; the bridesmaids exchanged nervous looks. Nora wasn't done: 'Stop using Nana and Daddy to push all your guilt onto me. I'm sure they'd just be happy that I'm happy. Because – you know what Mammy? – I'd marry Harry in my *own* living room before I married him in a church purely to please a whole load of distant cousins who have never met my fiancé, didn't send us congratulations when we got engaged, and generally don't give a toss about us.'

Eileen's face was ashen, but her mouth was tight. 'There's no talking to you when you're like this. You don't show any respect for your God, I'm not sure why I expect you to show respect for your mother.'

'Oh, enough of the sanctimonious bullshit,' Nora pleaded. 'I don't know why you worry so much about saving face. Considering Fin.'

Bea, who had sat in shocked silence up until then, made a little strangled noise. Even Daisy had to bite back a gasp. Nora had had fifteen years to bring up the elephant in the room that was her youngest sister, and she chose to do so five months before her wedding?

If Eileen's face had been grey before, now it was positively corpse-like. She had probably thought it had been so long that her family were never going to call her on it. She must have known they'd all been able to do the maths. A widow for twenty years, with a daughter of fifteen, and no explanation, no back story given. And none forthcoming, even now. Eileen rose stiffly from the table, gathered her handbag to her chest and walked off without a word. Even when she was out of sight, even after she was surely well down the road back towards the B&B, the girls didn't speak.

Until finally: 'Fuck. Nor . . .' Bea breathed. 'Are you okay?'

'What was that?' Daisy asked, still a bit shell-shocked.

'Should someone go after her?' Cleo worried.

'She's fine.' Nora resolutely saw off some more of her glass of wine. 'Just being a drama queen. As usual. Jesus.' She turned to Sarah, forgetting the pact the girls had made back at the train station. 'When you and Cole finally have that baby, please don't model your parenting on my bloody mother.'

There was an excruciating silence. Sarah went the colour of the rosé wine she'd been nursing all evening.

'Okay. That's you done for the night.' Bea rose from the table and dumped the remainder of Nora's glass of wine across the grass.

# Chapter 19

Breakfast was a somewhat tense affair. Upon rising, a hungover, horrified Nora had gone straight to her mother's room to apologise, but Eileen was still sour-mouthed and disapproving over her croissant and jam all the same. An apology to Sarah had immediately followed, but even so, Sarah was overly-quiet, avoiding eye-contact or the possibility that someone might bring up her imaginary baby again. Bea picked at her congealing eggs, feeling a bit ill, but not as ill as Nora looked; she was positively green. The idea of schlepping it to another one of those douche-bag boutiques and hauling herself in and out of fugly dresses all morning with so many elephants in the room to boot was not an appealing one.

The mood still hadn't lifted by the time they arrived at the bridesmaids' dress boutique – Nora driving again, albeit very slowly and carefully. Bea supressed a sigh as she unfolded herself from the car; the shop was so snooty that even the mannequins in the window looked bitchy. The leftmost mannequin was draped in a fabrication of bright tartan and stiff black taffeta; the centre, a red floor-length number with an impressively vampy split up to the thigh; the last one was in something that looked more like a nightie. This didn't bode well. Bea just hoped that the wine flu wouldn't addle Nora's otherwise reasonable taste.

Thankfully it appeared the more neutral dress options were kept in the back, clearly not showy enough for the stage of the shop window. After the now-familiar spiel about the 'feel' and 'tone' of the Dervan-Clarke wedding the four 'maids were allowed to roam the rails, pulling out anything they liked the look of.

'Sarah,' Cleo started, tugging out the skirt of a magenta drop-waist to better see its shape. 'Do you want to talk about it?'

Sarah paused midway through her inspection of a beaded burgundy beauty. 'There's nothing to talk about,' she said after a moment, faux breezily. 'A big, fat load of nothing.'

'I just don't want you to think we were talking about you,' Cleo winced. 'Well, we *were* talking about you, of course, but not in a gossipy way, you know?

'Stop digging.' Bea instructed, turning away from her consideration of whether black bridesmaids' dresses were classy or gothic. 'I am sorry though, Sarah,' she apologised, finding that she meant it. 'I didn't mean to overhear. And I shouldn't have spread it around; I was drunk and, well, surprised.'

'Surprised?' Sarah ran her fingertips down the roughness of a heavily brocaded gown. 'Why is it so surprising? We're married. We're in our thirties now. We've got the mortgage sorted. Why wouldn't we be trying to have a baby?' They'd come off birth control for the wedding. It hadn't been a big thing, not at that point. Just sort of a mutual agreement – they wouldn't be *trying*, per say, just not actively *preventing*. Cole had seemed quite excited at the thought – he always liked to be the first person to do something, after all, so the idea of fathering 'the group's' first offspring quite appealed. Whether the reality would have lived up to the anticipation, Sarah didn't know – maybe she'd never know.

'Just surprised that it was this Big Thing, I guess,' Bea tried, her tone suggesting the significant capitals on the words. 'You and Cole always seem pretty, you know, put together. So it was *surprising* to see you having a pop at one another in the hallway at a party. That's all.'

Sarah coughed back an unexpected laugh. 'Put together?' she echoed. 'That's nice to hear. Not quite the reality though, sadly.'

'It never is,' Bea agreed quietly, and the two women exchanged tentative smiles.

'Hey,' Daisy called, 'what do you guys think of this?' she asked, waving the hanger of a strapless champagne floor length gown.

In the end each of the girls picked out one option, and Nora selected another three. It became immediately obvious that what suited the fair-haired, curvaceous Daisy – such as the dusky lilac tea-dress – didn't quite work as well on the willowy, olive-skinned Sarah – who looked stunning in the forest green floor-length with an illusion neckline.

Bea stretched her arm out to hold her mobile phone closer to the thick piped window. She had the one smallest signal bar, and some H instead of 4G (whatever the eff H was meant to be) and it was driving her insane. She hadn't realised she was one of *those people*, the sort who felt vaguely unmoored when she couldn't check her Facebook or know for sure she didn't have any new emails. Back in the centre of the room Cleo was trying to keep a straight face in front of the shop staff as she turned dramatic circles in a bridesmaid dress that was so ostentatious if Elton John happened to be passing by he'd stop to tell them they should tone it down a little bit.

Bea must have managed to get her phone into the micro-metre-wide signal window; it buzzed against her hand as a few notifications got through and she felt the addict's guilty little rush as she checked them.

*Hope you lot are having a frocking good time*, Eli had text cheerfully earlier that morning.

*Frock off*, Bea shot back, stretching her arm out again to try and relocate the magic signal spot so that her reply would actually send.

There was a noisy rustling as Cleo moved across the room and stiffly sat in the armchair next to Bea's. 'So comfy, this,' she announced, sarcastically, flapping her arms like wings to exaggerate how the rigid material of the gown's wide skirt fanned up on each side and stuck up over the arms of the chair. Following Bea's cue she reached into her handbag and fetched out her own phone.

*Hey, what are you wearing? ;)*

Cleo burst out laughing. It took a moment but she remembered that she'd told Gray all about how she was going to be spending this morning modelling designer gowns; it was sweet that he'd remembered. She toyed with the idea of taking a selfie to show him the bedazzled monstrosity currently swathing her, pulling a jokey duckface, but the women from the shop had already told them they weren't allowed to take any pictures, and they were watching too closely for her to get away with it.

*Currently rocking a little bronze number – sort of a rhinestone meets taffeta affair.*

She could picture that little half-smile on his face as he read her response. She wondered if Claire had been texting him over the last week. He hadn't said anything about it at work, but then again she hadn't brought herself to ask. Cleo shot a look at Bea, currently just as engrossed with whoever she was texting – probably Eli, from the smiley little look on her face; would she know anything about whether Gray and Claire had been talking . . .?

*That sounds immense,* was Gray's response. *Any chance of a pic??*

*Sorry, the Dress Police say no pictures until you've paid a deposit,* Cleo explained. *But basically just picture Sexy Steampunk Gladiator crossed with Drag Queen, and you've got it.*

*Oh, I am!* was Gray's immediate reply; somehow the tone-less text was loaded with meaning and Cleo felt her face heating up.

'Bea, you're up,' Daisy called, holding up the last dress for trying on. Bea had been the one to pick this one out. It was understated, a soft shimmery silver knee length piece with a kick to the skirt and with one thick strap on the right shoulder. It was still only on the hanger but Cleo could already see how good it was going to look on Bea – her angular collarbone framed by the diagonal of the neck, her fashionable 'lob' haircut showing off that exposed shoulder to the best advantage.

She turned back to Gray, tapping the pad of her thumb distractedly against the hard case of her phone while she mentally tested out different answers. Face to face with Gray she had no choice but to flirt – conversation with the man was akin to being fish-hooked through the stomach and gently tugged closer and closer, bit by bit. Via text she felt she should probably have a shade more compunction.

She pictured what he would be doing on this sunny, weekend morning. Maybe he was enjoying the papers in bed, all crisp white sheets and sunlight in slants from the window, enjoying an Americano from a wide-mouthed cup, just like the good looking men in coffee machine adverts. Presumably there wasn't a long-limbed, bedheaded sex nymph dozing alongside him, or he wouldn't be texting Cleo. (She didn't think he was that much of a cad.) Or maybe he was just flipping between his text message inbox and Tinder, lining up a date with a nymph to be-bedhead later that night, cutting back to kill some time bantering with his work mate; after all, she always replied straight away. . . Ack. She did, didn't she? She locked her phone screen and slipped it back into her handbag, clicking the buckle closed for good measure.

(She bet Claire waited the perfect amount of time before replying to texts.)

'Oh, oh.' Nora piped up suddenly from the other side of the room. 'Oh, Mel, you look amazing!' she complimented

Bea as she slid from behind the privacy curtain, looking uncharacteristically shy; she hadn't bothered to take off her bright orange trainer socks, and she wasn't wearing a strapless bra so one black strap was showing on the left, but the dress was knock-out on her. It was perfect – modern, yet timeless, with a wintery feel. They'd freeze their arses off in December, but Cleo knew it was the one – and from the look on her face, Nora knew it too. It was the first time she'd had had any sort of spark all weekend.

# Chapter 20

*I was a guest at a wedding where the bride clearly (hopefully) forgot that she was wearing crotchless knickers, and playfully hooked her leg over her husband's shoulder when he knelt down in front of her to get her garter. 'Eyeful' doesn't quite cover it. . .*

Jamie, Essex

The penultimate appointment of the weekend was the smallest shop thus far: Grace Loves Lace. There was a new spring in Nora's step, a revival of purpose: she had a venue and her bridesmaid dresses; her mother hadn't stormed back to London following her elder daughter's outburst about her younger; she knew through trial and error that fit-and-flare dresses didn't really suit her stature (damn that Pandora Pritchard-Bailey for being right about that).

The eponymous Grace did things a little differently. She settled Nora and the others down with tea – real loose-leaf tea from a pot and served in tiny cups with matching saucers

– and after a little idle chit-chat disappeared into the rails herself, returning with only three gowns.

The other two weren't needed; conversation dropped away as Nora emerged wearing the first dress, the skirt sighing over her legs as she moved to the centre of the room. The bodice was simple, the back a deep scoop to a row of tiny, silk buttons. The skirt tumbled into soft tiers, full, but still elegant, Grace's assistant started forward with the finishing touch, a simple chapel-length veil scattered with winking crystals, and there she was: Nora the Bride.

Cleo rose to stand next to Nora; she was admiring herself in the mirror, hips slightly swaying to make the dress slide and move, a silly little beam on her face.

'You're going to be cold, you know,' Cleo pointed out, with a smile.

'So I'll be cold,' Nora shrugged.

The other girls crowded around – even Eileen's eyes were shining as she took in her daughter. Bea stood the other side of Nora, mindful of the slight poof of the skirt of the dress.

'Job done,' Bea announced, meeting Nora's eyes in the mirror, her eyes feeling embarrassingly hot. Harry would cry for sure, when he held his beautiful bride at the other end of the aisle come the big day on New Year's Eve. Christmas had felt ages away that morning, but suddenly Bea was all too aware of how close this wedding really was. Surely it was just last week Nora and Harry had announced their engagement, just a couple of months since they'd traded hearts? Time was racing on, and – as usual – Bea felt left behind.

But she remembered that night like it was yesterday, the night in the bar where Nora had met her to confess her and Harry's big secret. . .

\* \* \*

## 2 YEARS EARLIER

Nora pushed her handbag up on her shoulder. 'Are you sure you're going to be okay?'

Bea waved the hand that wasn't holding a glass of wine. 'Yup. I'll be fine. Fine.'

Nora hesitated. 'Are you sure?'

'I'll be FINE,' Bea repeated, bullishly. 'I don't want to leave the wine now we've paid for it. You head off though. Head off and see Harry. Your boyfriend. Your boyfriend Harry.' She was aware she was talking in circles and had not been in any way, shape or form cool with the news that had been visited on her tonight, but for now the Pinot Grigio was a buffer between her and caring too much about it.

Nora just laughed, and leaned forward to hug her oldest friend; Bea swayed awkwardly to stay on the bar stool. 'I'll text you tomorrow, okay?'

Nora and Harry. Harry and Nora. It turned her world upside down and yet made so much sense at the same time. Instead of leaving once she'd seen off the wine, Bea ordered another bottle. Harry had been out telling Cole at the same time; she wondered if he had taken the news with a little more dignity. Either way, if there was one person who was going to feel anywhere near where she was tonight, it would

be him. She pulled out her phone: *So, what just happened??
Call me ASAP.*

Fifth glass of wine down and Bea reeled further and further.
Theirs used to be the names people said in one breath – Bea-n-
Nora. And now it would be Harry-n-Nora. It didn't roll off the
tongue in the same way; instead it squatted there, threatening
to choke her. She poured the sixth glass of wine – way, way past
the little white line that made it a socially acceptable amount.
She thought about calling her mother to talk; she thought about
how nice it would be to have the sort of mother you could just
call up because you needed to talk. Nora and the Dervans were
the closet thing Bea had to family. They were Harry's family
now – Harry's *in-laws*. Bea topped up the wine again, again.

'Save some for me.' Bea blinked in confusion; Cole was
there, pulling out the barstool next to hers and making eye
contact with the guy behind the bar and mouthing that he
needed another glass. Had she text him?

'Where did you come from?' She pulled out her phone and
saw that at some point during her drunken introspection
she'd missed three calls from Cole.

'Nora told me where you were,' he explained, helping
himself to wine. He was drunk as well – Bea could tell from
the looseness in his frame, the generous, sloppy way in which
he poured the drink. 'So. Quite the headfuck, huh?'

Bea laughed. 'Quite,' she agreed.

'I mean, it's great,' Cole backtracked, after a long pause for
drinking. 'Really great. But still. You know? Wow.' At least Bea
wasn't the only one being a little bit crazy about it all.

'I can't believe it. Harry and Nora.' *Harry-n-Nora.*

'You know though, Sarah said something about Harry and Nora being cute together when she first met them,' Cole mused, referring to his new girlfriend of the last few months. Well, bully for freaking Psychic Sarah.

'Well, it came as a shock to me. My five year old self is whirling.'

'Well, as long as they don't go through a horrible break up. Christ, can you imagine how awkward that would be?'

Bea topped her drink up while she absorbed that new thought – when had they ordered another bottle? – that was something that hadn't occurred to her.

'Everything is changing,' she whined. 'Everything is weird! Cole!'

'Ahh, BeeBee. You've still got me.' Cole rubbed her bare arm affectionately. He knew her of old and he knew all her little idiosyncrasies, her shameful separation anxiety. She felt Cole's hand, steady and familiar on hers. When he took it back she felt alone. The last of the third bottle was shared out between their glasses. The last orders bell rang out into the dimness of the bar. The world dipped and swayed and Bea drifted along the threshold of insensibility, the wine now warm and tasteless, but still going down. *Harry-n-Nora*. She loved them; and now they loved each other, apparently.

'Have you got any wine in?' Cole asked; Bea's flat was a ten minute stagger away. 'Night cap? We're so fucked we might as well keep going!' he laughed.

'There'll be something,' Bea assured him; if not, she'd nick something from her flatmate Kirsty and replace it before she could notice. She absolutely, positively did not want Cole to go home and leave her to sober up, alone and thrown.

The walk didn't take the edge off their intoxication; if anything the fresh air had made her head spin even more. She'd taken off her heels and they dangled from their sling back strap from one hand while she fumbled drunkenly in her handbag for her keys with the other. The doorway where they waited was completely shadowed, the nearby overgrown hedging blocking out any street lights; beyond, night buses rumbled past. And then suddenly Cole pressed up against her, fitting around her curve, sliding his palms over the angle of her hips. His heart beat against her spine, she felt her pulse beat in answer. She half-turned back, wondering what the question was.

Cole pushed two fingers under her chin to tilt her face closer to his and kissed her. It was messy – he was drunk, and their bodies were at an odd slant to one another – but it felt right, right, right. This is what Harry-n-Nora had found; they'd fallen in love with a best friend. And, oh, Bea wanted it too.

Cole said something against her mouth; she felt the shape of it on her lips. It could have been her name. It could have been anything. They broke apart; Cole was breathing heavily. Bea bent shakily to pick up her handbag from where she'd dropped it at her feet to wrap her arms around her best friend. She gently probed at her heart, the way you'd agitate a tooth that's been aching, expecting something: regret, shame. She felt nothing; Cole said nothing.

She found her keys. Cole reached for her again; they fell through the door.

# Chapter 21

Cleo tapped her thumb and her forefinger together, giving the fetching impression that she was doing an impersonation of a crab. She winced at the flare of pain, immediate and sharp along the underside of her arm.

'I think its Repetitive Strain Injury,' she moaned at her colleague, Gray, who grinned into his mug of coffee.

'Wait, isn't that what teenaged boys get once they discover internet porn?' he smirked. 'Busy weekend, love?'

'You're not far off the mark, with "teenaged",' Cleo admitted, smiling as Gray spluttered on his drink. 'I've been helping to hole-punch heart shapes out of old *Smash Hits!* magazines from the nineties.'

'Right. Okay . . . Well, everyone's gotta have a hobby I suppose!'

'It's for the wedding,' Cleo clarified, laughing. 'It's quite sweet really. It's going to be used as the confetti.'

'Because it's not matrimony unless you have little heart shaped pictures of East 17 and Billie Piper thrown over the bride and groom?'

'Exactly.' Cleo helped herself to a second chocolate chip

cookie from the packet that Gray had produced when they first sat down. (She'd be good closer to the big day . . .)

'Okay, you know you really do need to explain . . .' Gray prompted.

Cleo swallowed her mouthful of cookie. 'Well, you see, when she was a kid, Nora LOVED *Smash Hits!* magazine . . .'

'Who didn't?' Gray allowed.

'But her mum was quite strict and didn't like her being in to all that.'

'All that?' Gray echoed, amused. 'What, pop music?'

'Apparently. So, anyway, Nora used to scrimp and save up her lunch money so she could buy it every fortnight. But she couldn't bring it home, or her mum would find it, so she gave it to her friend and he kept all of her issues for her. For years. That friend being Harry.'

'Ah.' Understanding dawned on Gray's face.

'And, years later – when they fell in love and moved in together and blah, blah, happy ever after – he turns up with three huge cardboard boxes stuffed full of old issues of *Smash Hits!* And they've been a right ballache to store, but they didn't just want to throw them away . . . so this seemed like a really good idea.'

'I'm not sure your wrist agrees.' Gray said, taking that wrist in his hand, almost like a doctor checking for a pulse, the broad pad of his thumb pressing gently against those fragile, birdlike bones, against the swell of her blood. Cleo scrambled back aboard her train of thought, plucking her hand back from his and using it to pick up her mug of cooling coffee.

'Well, you know how it is,' she shrugged. 'Bridesmaids are the dogsbodies of every big wedding!'

'Well, to be honest, I've never really been to a big wedding,' Gray shrugged, moving his own hands back to his drink, an easy mirroring of Cleo's own movements. 'Maybe a few family ones, but all my mates who've gotten hitched have done it pretty small-scale, registry offices and pubs, you know? Certainly no custom confetti hole-punched by the fair hands of beautiful maidens.' Cleo ignored the easy flirt, ignored the traitorous heartbeat shouting in her chest, pinched it down, right down. (She did not, could not and would not fancy this man, period. It was just a question of discipline.)

'What time are you getting there on Saturday?' she asked lightly, focusing on how Gray's fingertips were paler where he held his mug.

'I . . . I'm not sure if I'm going to be able to make it, actually,' Gray answered after a moment's pause. 'I was going to see if I could, er, move some things around, because it was really nice of your friend Claire to invite me, but, yeah.'

'Oh,' Cleo replied, tonelessly, her mind slow to decide how she wanted to react to this news. She'd been part mortified, part thrilled when Claire had informed them all that she'd invited Gray along to her 30th birthday dinner.

'Well, why not?' Claire had demanded, when the news had been met with an awkward silence. 'He got along really well with people at the engagement party, and at your birthday Cleo.'

'He got on really well with *you*, you mean,' Nora had teased gamely, but she'd still shot a worried glance over at Cleo. Nora was still utterly persuaded that Cleo and Gray were meant to be. (She'd even developed a celebrity-style nickname for their rhetorical relationship, which – unfortunately – was the rather unromantic 'Clay'.) The more Cleo railed against it, the more adamant Nora became.

'Well, if you've got something else on, I'm sure Claire will understand.' It felt like Gray was waiting for her to ask what his other plans were, but Cleo refused. (Because she didn't care. Honest.) 'But, you know, maybe you can just come for the dinner part, or meet us for drinks later in the night?' Cleo found herself saying. Gray regarded her, his expression smudgy, unreadable.

'Yeah, maybe,' he allowed, finally, with a half-smile. 'I'll drop you a text, yeah?'

'Yeah, sure. Or, you know, Claire.'

'Sure.' Gray unfolded slowly to his feet, gathering up the packet of cookies and folding over the packaging to keep them fresh for the next break. 'Guess I'm on washing up duty. Considering your wrist injury and all.' And with that he collected up their mugs and headed to the grotty old staff room sink, leaving Cleo with a full five minutes left of their morning break and her discipline bruised, but mercifully intact.

# Chapter 22

*I went away for my cousin's hen weekend – I didn't know anyone but the bride, and as the other hens were quite cliquey and serious it was a fair bit awkward when we arrived to do our life drawing class. It was even more awkward when the male model got a huge boner half an hour in. . .*

Lucy, Peterborough

'So I wanted to show you first,' Claire chirped. 'Just to check, you know; get the 'bridesmaid seal of approval and all that'. Claire was getting used to the idea of not being a bridesmaid, Bea thought, but there was still just the barest nip of real bitterness in her tone. 'But I think Nora's really gonna love these!'

To Bea, an invitation to Nora's hen do was probably going to be in the form of an email and/or text, once Nora had provided the finalised list of lucky gals. When she'd mentioned this to Claire last week however the girl had almost choked on her gin-and-slim and begged to take over the sourcing of 'proper' invitations. Already a little overwhelmed at the thought of marshalling twelve women into booking travel, accommodation and activities, Bea had readily handed over the invitation reins.

Now she was sincerely regretting it.

After a full minute's silence, she realised she'd better say *something*.

'Wow,' she just about managed.

'Great, aren't they?' beamed Claire. 'Do you want me to explain a little?'

Phew. 'Yes please!'

The invitations were much more of a . . . 'pamphlet' . . . than Bea had anticipated. The front cover was largely taken up by a close-up selfie of Nora, snagged from her Facebook page no doubt. Her mouth had been partially obscured by a bright pink lipstick print. Letters in a matching pink floating above her head proclaimed Nora to be **KISSING THE SINGLE LIFE GOODBYE!!!**

'That's actually my lip print!' Claire trilled. 'I did it on the back of the receipt at the copy place and got them to digitise it; it's amazing what they can do with computers these days, isn't it?'

'No kidding?' Bea flipped over to the inserts with a slight frisson of trepidation. Claire's skill at Facebook stalking was no longer in any doubt – each of the twelve hens were represented by a square-framed photograph snagged from their social media and washed over with a liberally applied pink filter. Nora was first and most prominent, as was natural, followed by Bea, Cleo, Claire, Daisy and Sarah (Bea decided not to comment on the fact that Claire had interjected herself in the centre of the row of bridesmaids). Then came Alannah and Aoife, Nora's twin younger sisters (or maybe it was Aoife then Alannah . . . ?) and four other friends made up the chosen dozen. **ONE LAST FLING BEFORE THE RING!!!** shouted the bright pink letters on this page. (Bea hated that. What, was Nora supposed to stop having fun once she became Mrs Clarke? Grr.)

At least Claire hadn't been able to do much damage with the main page; Bea had been very clear with her instructions that the information was just to be copied and pasted, and not embellished upon in any way, shape or form. Claire had still managed to jazz it up though, by using a silhouette shot of what appeared to be a gigantic woman pole-dancing up against the Eiffel Tower as the page's background and entitling the page **OOH LA LA!!!** (Did this woman ever use less than three exclamation marks for anything? Bea couldn't be sure.)

Bea and Daisy's carefully drafted information was intact, however offensively-fonted, so Bea guessed she had to be grateful for small mercies. The hens were duly instructed to assemble at St Pancras International for a weekend in gay Paris, where Bea had booked them accommodation on a pair of twin houseboats on the Seine, as close to the Eiffel Tower as possible. The Saturday night's requisite fancy dress was 90s-themed (naturally), and the four bridesmaids 'Backstreet Bea', 'Cleo-patra, Coming Atcha', 'Princess Daisy from Super Mario' and 'Clueless Cher-ah Horowitz' hoped that everyone would join them in heartily embracing it. At least Claire hadn't added herself to the bridesmaid sign-off. . .

The final page had a breakdown of upfront costs, with Bea's

banking details provided in a pink cloud shape for ease of reference and instructions to send RSVPs or questions to norasgettinghitched@geemail.com.

'Oh, the password for that email account is nora 1986,' Claire added, off-hand, before returning to chattering on about the many artistic decisions that had been taken in the invitations' journey. Bea flipped through the little booklet again. Okay, so it was *totally not Nora* and generally pretty cringe, but they definitely had their own certain charm, and Nora would probably be amused rather than horrified, which was the main thing.

'So, am I good to post them out?' Claire queried.

'Yeah sure, not long to go now and I need some money in ASAP as I've already paid off all the deposits,' Bea confirmed, wincing a little at the thought of her deflated bank balance.

'Great!' Claire fished under the table and pulled out a canvas tote shopper bag emblazoned with the logo of the estate agency where she worked; it was already stuffed with stamped and neatly-addressed envelopes. 'I'll post these now then!'

# Chapter 23

London was full of babies. Miniature chaps in chino shorts, pint-size princesses in sundresses: their fat little legs poking out, kicking merrily. Pregnant women in maxi dresses glided past her on the pavements, red-faced but serene, the globes of their fruitful bellies proudly leading the way. Every direction Sarah looked in, there they were.

The summer had burst like an over-ripe fruit and the days were starting to cool as they headed toward autumn; ironically, it was harvest time. Two more women had announced their pregnancies in the office, moaning light-heartedly about their 'bad luck' in having 'inconvenient' due dates around the Christmas holidays. Cole's younger sister and her boyfriend of only six months' standing had just yesterday afternoon publicised their own unexpected happy news by way of a grainy scan picture texted around the family before being uploaded straight to Facebook ('Oh, it was a bit of a shock! I was on the pill! But we're soooo happy!'). When she'd opened that text Sarah had felt like she'd just been eviscerated with her mobile phone. Numbly she allowed Cole to fold her against his chest, searching for comfort, squeezing her eyes shut, pressing down against the spiked ball of pain lodged somewhere deep below her collarbones.

'Well,' Cole had said, after a minute's silence, 'I guess at least this proves that my family is super fertile.'

Last night, Sarah had run the hottest bath she could stand, a favourite indulgence she'd long been avoiding since reading on the internet somewhere that the heat was detrimental to good ovum quality, and poured herself five generous fingers of whatever expensive whiskey Cole kept in his antique decanter. While she was waiting for the bath to fill she tidied the bathroom. The hideously complicated Clearblue Digital Ovulation Monitor she'd spent the better part of £200 on was quietly packed back into its box and away into the drawer unit under the sink. The His-and-Hers pre-natal vitamins that she kept next to their toothbrushes – so that they never forgot to take them of a morning – followed suit. The small plastic cup next to the toilet that she had dipped what felt now like a million home pregnancy tests into over the past two years she tossed into the bin.

Two years.

Raina, her heavily pregnant colleague, had inadvertently highlighted the length of time Sarah's womb had remained obstinately barren just that morning.

'Your wedding anniversary is coming up, isn't it?' she'd asked, after she'd finished complaining about how hard it was to be pregnant in the warm weather, and affirming just how much she was looking forward to September (and her maternity leave) arriving. 'How many years now; is it two?'

'Yes, two,' Sarah had confirmed politely, firmly persisting

in typing out her email, in the hope that Raina would take the hint and not continue to try to engage her in conversation.

'Time to start thinking about kiddies soon, surely!' Raina had chirped, leaning back in her desk chair and placing a protective palm atop her bump, as if her sentence somehow needed further illustration. 'Most married couples get cracking after the first year!'

Sarah recalled how she'd woken up that morning and not stuck a thermometer straight up between her legs to chart her basal body temperature for the first time in over a year. She'd expected to feel freed. Instead she'd just felt horribly, horribly empty.

'We're not quite settled enough yet,' she told Raina tonelessly; the standard line. 'We've got a lot of stuff going on.'

'Hmm, well, perhaps you need to re-evaluate your priorities,' Raina sniffed. 'You know fertility begins seriously declining after thirty. In fact, you will have already lost up to 90% of the eggs that you were born with!'

'I'm sure I'll be just fine,' Sarah had snapped, standing abruptly and walking off towards the tea point, mug in hand – not wanting the drink, just wanting to get away from smug Raina and her effective fucking ovaries.

Sarah wandered through the aisles of the library. Was there going to be a set of shelves somewhere in this building labelled Infertility? Surely not. Health, then. Sarah ran her forefinger lightly over the laminated spines of the books as she searched for what she needed, past countless books about what to expect when you're expecting (many of which – shamefully, painfully – she had pre-emptively already read).

She refused to make eye contact with the library assistant who stamped the checkout card of 'Get A Life: A Comprehensive Guide to IVF and Assisted Conception'.

\* \* \*

Daisy and Darren looked at one another. There wasn't much more to say.

Months and months of being in each other's lives, each other's flats, each other's bodies and here they were: an awkward silence and a Tesco carrier bag partially filled with odds-and-sods at Darren's feet. Perhaps the fact that their relationship had boiled down to a toothbrush, a rusted-up razor, a couple of pairs of underwear and some borrowed DVDs was a sign that Daisy was making the right decision.

Darren cleared his throat. 'So, shall I bring over your stuff from my flat sometime next week then?'

'I don't think I've got much in your flat Darren, so don't worry about it,' Daisy answered carefully. She, of course, had known this break-up was coming so she'd been able to subtly clear out her belongings over her past few visits.

'You've got shampoo and stuff in my shower,' Darren corrected her, mulishly.

'It's fine, you can toss it all.' That Bumble and Bumble shampoo and conditioner may be expensive, and still half-full, but not having to have another awkward meeting with Darren would be worth the sacrifice.

She'd given the usual spiel: it's not you, it's me, and all that. And it was actually pretty true. There was nothing particularly wrong with Darren, for all his oddities and irritating habits; Cleo was right – if Daisy loved him, really loved him, they'd be charming, not irksome. But there was no casual way of informing the man you were dumping that he was being chucked because you still dreamed of one day having someone who made your whole body feel like it was smiling.

'Okay then.' Despite his words, Darren looked in no rush to leave. He started towards Daisy, holding his hand forward almost as if he was going to touch her, but thought better of it at the last minute. 'I'd like us to stay friends, Daisy, if that's okay?'

'Sure thing,' Daisy lied. She'd give it a few months and then she'd subtly delete him from her Facebook friends' list. The key was to add him to a limited list for a little while before-hand, so he got used to not really seeing her updates on his feed. Sadly she'd had to do this many times before . . . 'But, in the circumstances, I don't really think it's appropriate for you to come to Nora and Harry's wedding in December. You understand.'

Darren's face crumpled a little further, but he rallied like a man: Daisy appreciated that about him. 'Sure. I understand. Yeah.'

'Thanks.'

'Okay then,' Darren said again, this time stopping to pick up his sad little plastic bag of lifely bric-a-brac. 'I'll see you around then, Daise, yeah?'

'See you around Darren,' Daisy agreed quietly, allowing herself to feel one last pang for one more aborted relationship. She remembered how flushed with anticipation she'd been before their first few dates, how once she'd not been able to get enough of him, how full of hope she'd been that this time it was going to be real and lasting, a grown-up love.

Later that night, Daisy popped her toothbrush into its holder, watching it spin and rattle on its end for a moment before falling still, alone in the ceramic pot once again.

# Chapter 24

A few months earlier, Bea had let herself slip past thirty with absolute minimal fuss. After all, the only real difference between that birthday and the ones either side of it was that her mother Hannah had felt obligated to actually send her a card (the so-called 'milestones' tended to have that effect on her). The actual day had been a Tuesday, and Bea had gone to Nora and Harry's for a home-cooked dinner, Eli making up the four. They had her favourite meal (spaghetti carbonara) and played her favourite board game (Articulate) and sank several bottles of her favourite wine. It had been low-key and intimate, like all of Bea's most favourite things.

Meanwhile, Claire was now turning 31, and it was more of an operation than Nora's bloody hen do. She'd booked out an area in one of the swankiest bars in Shoreditch, and was demanding all ladies in attendance do so sporting an 'LBD' (Bea assumed this meant Little Black Dress, and not the dementia disease her grandmother had had when she was younger). Bea – far more at home in a pair of skinny jeans and killer, colourful heels – had stood in generalised agonies in front of her fruitless wardrobe until she'd settled on the black jersey dress with the lace panel across the neck that she usually wore to funerals, obstinately teaming it with a pair of heels in watermelon-pink.

She loved Claire, she did, but these events were becoming so much of a faff. They'd have a booth reserved, yeah, but it would be way too small for everyone to sit down, and people would end up eating with plates balanced precariously on their knees, or slipping off the corners of the table. The drinks would cost about £14 each, and consist mainly of crushed ice and over-large sprigs of mint. The music would be obnoxious and booming and blare over any attempts at conversation. Meanwhile, the twenty-two year olds in eye-wateringly bodycon dresses would get served first at the bar and block the access to the sinks in the Ladies while they took endless mirror selfies. Bea glanced longingly at her bed before slipping her tired feet into their heels and trip-tropping her way along the corridor to the kitchen.

Kirsty, her flat-mate of the last few years, was wearing a Marvel Avengers tee, pyjama shorts and odd socks and was midway through making a cup of tea. Bea tried to control her jealousy.

'Wit-woo!' Kirsty called admiringly, as she turned her back to the kettle to better take in her dolled-up friend. 'You look lush! Super sophisticated. And I love the shoes.'

'Cheers!' Bea did an exaggerated spin, like she had reached the end of a catwalk. 'It's Claire's birthday and you know what she's like about people dressing up.'

'Oh yeah.' Kirsty rolled her eyes. In many ways she'd been the perfect flat-mate for Bea over the years because, unlike everyone else Bea seemed to meet, she had never been subsumed into the larger social group. She could bitch and moan and gossip about all of her besties with Kirsty without fear of it ever getting back to them. 'Where is it this year?' Kirsty asked.

'Some new place out east,' Bea answered dismissively. 'I can't remember the name. It's all in lower-case though, and you have to give a password to get in. The password is "Calloo Callay". They serve "deconstructed cocktails" . . .'

'Bloody hell!' Kirsty laughed, stirring sweetener into her tea. 'I hope you've activated your overdraft.'

'I know,' Bea groaned. 'Well, Eli is coming here first and we're going to have a quick pre-drink sharpener so we don't have to spend quite so much there.'

'And Eli isn't the one who you . . .?' Kirsty trailed off meaningfully. Bea sighed.

'No.' Kirsty did this on purpose just to be annoying; as much as Bea rued the night she'd slept with Cole, she might rue the fact that Kirsty had caught them together the next morning even more.

'Ah, Eli's the friend one,' Kirsty clarified, knowingly.

'They're both "friend ones",' Bea shot back, pulling her phone from her beaded clutch bag to check the time. 'Don't let me keep you from your Netflix commitments.'

'Message received, loud and clear!' Kirsty laughed, returning the milk to the refrigerator. 'I'll make myself scarce. Enjoy your poncey bar,' she called over her shoulder as she made her way to her bedroom and waiting laptop. The bell for the flat buzzed and Kirsty, much closer to the front door, pulled

Erin Lawless

it open before Bea could even make a move towards it.

'Hi!' she greeted Eli brightly, pushing the door wide in invitation. 'Eli, right?'

'Yeah. Hi Kirsty,' Eli answered politely, fidgeting with the bottle of wine he was holding by its neck.

'Sorry, I always get you guys mixed up,' Kirsty smirked; Bea shot her a murderous look. 'I'll get out of your hair. Have a good night, guys!'

'One of Londis' finest vintages, madam,' Eli joked, moving down the corridor to join Bea in the kitchen. 'You look nice.'

Bea rolled her eyes. 'Don't you mean I scrub up well?' She snatched the bottle of wine from her friend. 'You old charmer.'

Eli plucked it back. 'Just take the compliment will you. And get some glasses. We've got to get going soon.' Bea obediently fetched down two wine glasses while Eli opened the screw-top on the cheap bottle of plonk.

'So, how's hen prep going?' He asked conversationally as Bea poured generously.

'There is other stuff going on in my life you know!' Bea snapped, as she slotted the wine into the shelf on the fridge door. 'It's not all about the bloody Dervan-Clarke wedding.'

'Sorry.' Eli looked genuinely abashed. 'Er. How's work?'

'I don't want to talk about work.' Bea kicked off her heels and sank into one of the little dining table chairs, knowing as she did so that she was only making it worse for herself when the time came to put the shoes back on.

Eli laughed. 'Okay.' He joined her at the table. 'Well, can we talk about my work?'

'Sure. Shoot.'

'Well, I got called into a meeting with my boss yesterday.'

'Wait. Is this a story with a happy ending or a sad one?'

'Er, happy, I guess.'

'Good. Okay, go.'

'So, they chose my design to be used for the headquarters of that charity, do you remember . . . ?'

Bea sat up straighter. 'Oh, Eli.' She put her hand over his. 'Yes, I remember.' Eli had talked about nothing else for about a month, working hour after hour of pro bono overtime to finalise his architectural plans for an international children's charity. Bea's heart strained with pride. How had that skinny, curtain-fringed kid who endlessly doodled in the gridded margins of his maths exercise books grown up to be such a bloody spectacular man?

'Yeah.' The tips of Eli's ears and the plane of his cheeks were flushed an excited pink. 'My manager said I was really going places with the firm.'

'That's amazing! I wish we had something more exciting to be toasting with!' Bea laughed. 'But it's this or water. So, congratulations!'

'Thanks,' Eli beamed, clinking his wine glass gently against hers. 'Does this call for a Bea Hug?'

Bea laughed. 'Go on then.' She had always been infamously un-huggy, the opposite of Nora, but Eli had always insisted that made her hugs all the more special. She put her drink down and jumped to her feet. 'Come here then!' she grinned, holding out her arms. Eli hopped up and into them, pressing his face lightly against the hair she'd just gently tonged and spray-set. 'Big, huge, giant congratulations!'

'Thanks Beebee,' he murmured into the side of her neck, that old school nickname, just how Cole had done: against her breasts, into her mouth; Bea felt the pooling of lust and shook it off, feeling disgusted with herself. She peeled away from Eli, literally holding him at arm's length.

'Anyway, better drink up,' she nodded towards their abandoned wine on the table, their wine glasses set down so close the globes of the glass were kissing. 'We're going to be late.'

\* \* \*

Sarah fumbled with the uncooperative clasp of her necklace, willing it to slide into place already. Finally it did, and she centred the pendant on its chain in the middle of her collarbones. She smoothed her dress out over her hips. Black didn't really do anything for her: her dark hair and dark eyes popped more against strong colours. But the Birthday Girl had spoken, so Sarah had grabbed an inoffensive black skater-style dress from New Look over lunch the day before.

'You look nice,' Cole complimented from where he stood in the bedroom door, arms folded across his chest, head slightly cocked.

Sarah looked up at him from where she was fishing underneath her bed for her shoes. 'Not like I'm in mourning?'

Cole smirked. 'Maybe you look a little bit like a mourner. A sexy mourner.' He moved into the room, his big hands possessively stroking over her as she straightened up. 'Say, what time did we say we'd be at this thing anyway?'

'Eight.' Sarah moved away to sit on the end of the bed and slip on her black heels. 'So are you ready to go?'

'We can be a little late, can't we?' Cole murmured suggestively, sitting heavily on the end of the bed next to her, running those big hands over her again, pressing his face into the bare skin of her neck, his fingers plucking at the hem of that unfamiliar dress.

Sarah hopped to her feet. 'Not really, no.' She grabbed up her smaller 'going out' handbag from the armchair in the corner of their bedroom. 'Seriously, are you ready?'

Cole sighed. 'Baby, seriously, what's up with you? Are you okay?'

Sarah tossed a lip-gloss into her handbag with a little more feeling than was strictly necessary. 'I'm fine,' she intoned, not even bothering to put any real insistence into her voice. *Baby*. Cole had called her that since day one. She'd used to joke that it was because he couldn't remember her name, but secretly she'd quite liked it. Recently though, it had started to make her skin prickle, like he was mocking her: *baby, baby*.

'Are you sure?' Cole pressed, 'because you're not, you know, acting like yourself.'

'And you're the world authority on me being me, yeah?' Sarah shot, throwing a compact in to join the lip-gloss.

'Well. Yeah? Sar, I am your husband, you know!'

'I know.' And he was, he was. But he'd known her for only two and half years, after all – she'd had the black heels she was wearing for longer than that. And when he said she wasn't being herself he wasn't referring to the depression, or the weight loss; he meant that it wasn't like her to turn down sex.

For the last two years she hadn't been able to get enough. Even on cycle days she knew were non-fertile – well, you never knew, did you? In fact, in recent months, it was Cole who had cooled off their sex life – claiming he felt like a stud horse, a performing gigolo – frowning at his wife as she lay there post-coitally with her bum propped up on a tower of pillows, giving his sperm the downhill advantage.

'Is this because I said I wouldn't go to the doctors?'

Sarah gave a bitter little laugh, clipping the clasp of her handbag shut. 'Look, can we not do this right now? I have been trying and trying and trying to get you to talk about going to the fertility doctor. For *weeks*. But, right now, we have to go to your friend's bloody birthday party, so *please*. Are you ready to go?'

'I told you I'd go if all your tests came back fine,' Cole continued, as if he hadn't heard her. 'It just doesn't make any sense for both of us to faff around with it at the same time. So, you know, if your stuff turns up okay, then, yeah, maybe it's the swimmers – but we can do all those checks then, baby.'

Sarah rounded on him, her eyes flashing. 'Oh, you want to talk "faff"? Faff'. Well, okay. So, when I go in next week I will need to have a blood test. I will need to have an ultrasound. I'm going to have speculums and swabs and a stranger's bloody hand shoved up inside me. I will need to be tested for STDs. And then, after all that, they are going to flood my fallopian tubes with dye and watch what happens. And that's just *phase one*.

'Whereas, all you would need to do, is to wank into a plastic cup. It's not exactly the same thing, is it? No. Okay, so, can we please go?'

Cole stared at her from where he still sat at the end of the bed, stared at her like he wasn't entirely sure who this woman in the black dress ranting about wanking was. Sarah felt the indignity bite inside her chest and hated it, hated herself.

'Sure. I'll just get my wallet then,' Cole finally said, meekly, skirting around her as he left the room, like a man giving a wide berth to an unexploded bomb.

# Chapter 25

'I can't believe you had sex with him after you'd already decided you were going to break up with him!' Nora squealed. 'You heartless bitch!'

'Hey, it's only polite!' Daisy insisted. 'Plus it gives you a chance to really go out on a high, and all that. Nobody wants to be remembered as a crap shag, do they?'

'Please forgive her,' Nora laughed, leaning towards Gray as she spoke. 'She's more open than a Tesco Metro.'

Gray smiled winningly at her over his £17 Old Fashioned. 'No, it's cool, I'm learning a lot! So the next time I have really mindblowing sex, I'm going to be thinking: uh-oh, I'm about to get chucked!' Nora and Daisy giggled; Cleo busied herself with chomping down on an ice cube from her drink – Gray plus the words 'mindblowing sex' was doing funny things to her body temperature.

Across the other side of the booth Cole and Sarah were doing their best to ignore one another whilst sat next to each other and engaged in conversation with the same person. Cleo noted the half-drunk martini glass of cocktail in front of Sarah. She'd done this for almost as long as she'd known her

– tee-total for half of every month, drinking socially along with the rest of them for the rest of it. Cleo had always just taken it as a quirk, like yo-yo dieting. Now she recognised it for what it was, what it always had been: Sarah only drinking during her period, when she knew there was no way she could be pregnant. She guessed there'd be no little Baby Norris nine months from now, once again, and her heart gave a pang for her friend.

'I think they're fighting,' Eli said, having followed her gaze across to Cole and Sarah. 'When I was sat with them earlier, brrr, it was like the Arctic.'

Eli was a weirdly empathic guy. He'd picked up on Nora and Harry long before being told about it and he always knew when somebody was hurting. It was like the universe's most tasteless joke that he had spent most of his life head-over-heels for the most oblivious woman in the world.

Maybe it was because Cleo had originally been an outsider, but she'd noticed it right away. The way that Eli turned his face to Bea no matter where she was in the room, like she was always calling his name. The way that he was always fabricating reasons to touch her hand, to trap her in a hug. The way he paraded his unsuitable girlfriends in front of her like a misbehaving child playing up for the attention. They'd only ever discussed it obliquely, of course, so Cleo was still left wondering what Eli was waiting for; maybe he was going to end up waiting forever.

Bea sat the other side of the table, deep in conversation with the birthday girl, Claire; from the slightly strained look on the face of the former and the eager gesturing of the latter,

Cleo guessed it was about the upcoming hen do, once again. She didn't know why Bea had involved Claire so bloody much – it was meant to be a joint organisational effort between all four bridesmaids, which was already a little 'too many cooks' for comfort. . .

'Can I get you another drink?' Gray butted in to her internal musing, smiling expectantly, leaning close to be heard better over the thump of the music. 'Do you want to come up to the bar with me and pick something, maybe?' Cleo felt Nora and Daisy's eyes on her. Her own cocktail was mostly finished, and mainly melted ice at this point. And by god, did she want another drink.

'I'm fine,' she assured Gray, hurriedly. 'It looks like the birthday girl might need a top up though?' she pointed out, motioning towards Claire at the other end of the table. Gray hesitated for the smallest instant, before reasserting his smile.

'Okay. Let me know if you want something though.'

Not willing to face Nora's judgement, Cleo hurriedly turned her attention back in Eli's direction. He was looking at her like she was quite insane.

'What's that face for?' Cleo asked him, alarmed.

'Nothing. Well, to be honest . . . I know it's none of my business, but – I've just gotta ask – what the hell is the deal there?'

Cleo laughed despite herself. 'Deal? What deal?'

Eli gestured towards where Gray, having taken Claire's drink order, was making his way over to the bar. 'You know. With Fifty Shades.'

Cleo rolled her eyes but didn't bother protesting at the use of that stupid nickname. 'Eli, please. I get enough of this from the girls. There is no *deal*. He's a friend, is all. My mate from work.'

'Uh-huh.' Eli's eyes on her were calm and disbelieving. 'Because nobody falls in love with their friend, right?' he teased gently. (He could be talking about Nora and Harry, of course, but Cleo knew better.)

'He's dating half of London,' Cleo found herself confiding, the loud background music somehow acting as a cover, making her a little more daring.

'Meanwhile, you haven't been on a date since you met him, have you?' Eli pointed out, irritatingly on point and aware, as ever. 'So what? Who cares?'

'Well, why would he date a different girl every week if he wanted to date me?' The words left Cleo's lips, and left her cringing.

Eli's eyes flicked across the table to where Bea sat, looking uncharacteristically done up that night in a black lace dress, her normally straight hair tonged into soft waves. She threw her head back laughing at a joke Claire had made and Eli's jaw tensed; he looked away.

'Does he even know that he *could* date you?' he asked Cleo curtly. 'How can he, when you flash hot and cold on him like you do?'

'Excuse me? Hot and cold?' Cleo echoed, slightly horrified at the direction her night (and this conversation) was taking.

Eli gestured impatiently. 'One minute you're leaning on his shoulder, whispering in his ear, and you're looking at him like he's the only guy in the world. Then the next – you're turning down drinks; you're pushing him on your mates. I don't blame the guy for dating other women. You're not exactly giving him any reason to wait around on you.'

Cleo drew herself up, refusing to take the offense that was being so blatantly offered. 'Hey, that's unnecessary,' she hissed. 'Don't take what Bea's always done with you out on me.'

Eli's tension deflated all at once. He tilted his fair head back against the leather of the booth's seating, like he was praying for strength. He decided he'd find it in the JD and coke in front of him, which he grabbed up and finished off with two long swallows.

'Yeah. Sorry,' he said eventually, gruff and aching. 'Anyway. Let *me* get you that drink, at least.' And before Cleo could answer, he was manoeuvring his way through his seated friends and out towards the bar, nodding politely at a returning Gray as they crossed paths.

# Chapter 26

Sarah finished unfurling her mat and settled down, trying to centre herself, pushing the soles of her bare feet together and pulling them back into the lotus position. This was the second yoga class in a row that Daisy had missed, pleading illness; Sarah hadn't realised how used to the routine she had become, having those quick, quiet little catch ups of a morning. With the hen do of the year coming up at the weekend she was also looking forward to discussing logistics without bossy school marm Cleo or constantly sarcastic Bea stressing her out. She and Daisy often grabbed a drink and a chat at the gym's juice bar after the class; Daisy was pretty much her own boss at this point and Sarah – well, nobody really seemed to give a crap what time Sarah made it into work, if she was honest.

She'd started to do yoga classes over a year ago, back when her late night internet searches on ways to naturally boost female fertility had her convinced that all she needed to do was increase blood flow to her pelvis area with the Cobbler's Pose. That conviction had waned, but she found she was enjoying the new little stress-free pockets in her life and kept at it.

Some wise yogis insist that emotions are stored in the body: that bad childhood memories sleep on in our bones; the butterfly-feeling of complete happiness you have had, once or twice, sits stored in your cells, waiting to be tapped; that sadness and tension lay twinned in unused muscles, needing to be stretched and released. Sarah didn't know about any of that; all she knew is that once, a few months after starting the classes, she lay on her mat in the neutral position of Savasana and felt *whole* for the first time in a long while.

'Good morning, everybody,' greeted the class instructor, serenely picking her way through the mats spread out on the gym studio floor to the mirrors at the front, her own rolled up exercise mat over her shoulder like an adventurer's pack. 'Just before we get started, I just wanted to let you know that I am now fully qualified in Pregnancy Yoga! I'll be starting classes here on Thursday afternoons. Please do tell any of your friends who are expecting!'

Sarah pulled her feet a little further back, opening up her pelvis that tiny fraction more, pulling air deep into her lungs, feeling her chest expand, calm and controlled. A few weeks ago, hearing that might have floored her, clawed at her heart and left her gasping. But yesterday she had received her referral through to have a hysterisalpingogram – and her GP had riled up hope where Sarah was convinced no more existed, telling her all about the scores of mysterious infertile women who, as it turned out, just needed a good flushing out. All that was needed now was for Sarah to get her period and start a new cycle, so the HSG could be scheduled in.

As the gentle background music tinkled into life and the

class was urged to move into their first position, Sarah couldn't help but smile down at her yoga mat as she placed her forehead against it for the Balasana pose – the irony that she now desperately wanted her dreaded period to arrive was not beyond her. . .

# Chapter 27

*I was once forced to participate in a game at a hen do
where we had to carve penises out of cucumbers, using
only our teeth. The cucumbers were then judged and the
most realistic won a prize.*

Olivia, Warwick

Two and a half hours out of London St Pancras, twelve
women spilled out into Gare du Nord, already more than
a little merry on cans of gin and tonic from the bar carriage, the
late-morning autumn light soft but strong through the big
windows. The group drew wearied looks from passers-by, obvious
as they were with their pink matching tees and loud voices,
giggling and bouncing their way through the station, Cleo faffing
with the itinerary print out that told them which exit they needed.

The house boat idea had started off as a joke – it had
begun to come up in sidebars as automated advertising after
Bea had started searching accommodation in Paris. 'Jesus,
whose idea would it be to stay on a pokey boat?' Bea and
Nora had laughed. But after a few weeks they found they

couldn't quite picture anything else and so they'd made the booking.

The boats were virtually identical, moored head-to-toe parallel to the riverbank, one painted in British racing green and the other in a burgundy like Christmas port, both pleasingly shabby, with years' worth of water lines criss-crossing the hulls and little tangles of green garden taking up one half of each of the decks.Bea didn't know whether it was as standard or just for them, but each of the boats was strung with cheery Union Jack bunting, bottles of champagne sat waiting in fresh ice buckets and towers of cliché but delicious-looking croissants piled haphazardly onto cake plates.

'Ooh la la!' Nora squealed, grabbing the topmost pastry and throwing herself down on the galley-style seating in the living area. The green boat was home for the weekend for Nora, Claire and the four bridesmaids, the other six hens taking up residence on the burgundy one. Out through the portholes, couples walked hand-in-hand along the cream stone walls, friends sat drinking coffee underneath the periwinkle blue parasols of street cafés; it was just like a movie. 'Ohmigod, I'm so excited!'

'*Sacre bleu!*' Daisy laughed, joining her friend and tearing off a corner of her croissant for herself.

'Right, ladies, let's get sorted. *S'il vous plait.*' Cleo clapped her hands at them all, already in full teacher mode.

'Hey guys!' Claire was standing outside on the upper deck, in between the sun chairs, waving madly at the hens on the other boat.

'We can fit in a few hours of sightseeing before we need

to get back and dressed for dinner,' Cleo continued, ignoring her, reaching for one of the bottles of champagne and fiddling with the twist key.

'Oh, and my scavenger hunt!' Claire bounced down the wooden steps that led to and from deck-level. 'It starts from now, and you have until we get back to the station tomorrow night.' She fished down the side of her Ted Baker weekend holdall and passed a folder full of print outs across to Nora, who brushed croissant flakes from her fingers and took it.

'Oh, it's like Bachelorette Bingo!' Daisy realised, brightly, cocking her head so she could read some of the dares. 'Okay, so she's got to get a kiss from someone called Harry – Claire, hun, that might be a little difficult in France? Selfie with another bride-to-be, mmhmm.'

Nora turned over one of the print outs to keep reading on the reverse side, looking a little pained. 'Wow, there's a lot here, Claire.'

'I know,' Claire beamed.

'I need to get a condom from a stranger's wallet?' Nora read, slightly alarmed. 'How would I even go about that?'

'You ask?' Bea suggested, lining up plastic champagne flutes for Cleo to fill.

'I ask?' Nora echoed with a scoff of disbelief. 'What the hell is French for 'condom' anyway?'

'Le sac?' Cleo giggled.

'GCSE-level French, once again proving useless in actual life,' Bea teased. 'I can't believe Madame Moreau didn't adequately prepare us for talking about contraceptive sheaths with strangers!'

'And check out the bonus round,' Claire urged, gesturing to the bottom of the back page.

'The Spice Boys Challenge,' Nora read aloud. 'I have to take a picture with five different guys – one sporty, one baby, one scary, one ginger and one posh. Oh my god!' she laughed. 'Cleo, you'd better pass me that champagne.'

* * *

The hens, having dumped their bags and changed out of their travel clothes, all congregated, crowded, in the green boat, the hems of their sundresses sticking to their sweaty legs, hair going limp and flat under the thematically-appropriate pink berets that everyone was being forced to wear.

'Okay!' Cleo called for order, pulling at her beret so that it was fashionably off-centre with one hand while she used the other to hold her drink aloft. 'So, here we are, Nora's HEN DO!' The other eleven girls echoed back a cheer. Sarah snapped a picture of Cleo with her phone, and Cleo subconsciously fiddled with her beret again. 'So before we get going and try and do most of Paris' tourist sights in – ooh, six hours! – we're going to go over some ground rules.' She laughed at the resounding chorus of groans.

'So, rule number one, the Golden Rule if you will: no texting boys. *Particularly* no texting boys who are currently on the stag do.'

'Even if they are your husband,' Bea said pointedly, looking at Sarah. Harry and his lads were currently stagging it up in Barcelona. Nora had been emphatic that she didn't want to know a single thing about what was going on – as long as he came back with two eyebrows and zero tattoos, she'd be fine.

'Rule number two. No pictures on Facebook without the *express permission* of *everyone* in it!'

This was a firm but fair rule. Some of the girls had gone to the hen do of a friend the year before, where selfies were being uploaded hard and fast to social media throughout the night. Unfortunately there had been a couple of shots where one of the bridesmaids was pulling a bouncer in the background. (She'd been married. She wasn't any more . . .)

'And finally, rule number three: make sure Nora always has a drink in her hand!' Cleo shouted. 'To Nora!'

'TO NORA!' the hens echoed en masse, glass flutes tinkling together as they cheersed.

Nora jumped to her feet and hugged her hens at random, eager and excited, looking as sweet as ice-cream in a pale mint sun dress with cream sandals and – of course – the requisite pink sash diagonally across her torso proclaiming her to be the BRIDE-2-B!

The girls all spilled out into Les Berges, craning their necks and shading their eyes to appreciate the iconic Tower, where it was just visible as the river started to bend, Cleo already consulting the print outs of Google Maps she'd prepared. They made a beeline to the Pont des Arts, the love lock bridge. Nora had always found that sort of thing stupidly romantic, and Bea knew that she and Harry had taken their first holiday alone in Florence, where they'd duly scrawled their names on a padlock, tossing the key down into the Arno River, locking themselves into love eternally, or some such bollocks.

The bridge wasn't as romantic as Bea had anticipated. Most of it had been restored with glass panelling, rather than the traditional metal railings. The council had obviously just done a mass removal of the padlocks; the railings were patchy. They had to – the weight of all that scrap metal was buckling the old pedestrian bridge. But the lovers of Paris didn't care. People leant out over the Seine, over the new glass panels, to reach the metal fittings behind them – clipping padlocks on to other padlocks if there was no other space. Even now, a street peddler was calling to them – his French even more broken than theirs – trying to hawk his cheap looking locks for ten euros each.

'Wait,' Cleo instructed, seeing that Nora was tempted, digging in her handbag and presenting her friend with a hefty padlock, already thoughtfully Sharpie'd with Nora and Harry's names. Nora, laughing, posed for a photo as she bent to close the shackle of the padlock, finding a tiny bit of bare space on one of the tall cast-iron streetlights: another thoughtless tourist in love in the City of Love. Bea thought about the weight of Nora's love; she wondered how the Earth didn't just dip out of orbit with the heaviness of all the people and their padlocks of love on it.

They raced through the Louvre – Cleo cheerfully informing them that if they were to only spend three seconds gazing at each object it would take them three whole months to get through it. The weekend crowds were thick and intimidating, but they paused a while in order to get as close to the barriers around the *Mona Lisa* as possible, the famous portrait so much smaller and unassuming in real life than they'd expected that they might have missed it altogether if it wasn't for the queue of tourists massed in front of it. They giggled and dithered, too embarrassed to take a blatant selfie with said Lisa, until finally – rolling her eyes at everyone's Britishness – Daisy did the honours.

Back outside in the fug of the autumnal city, there was a brief pause for group photographs in front of the iconic Pyramide du Louvre, taken by a very obliging Frenchman, who in turn seemed quite taken with the be-sashed Nora.

'It's her hen party,' Cleo attempted to communicate. 'Er. Le fête de poule?' she tried, flapping her arms at the elbow in a reasonable, yet inadvisable impression of a chicken. She wasn't sure if it was that, or her clearly appalling French that left the man crying with laughter.

'Do you think he's ginger enough to be one of my Spice Boys?' Nora tried.

'No way!' one of her sisters had protested.

'He's strawberry-blonde, at the very least!' Nora had insisted. 'Bridesmaids' adjudication?' she requested.

'Denied!' declared Claire, not seeming remotely bothered that she wasn't technically a bridesmaid.

They didn't have time for another museum and its queues, but they made sure to wander back towards the Seine and past the Musee d'Orsay, where they found another very obliging Frenchman to take photographs of the group posting alongside the sculptures representing the continents, two girls to each (Daisy insisting on and receiving rights to the Americas statue, naturally). Happily for Nora, this time the bridesmaids' adjudication found this Frenchman to be appropriately sporty (well, he was wearing Nike shorts anyway) and allowed Nora to take a photograph with him as one-fifth of her Spice Boys challenge.

Next was a refuelling stop in a Montmarte patisserie, where they drank deeply from bowls of hot coffee and lined their stomachs for later by sharing huge loaves of brioche with dishes of dark yellow butter, honey and jams in every colour, having to sit leisurely chatting for almost an hour afterwards, purely to recover from the food coma they'd put themselves in to. Their friend Bec brought her beautician skills to the fore and gave each of the eleven hens a 'tricolore' manicure while they rested.

'Who was it that said 'Paris is always a good idea'?' Nora laughed happily, as she purchased a box of pastel macaroons on her way out of the patisserie. 'Because they knew what they were talking about!'

They dragged their carb-heavy bodies up to the dome of the Sacré Cœur Basilica, the highest point in all Paris, where even the point of the Eiffel Tower hung far below them, looking like a toy. Then, finally, the afternoon already old, they got the metro back across the city to the Avenue des Champs Élysées and the L'Arc de Triomphe.

They sat on the side of one of the fountains in the Place de la Concorde to rest their aching feet, eavesdropping on an English-language tour group that had helpfully stopped near them, soaking up some of the square's tumultuous revolutionary history: the site of the guillotine and where notables like Queen Marie Antoinette herself had lost her head.

'Let them eat cake,' Nora joked, offering her box of maca-

roons around amongst her hens. Cleo just about bit back the
know-it-all urge to tell her friend that that was a complete
myth; History teacher Gray had insisted on giving her a run
through of important dates, facts and figures ever since finding
out she was off to France's belle capital. Cleo slipped her phone
from her bag – Gray wasn't at the stag do, of course, so this
wasn't strictly breaking her own rules.

*Been here for five hours*, she complained, *and we've already
had the let them eat cake joke. . .*

*Poor old Marie A.*, Gray shot back almost immediately, with
an eye-rolling emoji for good measure. *It must be so frustrating
to be remembered for that shit!*

*We're just in the square where she died, too*, Cleo replied.
*Her ghost is clearly here, and pissed off.*

*I'd like to think her ghost is at the Palace at Versaille*, Gray
countered. That was another thing Cleo loved about him – he
was thoughtful and considerate of even the most stupid topics
of conversation. *Or at least at the Petit Trianon? I don't suppose
you're going to get enough free time before evening hen shenanigans to jump on a train to Versailles and go and find out??*

*Ha, unlikely*, Cleo told him (but getting a little thrill at the
thought that he believed her a woman capable of *shenanigans*).
*At this rate we're going to have about ten minutes to change
before the dinner booking. Have I mentioned how we are twelve
girls with only two bathrooms?? I would have loved to have
seen Versailles though. Next time!*

*You would totally love it there*, Gray agreed. *I've been twice
– it's one of my favourite places in the world. When you go back,
please take me!!*

Cleo dropped her phone back into the side pocket of her bag like it had burnt her hand. The jerk of the movement caught Bea's attention; she frowned.

'Not texting anyone you shouldn't be, are you?' she asked Cleo airily. Cleo just sent her a mute but withering look in response. There was literally no way that Bea would make it to the end of the day without texting Eli – she doubted there had been a day since mobile phones were bloody invented that Eli and Bea hadn't text one another – and texting groomsman Eli *most definitely* violated Rule One.

When all the feet were rested, and all the macaroons finished off, the gaggle of hens finally started to make their way back to the river and the boats, walking between the legs of the Eiffel Tower, craning their necks again to fully appreciate the engineering – and the *height* – of the venerable iron lady. Actually climbing up there was due to be their Sunday morning activity – they'd have a fair bit of the day before the evening Eurostar home. And climbing was exactly what they were set to do – not having realised until it was too late that you needed to pre-book tickets for the lifts between the levels. Cleo had looked up how many steps they were talking about – 1,665 from the bottom to the top – and had decided to keep that particular piece of Parisian trivia to herself. She hoped the hangovers wouldn't prove too debilitating when the time came. . .

# Chapter 28

*A friend of mine went to an amazing hen party where she proceeded to get very drunk. She needed a cigarette, so she went outside to have one. Wanting to sober up a little, she decided to go for a little walk, but ended up getting lost and walking across a muddy field, then walked back to the house. Too drunk to wipe her feet at the door, she trailed mud up the stairs into the bathroom, where she promptly threw up in the toilet. Feeling a bit better, she decided to borrow a toothbrush and clean her teeth before returning to the party downstairs. It was only when she got back out onto the landing that she realised she couldn't hear her friends, or any music . . . You guessed it, she'd walked into completely the wrong house. Needless to say, she legged it. . .*

Nicole, Hemel Hempstead

As anticipated, they hadn't left themselves quite enough time. Cleo went outside to stand on the deck of the boat while she called to push their dinner reservations back in her basic and stumbling French, while the five girls she was sharing the accommodation with squabbled below: someone had taken some else's phone charger out of the European plug adaptor to use it for their hair straighteners.

'We've got 45 minutes, tops,' she informed her friends as she descended back into the belly of the boat, grabbing up a luminous pink bottle of setting spray and squirting it liberally on her curls. 'This is so counter intuitive,' she complained. 'Normally before going on a night out I'm trying to flatten my hair, not make it wilder!'

Bea shot her an impatient look from where she was attempting to scrape her long shoulder-skimming bob into an unfashionably high ponytail. 'Poor you. I've been doing 50 sit-ups a day for the last month. Crop tops are not designed for thirty-year-old bellies,' she shuddered.

'Hey, at least you guys don't have to wear a wig!' interjected Daisy, voice distorted as she attempted to draw on lip-liner at the same time as speaking. 'I'm going to sweat like a pig.'

Sarah was the first ready, but then her costume was the easiest. Although her straight, dark hair was a little too long for her to truly pass as a nineties-Victoria Beckham lookalike, her willowy frame in a black bodycon dress was otherwise en pointe for Posh Spice.

Daisy was next, probably by virtue of her not having to worry about doing anything to her hair. The only one of them who'd had to resort to actual fancy dress rather than high street shops for her outfit, her Union Jack mini-dress definitely covered a lot more surface area than Geri Halliwell's infamous original from the 1997 Brit Awards (however still left her ample assets very much on display).

Daisy flipped at her overly-red synthetic hair and practiced a cheeky pout while looking into her compact mirror. 'I don't get lip-liner,' she complained. 'I especially don't get lip-liner that's a completely different shade to the lip-stick?'

'Hey, that's just the nineties look!' Sarah reassured her.

Daisy looked back at her reflection, dubious. 'I look like a nutcase.'

'No, you just look like someone in Ginger Spice fancy dress,' Sarah pointed out. 'Trust me, nobody's going to think this is somebody's genuine casual evening look, hun.'

Nora was next, having raced through her beauty preparations so she could have another glass of champagne without risking wobbly make-up application. There'd been some debate over if *she* should have been Ginger, with her hair dye bottle-enhanced auburn hair, particularly as the natural-blonde Daisy could then have been Baby Spice. They'd all decided, resignedly, that Nora just simply didn't have the required physique (aka the required cleavage) and so it was Baby Spice for the Bride-to-Be.It worked out okay, because it meant that she could wear a white skater style dress and feel suitably bridal (even if the baby pink patent platform-heeled knee-high boots ruined the virginal look somewhat).

'Has anyone seen my lollipop?' she demanded, rifling through bags with one hand while she held her drink safely aloft with the other.

Fighting against her natural instinct to smooth her hair down against her scalp, Cleo joined the finished articles out in the boat's long galley seating area, pouring herself a glass of room temperature sparkling wine and picking at a grown-stale croissant. Okay, so it wasn't her usual look, but her grandmother's Caribbean genes leant themselves quite well to the Scary Spice afro. The leopard print leggings and black satin bustier were much more out of her comfort zone however, so she chugged the lukewarm Prosecco for courage.

'LOOK SCARY!' bellowed Nora, as she angled her phone to take a posed snap of Scary Spice-Cleo.

'LOOK SEXY!' Daisy demanded in the same moment, leaving Cleo caught looking a bit like she needed the toilet in the final picture. It was a fun shot through – the leggings made her legs look super long, the top lifted her breasts scandalously, and her eyes shone dark and knowing; she looked like a woman full of the sort of secrets that men want to learn.

'Hey, can you WhatsApp me that?' Cleo asked Nora; maybe she'd decide a little later to forward it into her chat with Gray – see what he thought of the mild mannered Miss Adkins gone a little scary.

Bea exited her bedroom with only minutes to spare, looking thoroughly miserable, having waited until the last possible second to don her outfit. She was lucky that crop tops were unfathomably back in fashion (with prepubescent tweens, anyway) so she'd been able to find what she needed on the high street relatively easily for her Sporty Spice ensemble. The bottom of her costume was, appropriately, a pair of Adidas popper-style jogging bottoms that she'd had lurking at the bottom of a drawer since she was about nineteen. Bea had never been to Paris; she hadn't anticipated that her big night out in the beautiful old city would be spent wearing joggers and Reeboks. But Nora had thought it would be hysterical for her and her four bridesmaids to rock Spice Girls fancy dress and nobody – least of all Bea – said no to Nora.

'Hey, would you mind getting some quick group pictures?' Nora begged Claire, even though they were already running late; mutely Claire took Nora's phone and dutifully snapped away as the other five hens posed with high-kicks and Girl Power peace signs.

Claire, ostracised from the group fancy dress of course, as she wasn't a bridesmaid, was dressed as a Teletubby. Bea had spat out her gin and tonic laughing when her friend had informed her that this was her plan. In reality however this meant she was wearing a wickedly tight red mini dress with a sheet of reflective silver card fastened across her stomach and a wonky homemade-looking 'antenna' on a red headband. Bea swore under her breath. Even someone dressed as a fecking Teletubby was showing her up. She pulled her ratty Adidas trousers a little lower, letting her hipbones jut out over the waistband – at least with a month's worth of sit ups and a reasonably severe crash no-carb diet her stomach was looking suitably sporty in the heinous crop top.

Nora, laughing, twirled one of her pigtails around her forefinger while she posed for a photo. Bea smiled; take away the booze and the boobs, and this could be twenty years ago. Ten-year-old Nora had gone through a stage of attempting to dress like Baby Spice – well, she'd favoured a lot of pastel colours, wrangled her hair into lop-sided pigtails and worn a pair of wedge flip-flops made of foam she'd bought from Tammy Girl until they quite literally fell apart.

'You're bloody obsessed with those slappers!' Bea's mother Hannah had once snapped at them; in retrospect, she'd been right. In the days before the internet the two pre-teen girls had had no other choice but to glue themselves to the cable music channels – flicking impatiently between MTV and The Box – waiting for a Spice Girls video to be requested. If – thrillingly! – it was a new one, it was immediately recorded to a VHS Nora kept for that express purpose, so that they could examine it closely at their leisure; Nora painstakingly jotting down the lyrics for later memorising, whilst Bea beadily reviewed the required choreography.

They'd kept a scrapbook too – Bea had almost forgotten! – and passed it back and forth weekly in a ceremony of sorts almost as formal and revered as the Changing of the Guard. Whichever girl had the book that week was in charge of snipping out any newspaper articles or pictures of the Spice Girls and carefully pasting them in. Bea's mum unfortunately never bothered with newspapers or magazines, so Bea's week was always light for new additions. Eventually Eli had decided to help out (despite proclaiming that the Spice Girls were RUBBISH and that East 17 were AMAZING) and regularly produced carefully cut clippings for Bea, even after his father had smacked him round the head for ruining the Sunday papers before he'd gotten a chance to read them.

Simpler times, thought Bea, heeding the call to grab up your bag and get going, the other half of the hen do already bankside and hollering about how late they were. It might be a cliché, but – still – Bea wasn't entirely sure where the first third of her life had gone. It seemed like one minute they'd all been stressing about feeding and cleaning up after her Tamagotchi, and suddenly life was all shit bosses, expensive shoebox-sized flats, unexplained infertility. Bea checked that there was no lipstick on her teeth one last time before alighting from the boat (she knew Nineties Mel C had never really worn all that make-up, but there *really was a line*) and girded herself for the night ahead, putting aside memories of the days of Panda Pops and cheap nail-varnishes from the corner shop that always stained her nails green, of ten year old Eli passing her envelopes of newspaper cuttings and smiling just because he'd made her smile.

# Chapter 29

*My best friend insisted she wanted a 'traditional' hen party, so I searched high and low for the buffest male stripper around to come to the cottage we were staying in – to serve us drinks with his bum out, that sort of thing. I obviously misjudged just how seriously he took his job; the minute he arrived the clothes came off, the baby oil came out, and my poor friend was pinned to a chair while he performed a reasonably aggressive lap dance for her. About halfway through though, his energetic dancing managed to flick baby oil in her eye (we're still not sure what part of the anatomy it came from) and we had to spend the next hour and a half washing it out with bottled water in a shot glass.*

Rachel, Milton Keynes

Daisy felt faintly embarrassed as the dozen hens formed an orderly English queue in front of the bouncer. Spice Girls and Teletubbies aside, there was a Baby-One-More-Time era Britney Spears, a Marge Simpson, a Sexy Beanie Baby (props to Bec for coming up with that beauty) and more. She was sure the bouncer must have seen it all before – and worse – but still, it felt a little odd, stood outside that venerable establishment; Daisy surreptitiously attempted to pull her dress both up and down simultaneously.She was getting old. In fact, if she was honest, she was already ready for bed. She stifled a yawn and hoped very much that the bouncer wasn't going to demand to see ID, as she wasn't bearing a terrible amount of resemblance to her passport picture at that moment in time, and she really couldn't be bothered to take her wig off after all the efforts to stuff her real hair in neatly underneath.

The bouncer took a disinterested glance at the booking confirmation print-out Cleo had presented him with and waved them past.

'Ladies and, ladies!' Bea cheered, turning around to face them and walk backwards through into the entrance lobby, her pale skin rosed over with the wash from the red lights. 'Welcome to the *Moulin Rouge!*'

They were a good fifteen minutes late, even after the time that Cleo had called and put the table reservation back to, and the hostess sat them with a polite impatience before heading off to collect their pre-ordered, pre-chilled drinks.

The entry, three-course meal, drinks and seats to the cabaret act at the *Moulin Rouge* had not been particularly cheap – especially as each hen was paying one-eleventh of Nora's share – but they'd all agreed quite quickly that it just had to be done. Fifteen year old Nora had been faintly obsessed with the Baz Lurhmann film when it had first released and had quite convinced herself that in a past life she had been a dazzling courtesan in turn-of-the-century Paris, coughing prettily into handkerchiefs, dying stylishly of consumption.

To Daisy's relief their table was quite private, more of a booth with a high back, and she felt less like an A grade dickhead as she wiggled into place along the leather seating, keeping the hem of her Union Jack mini-dress at an acceptable mast. Nora, of course, was sat in the very centre of the curve; Daisy hoped she didn't need to go to the bathroom too often during the course of their evening.

'Okay, presents or a game first?' Bea asked the Bride-To-Be, as the hostess finished ferrying over their carafes of fruit purees and juices to mix with the three litre bottle of vodka they'd pre-ordered and the hens impatiently began pouring themselves cocktails.

'Presents!' Nora echoed in a squeal. 'What presents?'

'You've got a few small things,' Sarah informed her, with a smile.

Nora looked around at her grinning hens. 'Oh, guys, no. It's too much! Presents as well!?'

'Don't thank us yet hun,' Daisy warned, fishing under the table for the tote shopper she'd been carrying that had most of the gifts inside.

For all that she'd immediately said she couldn't possibly accept any presents, Nora tore into the first with gusto. It took her a few turns of the see-through plastic envelope of rubber to work out exactly what it was; when she did she burst out laughing.

'My date for the evening?' she asked, as she freed the

currently flattened blow up man from his packaging. 'Hardly Ewan McGregor though, is he?'

'I reckon he could give Ewan a run for his money though,' Bea laughed dirtily, reaching over to highlight the doll's impressive manly appendage (which would no doubt be even more impressive once, erm, *inflated*).

Nora's eyebrows almost disappeared into her hair. 'So I see!'

'Is that what you're going to call him then?' grinned Claire. 'Ewan?'

'I think he should be called Dickie!' shrieked one of Nora's sisters, already half-a-glass of cocktail down and still going strong.

'Horny Harry?' suggested Bec, in a nod to the absent groom.

'Roger!'

'Randy!'

Nora spluttered laughter into her drink. 'Okay, Randy it is!' The girls all cheered, giddy and silly, clinking their drink against that of the friends closest to them. At home they might be teachers, or mothers, or line managers, and there might be a full in tray at work, or a full laundry basket in the house, but right here, right now they were in Paris, with the ceiling of the *Moulin Rouge* soaring above them, and what felt very much like bottomless vodka to make their way through.

'Okay, next one!' Claire passed across a rectangular shaped box, grinning wickedly.

Nora was briefly stunned into silence once she'd unwrapped it – 'it' being a bright blue vibrator with more moving parts than seemed feasible (or necessary).

'Wow guys, this is so funny!' Nora joked, deadpan. 'Because, just the other day I was saying that I had always wondered what it would be like to be shagged by a Smurf!' The hens howled with laughter.

'Okay, last one,' Cleo promised, handing the third gift over. 'You, er, might sense a bit of a running theme.'

'The running theme being "cock"!' Daisy crowed, frankly.

'Wow guys, this is almost beautiful!' Nora laughed, as she unwrapped a delicate glass dildo shaped like the Eiffel Tower.

'Well, just don't put it on your mantelpiece,' one of Nora's sisters warned. 'You don't want to give poor Mammy a heart attack!'

'Like she'd have a clue what it was!' guffawed the other Dervan twin.

'Well, thanks so much for those, guys. Although, of course, now I'm wondering if I *really need* Harry at all!' Nora teased.

'Yeah, you do sweetie,' insisted an already more-than-tipsy Sarah. 'Because these things can't cut the grass. Trust me!' she burst into peals of laughter.

'Okay, a game, a game!' cheered Cleo; Bea noticed that at some point during the distraction of the present-opening, Cleo had been checking her mobile phone – it was sat quietly next to her drink.

'Okay, how about *Truth or Dare?*' Bea suggested; they'd already played *Mr and Mrs* and *Never Have I Ever* on the Eurostar over. *Truth or Dare* had been another big Nora obsession around the last few years of primary school and first few years of secondary. She'd insisted Bea, Claire and her other girl friends play it with her ad nauseum; they'd mainly only done dares because at eleven they didn't really have any decent secrets.

Bea didn't much care for the game – considering she'd grown up to be rather a creature of secrets – but this was Nora's weekend after all.

'Okay, who first?'

Daisy solved the conundrum by grabbing up one of the plastic cocktail stirrers and spinning it in the middle of the table; the rounded end landed on Bec.

'Oh, I can never think of anything good!' Bec whined. 'Nora, truth or dare?'

'Dare!' yelled Nora without hesitation.

'Ooooh,' Bec, wiggled in place, thinking hard. 'Stand up and shout I'M ON MY HEN DO!'

A giggling Nora acquiesced, awkwardly slipping off her platform shoes so she could safely stand on the leather of the seating.

'Oh, Christ,' Cleo murmured, hand over her face but still laughing, 'I hope we don't get kicked out.'

'I'M ON MY HEN DO!' Nora bellowed obediently, arms spread wide, to a chorus of polite applause from the rest of the tourists in the hall (thankfully the staff seemed supremely unfazed) while her hens snapped away below, taking pictures on their phones.

'Right!' Nora announced as she returned to a sitting position. 'Claire. Truth or dare?'

'Truth?' Claire answered, like she wasn't quite sure.

'Where is the weirdest place you've ever had sex?'

Claire's face pinked. 'You know where,' she protested.

230

'Tell the group!' Nora insisted, drunk and merciless. Bea, who knew too, added a little more of the vodka to her glass.

'Umm ner mm cow,' Claire murmured.

'So we can hear!' Daisy insisted, laughing.

Claire rolled her eyes and steeled her hand on her drink. 'I said *under a cow.*'

'Wait, wait,' Sarah protested, over the tide of screams and laughter from the hens. 'How does that even happen? *Under a cow*? What do you even mean!?'

Claire sighed. 'I was on a team building weekend, back when I worked for that really poncey Estate Agents in Chelsea? They sent us to a working farm. It was *disgusting*. Anyway, they told me and one of the Lettings Negotiators to go and muck out the stalls where the cows were. And when we were done with that, we . . .'

'Got a little mucky yourselves!' Daisy crowed with undisguised delight. 'Good on you, girl.' The rest of the hens agreed, gifting Claire with a smattering of impressed applause. Slightly mollified, Claire sipped at her drink and deliberated who was next in the firing line.

'Cleo,' she announced. 'Truth or dare?'

'Truth,' Cleo requested immediately. Claire tilted her head, like she was considering how best to phrase the question that was rolling on her tongue.

'What's really going on between you and Gray?'

Cleo's eyes flashed on her phone, just once, and Bea knew she'd been right to assume the girl had been texting her colleague.

Cleo felt all the champagne and the vodka sitting heavily

somewhere under that black satin bustier and all the bravado she could usually muster.

'There's nothing "really going on" between me and Gray,' she insisted.

'Oh, come on, the name of the game is TRUTH or Dare,' Bea immediately – and loudly – complained. Nora shot her friend a censorious look, but sent another one Cleo's way straight after.

'What do you want me to say?' Cleo didn't know if it was her laughing, or the champagne. 'Tell you that I fancy him? That I'm like an obsessed teenager? That I'm so fantastically over-the-top in love with him I'm considering looking for another job and I pretty much want to drown myself in my morning coffee every time he tells me all about the date he went on the night before? Is that what you want to hear?'

There was an awkward silence, and Cleo belatedly realised that halfway through her jokey-outburst, she'd stopped laughing; Nora looked at her with soft eyes.

'Something like that,' Bea joked weakly, in an attempt to break the tightness of the moment. Thankful, Cleo took a deep drink and began thinking about what good truths or dares she could come up with for the next round in order to distract the hens (and herself) from her and her embarrassing eruption of love.

But Claire wasn't letting it go. 'You told me you didn't fancy him, that you were just friends. You know, he talks about you all the time. All the time. But I didn't think anything of it, because you said you were just friends,' she repeated. Cleo looked at her, mutely apologetic. 'Obviously I won't try anything with him though if you're in love with him? If you'd rather I didn't?' Claire finished, looking faintly mutinous but resigned.

Cleo cleared her throat. 'Would you mind awfully?' she asked, polite to a fault.

All at once Claire seemed a little deflated; even her little Teletubby antenna headband seemed to hang a little lower. 'No problem,' she managed, with an attempt at cheer, mixing herself another drink, a little stronger than the one before.

'Right Bea,' Cleo announced hurriedly, wanting to move along as quickly as possible. 'Truth or dare?'

'In the interests of us not getting kicked out, I'll go with truth.'

'How many men have you slept with?' Cleo asked; not the most imaginative of questions, but all she wanted at that moment was distance between the group and the Gray awkwardness.

Bea seemed to agree, because she answered immediately. 'Twelve. Okay, Alannah—'

'Twelve?' echoed Nora, before Bea could get the question out to her sister. 'Twelve?' Her forehead creased in a light frown. 'Have you slept with anyone new recently?'

Bea rolled her eyes. 'Chance would be a fine thing, trust me.'

'Well then you must be eleven,' Nora argued. 'I remember when you got to ten and you were all, double figures, oooh. And there's been that one guy since then. Eleven.'

All at once Bea went decidedly pale and fidgeted with a set of midi-rings on her index finger.

'Yes. You're right. Eleven. Haha. I'm glad one of us is paying attention!' Her joke was as weak as her fake laughter. Nora eyed her oldest friend doubtfully. 'Anyway,' Bea continued, doggedly, 'Alannah, truth or dare?'

Nora thought she saw a strange look pass between Bea and Claire, but she must have imagined it. No way would Claire know something about her oldest friend that she didn't.

Alannah was saved from having to answer – and Bea from any further suspicion – by the timely arrival of the round of starters.

\* \* \*

The desserts arrived just as the heavy curtain raised to reveal the dancers readied on stage for the 11pm cabaret show, an acceptably sumptuous riot of feathers, rhinestones and barely-concealed nipples.

'I expected there to be nudity on my hen do, just not other women's!' joked Nora. 'Ou et la penis dans le Paris?'

'I think you've got quite enough Parisian penis there,' pointed out Daisy, nodding towards the tote bag holding a still deflated Randy, the Smurf-coloured vibrator and the Eiffel Tower dildo.

'I'm glad you didn't decide to go for *Moulin Rouge* fancy dress,' Cleo told her friend with feeling.

'Maybe next time,' Nora winked.

The show was spectacular, the entire room was entranced – but Cleo found she couldn't ignore the blinking LED at the top of her phone that signalled she had a message notification. It was probably nobody. It was probably her mum. It was probably o2 telling her that she'd already gone way, way over her agreed data package. (She shouldn't have sent all those pictures to Gray.)

Up on stage a ventriloquist was jabbering on – impressive, but not as interesting as the impossibly beautiful women who'd been dancing around with snakes, and a lot of it was lost in translation – and that little green light was blink-blink-blinking her to distraction. Cleo knew she should put the phone away in her bag – or give it to Bea and beg her to keep her away from it – but she didn't do either.

Gray had sent her the emoji of the screaming face with its hands up. Cleo blinked.

*Look at you!!* The text followed. *Thank god you don't dress like that for work!*

Stung, Cleo immediately forgot her promise to check but not reply.

*I think the kids at the Academy are a little too young to even know who Scary Spice is, to be fair. Surely I don't look that mad??*

*Mad? You look amazing!* Gray shot back, before Cleo even had the chance to put her phone down, and kept going. Cleo stared at the little *Gray is typing . . .* line at the top of the chat box and felt her mouth go a little dry; she resisted the urge to take a deep swallow of her vodka – she didn't need any more embarrassing outbursts.

*If you wore that to work, little learning would get done. Or teaching, for that matter.*

*Well, there's no fear of me turning up in this on Monday*

*morning, don't worry . . .* Cleo tapped out. *This is much more of a 'Saturday night' sort out get-up.*

*Well, we need to get a Saturday night in the diary ASAP,* was Gray's immediate response.

Cleo was holding her phone so gingerly that it almost jumped clear out of her hands when Daisy elbowed her in the ribs.

'No texting boys!' her friend reminded her, shouting over the roar and crash of the music as the cabaret show built towards its climax.

Guiltily, Cleo immediately slipped her mobile into her handbag, before snatching it back out the minute Daisy's attention was back on the stage.

*If you can fit me into your busy schedule. Hey, G, out of interest, do you flirt this much with everyone or am I meant to think I'm special?*

This time Cleo did put her phone away in her handbag – switched off for good measure.

# Chapter 30

It was the early hours and probably too brisk and autumnal to be sitting outside, but the hens had thick enough beer-jackets and the little bistro-style courtyard under the stars had been too charming to resist. The proprietor had brought out armfuls of warm but scratchy blankets for *les jolies dames* which they draped over their knees to ward off the last few bites of the cold.

'So, back to the boats after this?' Nora asked the group as she poured out the dregs from the most recent bottle of wine.

Daisy gave such an emphatic yawn that Bea swore she could hear her jaw clicking as it stretched. 'Yes please. I'm dead on my feet. I can't party like its 1999 anymore.'

'Well as we were like, 13 years old in 1999, I very much hope your parties weren't like this,' Nora pointed out, waggling the empty bottle of red for emphasis.

'Oh, I seriously doubt I'm getting up to the top of the Eiffel Tower tomorrow,' groaned Abbey, Nora's best friend from work, even as she picked up her recently replenished wine glass. 'Great evening. I can't wait for the wedding!'

'Yeah, it's been amazing,' Bea agreed with her, feeling a little frisson of pride at her stake in throwing her best friend a truly worthy hen extravaganza. Even if they were all a little too hanging to fully appreciate the sightseeing they'd left for tomorrow, tonight had truly been a success.

'I mean, I've gotta admit, I was a little worried when I saw the invitation . . .' Abbey laughed, carelessly loudly, over the rim of her glass.

'Oh, I know,' Bea rolled her eyes. 'You know that was nothing to do with me, right? Claire totally railroaded us with them and we couldn't find a way to tell her they were naff. At least Nora saw the funny side!'

'Yeah, what is with Claire? She's not a bridesmaid?' Abbey asked, curious.

'No, she's not, and she's got a massive stick up her arse about it,' Bea confided. 'She's being a bit of a nightmare to be honest—'

'There's no need to be a bitch,' snapped a tremulous voice, and Bea realised far too late that they hadn't been being as quiet as she thought they were. Claire was wasted, but her eyes were alive and blazing, the drink she'd just knocked over bleeding a darker red patch across the spread of her dress.

Mother Cleo was on her feet and moving towards Claire immediately, palms raised, placating. 'Claire, she didn't mean it like that—'

'Yes she did. You think I haven't seen all those emails coming in and out of the RSVP email?'

Nora looked between them. 'What RSVP email?'

Bea swallowed. 'Claire set up a gmail for people to email RSVPs and questions about this weekend and stuff to.' And more than a few of those emails had been less than flattering about the cringey invitations, which had lead on to discussions about Claire's embarrassing over-involvement. Bea racked her memory – had any of them been that terrible? The champagne and the vodka and the wine and the long night had left a frustrating fog where her brain should be. Damnit – it had never occurred to her that Claire might be lurking around in the background of the inbox she'd set up.

'Hey Nor.' Claire was smiling, and for a moment Bea thought the coming storm had broken before it arrived. 'Do you want to know who Bea's *real* number eleven was?'

That pierced through the fog padded inside Bea's head; she shot to her feet. 'Claire.'

Claire didn't break her stride. 'It's probably the only thing she's never told you. But she told me.' Her eyes flicked to Bea. 'Didn't you, Bea?'

'Claire,' Bea said again, desperation bleeding into her voice. 'Let's not do this, okay? I'm sorry. We're all really drunk. Let's not ruin the whole evening. Please.'

'Why would it ruin the evening?' Claire asked dismissively. 'We're all just friends being truthful with one another, right? It's just a game.'

'This is not a game,' Bea said between tight lips. 'Come on.'

Nora overcame what must have been raging curiosity to intervene. 'Okay, everyone calm down. Shall we get another round of bottles of wine?' she attempted to diffuse the situation, while her eyes still flicked to Bea.

'Well, one person around this table deserves to know

anyway,' Claire continued, unheeding. 'Probably the one person who hasn't been a bitch about me behind my back. Sarah. Don't you want to know who Bea's mystery shag was?'

Sarah glanced at Bea, nervously. 'I think that's really Bea's own business, Claire. I—'

'Well no, sorry, it is your business, because it's your husband, after all.'

Bea's eyes flickered closed. The courtyard was so quiet, so achingly quiet – there weren't any sharp intakes of breath, or any gasps or cries, and for a moment she could almost pretend that nobody had heard Claire's words.

'Cole?' Sarah's voice was slightly strangled. 'Cole?' she repeated. Bea opened her eyes; Sarah was looking right at her. 'Was it when you guys were at school or something?'

'No,' Claire interrupted, denying Bea even this small attempt at firefighting. 'In fact I think it was just before you two got engaged. It was the night you came clean about you and Harry,' Claire informed Nora. 'So, in a way, it's almost like you have Nora to thank for your marriage, Sarah!'

Sarah, to her credit, didn't say anything at all. She just looked at Bea with eyes impossible to read. The rest of the hens shifted uncomfortably – a few even looked at Bea with open distaste, the mirror of what Bea had long felt towards herself; she felt her stomach curdling. Of all the many mistakes she'd ever made in her life, this was the one she'd always been most afraid of. When Nora had fallen into bed with her best friend, she ended up engaged. When Bea did it, she just ended up with even more self-loathing.

'Anyway, now that's out in the open, I think I'll head back

to the boats early. Bec, do you mind if I bunk in with you guys? I don't really feel welcome on the bridesmaids' boat. Not being a bridesmaid and all. I really wouldn't want to *embarrass* myself by overstepping the mark.'

And with that, heels dangling from one hand, dress impossibly stained, make-up smeared underneath her eyes, Claire exited the courtyard without pausing to look back.

Cleo was still standing and she moved quickly, pulling her own discarded heels from underneath the table and cramming her feet into them. 'I'll go with her, make sure she gets back okay,' she offered. A few of the other girls took the opportunity to join her, keen to get out of Bea's earshot and commence the discussion and dissection of what the hell had just happened, no doubt. In the space of thirty seconds it was just Nora, Bea, Sarah and Daisy sat at what had minutes ago been a happy and bustling table, surrounded by a dozen abandoned glasses of wine, Claire's overturned drink still dripping slowly and thickly onto the cobbled slabs of the courtyard.

Nora and Daisy were looking at Sarah; Sarah was looking at Bea.

'I know you're probably thinking it was some epic love story,' Bea managed. 'It wasn't. I can promise you that. We were so drunk we didn't even know what we were doing. And we'd had a really weird day.'

Nora gave an almost imperceptible shake of her head at this, a 'don't blame this on me' gesture.

'And that made it okay for you to sleep with my boyfriend?' Sarah asked carefully, still frighteningly calm.

Bea shifted uncomfortably. 'Of course not. But you weren't like a real thing to me. I'd met you like twice. And Cole's girl-friends were always this big nothing, even to him. You were obviously different though. He loved you. He was d-disgusted in the morning,' Bea stuttered, her voice breaking on the word. 'He made me promise I'd never tell anyone ever. He was so afraid of losing you. I think it really made him realise what you meant to him and that's why he proposed a few weeks later.'

'Are you seriously telling me that I should be grateful my marriage exists thanks to you sleeping with my boyfriend?' Sarah bit back, voice rising.

Bea shrank in her chair. 'Of course not. Of course not. Jesus, Sarah, I'm so sorry. But please don't blow this out of proportion. It was over two years ago. And Cole loves you more than anything, don't let this stupid drunken thing that meant *nothing* impact on your relationship-'

'Thank you Bea,' Sarah interrupted, back in control, her voice calm. 'But I think you should really uninvolve yourself from my marriage, if you don't mind.' With a poise that even Bea had to admire in that moment, Sarah finished off her glass of wine with a controlled swallow and got fluidly to her feet. 'Shall we head off?' she asked Nora and Daisy. 'It's gotten really cold.'

They began the walk back towards where the boats were moored, keeping an eye out for an available taxi as they went, Sarah leading the way with her arms linked through Daisy's, their heads – one fair, one dark – bent together as they talked quietly. Nora watched from behind with concern etched across her face.

'Well, it's certainly a hen do memory,' she said eventually, the first thing she'd said to Bea in the five long minutes they'd been walking side by side. 'I can't believe you never told me.'

'Cole made me promise I wouldn't tell anybody,' Bea repeated.

Nora shot her a sideways look. 'But you told Claire. That worked out well.'

Bea sighed. 'I didn't tell her straight away. I only told her last year. I just had to tell someone. It felt like it was eating me up inside.'

'But why not me?' Nora asked again.

'Because. Because I couldn't bear the thought of you looking at me in the way you're looking at me now,' Bea choked out.

Nora sighed. 'You are so self-destructive – you know that Bea? And I can't help you. Not when you insist on just making your life into shit.'

Despite the bruising she'd already taken that night, Bea bristled at that. 'Making my life into shit?' she echoed, incredulous. 'My life is already shit! We're not all so lucky as you, Nor.'

'And you need to stop that!' Nora snapped. 'My life's no fairy-tale. The only difference between you and me is that I have gone after what I wanted. I took chances.'

'And what's that supposed to mean?'

'What's the real reason you didn't go to university, Bea? Why don't you ever apply for any of the jobs I email you? Why didn't you give Eli a chance when he came back after graduation and asked you out?' Nora shook her head. 'It's like you're frightened to be happy. I will never understand

243

you.' And those words, from the person she loved most in the word, stung Bea deeper than all of the slurs she'd slung at herself over a lifetime. Shocked into silence, Bea fell quiet; the pair of old friends walked the entire way back to the riverbank listening to the rise and fall of Daisy's voice ahead of them.

# Chapter 31

'Hey, are you back yet?' Cole called through the house before he slammed the front door and let his weekend bag fall to the floor with a soft thump.

'In the bedroom,' Sarah called back, calmly. She checked her appearance in the mirror, making sure her lips still appeared freshly glossed. Makeup was a sort of armour for things like this.

'Hey beautiful,' Cole rushed into the room, filling up the small space with his big frame, putting those hands all over her. Sarah allowed him to kiss her, knowing once he did that he'd release her. 'Did you have a good time?' he asked, turning to sit on the edge of the bed and take off his shoes. 'I've got to admit, I think I'm still a little drunk!' he chuckled. 'Harry still has all the body hair he came with though, I'm a man of my word.'

'Were you ever going to tell me that you'd slept with Bea?'

An expression of pure panic bled across Cole's face in an instant. 'What?'

'Don't insult me by buying time while you try and work out if you're going to get away with denying it.' Sarah knew her husband far too well. 'Well? Were you ever going to tell me?'

Cole's face darkened. 'That bitch. How dare she tell you that.'

'Don't take this out on Bea. She didn't tell me. And she's not the one who cheated on me. That was you. That was all you.'

Cole was on his feet. 'Baby, it meant nothing. We were fucked off our faces drunk. I regretted it the minute it happened.'

Sarah waved her hand dismissively, stopping Cole from approaching her any closer. 'Oh I've already heard all this from her. Don't you have anything new to say?' She waited a beat. 'No? Okay then.' She moved towards the bag she'd repacked since arriving back from Paris; Cole caught sight of it and his panic flared again.

'Baby, don't do this,' he begged, grabbing both of her wrists in his hands and holding her facing him, even as she strained to turn away. 'It was years ago. You're my wife and I love you. We're going to have a baby. Come on, Sar.'

Sarah stopped struggling; she looked her husband dead in the eye. 'Do you know what? It's funny. I never in a million years thought these words would ever, ever come out of my mouth, but, I'm glad I'm not pregnant. I'm *so glad.*'

Cole let go of his wife's wrists all at once, like he'd been burned. And he didn't follow her out of the bedroom, or out of the house, or out of the city.

* * *

Life was always interesting, she had to give it that. Just when you think you've got your feet underneath you, the rug will get swept away, the ropes will be cut. Bad things keep on happening to good people and the best laid plans keep on going awry.

Why now. Why her? The timing was unbearably cruel.

One lone toothbrush in the holder; Daisy stared at it as the two pink lines on the pregnancy test just got darker and darker.

# Chapter 32

Cleo studied the top of Gray's bent head; the harshness of the overhead strip lights threw a halo of paleness around his crown. He sat in quiet concentration, his bottom lip sucked in between his teeth, click-click-clicking his pen absent-mindedly as he read through his student's essay. He'd been doing this lately, bringing his marking along to breaks and lunch, a not-so-subtle but ever-so-polite barrier between them.

For the millionth time in her life – and at least the hundredth time since she got back from Paris – Cleo reflected on how very, very much alcohol was *not* her friend. Oh, how she rued that message she'd sent him, that split second while she'd been spangled on champagne and frankly giddy from being at the Moulin Rouge, but most of all she rued the fact that she'd turned her phone off for the rest of the evening and missed the three attempted calls he'd made to her in response.

A combination of hangover, embarrassment and dealing with the fall-out of the Bea / Cole big reveal had eaten up much of the next day, but – after bidding the rest of the (slightly subdued) hen party contingent goodbye at the Eurostar terminal – Cleo had sat on the tube back towards

Acton, her phone heavy in her hands, a message to Gray resolutely undrafted. Copping out completely, dreaming of a chip butty and her blissful king-sized bed, Cleo had decided that a cheerful, face-to-face chat over coffee during Monday break time, where she could play down her slight Single White Female craziness, perhaps even distract Gray by telling him all the hen do gossip.

As it turned out, she needn't have worried. Gray had appeared at their usual spot, armed with an over-done smile and a sheath of coursework. He'd gone through the motions all right, asking if Nora had enjoyed her spinsterhood send-off, making all the right noises as Cleo showed him some of the funniest snaps on her phone. He hadn't mentioned Cleo's particularly passive-aggressive beauty of a message, or how it could neatly be translated into a caterwauling WHY DON'T YOU FANCY MEEEE? And so Cleo didn't bring it up.

And here they were, three weeks later, still not talking about it, Gray still pretending to mark essays over his break (the end of term was approaching, he'd pointed out when she'd tentatively asked him what was up with the teachery diligence).

And to think – she'd been so concerned about her stupid crush ruining a great friendship. Seems like it had always been a self-fulfilling prophecy.

Cleo drained the lukewarm dregs of her coffee. Past Hallowe'en the staff room – along with everything inside it – retained absolutely no heat whatsoever. 'Oh, man, I cannot wait for this term to be over!' she admitted, with feeling. With January and the mock exams looming just the other side of Christmas she'd found herself doing more marking, revision planning and tutoring than perhaps hours in the day strictly allowed.

'Just got to get through the big party first,' Gray pointed out, looking up from his papers with a flash of his former smile. Was it really a year since they'd properly met, over a glass of too-strong Disaronno and cranberry and a queasy, protesting stomach too-full of questionable canapés? None of that this year, Cleo promised herself (reminder again: *alcohol is not your friend*). Going by her track record she'd probably hitch up her cocktail dress and rugby tackle him to the floor. She looked up and met Gray's eye-contact; he was still smiling.

In fact, maybe it would be better if she didn't go to the Christmas party at all this year. . .

The house still smelt and felt the same as Sarah let herself in the front door; she didn't know why, but she realised that she'd been expecting some sort of discernible difference. She let out the breath that she'd been holding as she'd fumbled over-loudly with her keys at the lock – it was clear from the stillness of the air that her former home was indeed empty, as she'd hoped. It was 2pm on a Tuesday – Cole was sure to be at work – but she knew that for the first week or so after she'd moved out he'd taken sick leave and hung around the house, hoping to catch her. Obviously his bosses' patience had run out.

The pressure somewhat off her, Sarah lingered in the entrance hall, noting with a little satisfaction the furring of dust laying across the glass of the wall mirror, for all it was dim, the wintery mid-afternoon not allowing much light through the windows. She ran an experimental hand over the curl of the bannister – remembering idly that it was probably due its six-monthly oiling and varnishing. She supposed if she and Cole really did get divorced, then the house would have to go on the market sooner rather than later. Cole had fronted the entirety of the initial deposit, and paid about 75% of the mortgage – Sarah wondered if she'd even get anything from the proceeds.

She remembered their first viewing of the house. Cole had been more or less happy to let Sarah take the lead on house-hunting, but she had insisted that he make time for each and every appointment. Even though their budget was reasonable (thanks to Cole's salary anyway – Sarah wouldn't have had a hope of getting a mortgage on a garden shed without his uplift to their combined income) they'd quickly grown pretty disillusioned. Everything decent was too much of a commute to work. Everything more convenient was boxy, or damp, or in what her mother would have called (with a little sniff) a 'rough neighbourhood'. So, when they found it, their two-bed, two-reception little town house had seemed like some sort of mirage. Cole had spent hours combing over the Homeowner's Survey documentation, trying to work out where the catch was.

But – no catch – a few weeks, a few signatures and some eye-wateringly large bank transfers later, and the little town-house was theirs. Sarah tried to picture another newly-engaged couple coming hopefully through that same front door grasping glossy particulars and floorplans, accompanied by an equally glossy estate agent. Her stomach rolled over itself in protest.

Feeling heavy and old, Sarah slowly climbed the stairs, distracting herself with yet another mental inventory of the bits and pieces she needed to pack, trying to focus on the task at hand. Still, she found herself hesitating at the threshold to the master bedroom and turning right, standing in the doorway she'd lost long minutes to the past. The absolute sadness of a purposeless space, of a nursery waiting for a crib – she'd flat out refused to allow Cole to buy a spare bed for overnight guests, no matter how many times he assured her it would just be temporary.

Christ. Sarah felt her top lip curl. The person she'd been in her youth would absolutely despair at the whinging, sopping woman she'd become. She turned her back on the empty second bedroom, and went to pack up the jewellery she'd left behind.

\* \* \*

'Okay, Daisy,' the nurse was saying in a perfectly practiced NHS-tone as she matter-of-factly tucked a wodge of blue tissue paper into the elastic of her undies. At least this was validation that Daisy had been right to spend a little extra time on bikini line maintenance the evening before. 'Now this might be a teeny bit chilly, but it will warm up, I promise!'

Despite the warning, Daisy flinched as the woman squirted a clear stream of gel from a tube directly onto the skin of her exposed abdomen; it felt like a knife of ice. The hard head of the sonographer's wand wasn't much better; it pressed insistently into the softness of Daisy's belly like it was trying to iron out the folds of skin there. Somewhere, deep inside, her supposed foetus was in there, and according to the pregnancy app she'd downloaded, currently the size of a lime. Daisy held her breath, with no idea why.

The sonographer's brow creased ever-so-slightly as she peered at the screen, maddeningly angled away from Daisy. The wand pressed in a little harder, rolling over from right to left, and then back again, before being abruptly withdrawn. Daisy felt hard, spiking panic gripping at every part of her. Oh shit. Shit. She'd only known about this baby for two weeks. She'd not really been thinking of it as real, if she was honest, but suddenly – with that faint furrow of concern between the nurse's eyebrows – it was the realest, realest thing that could or would ever exist for her.

'Okay, Daisy,' the woman repeated, all cheerful business. 'Now what I need for you to do is to bend your legs, bring your heels up to your bum for me, then lift your hips and give everything a good shake.'

Daisy, who was halfway through complying with the instructions to bring her feet up to her middle before the nurse got to the end of her sentence, almost fell off the table.

'A good shake?' she echoed, panicked. 'Why? Is there something wrong?' Was this how they encouraged along miscarriages of unviable pregnancies? Surely not. Daisy felt sick. For the millionth time in the last fourteen days she cursed every single alcoholic drink she'd consumed, every ibuprofen pill she'd popped, all of the hundred foetus-unfriendly things she may have done while she was still unknowing.

'Nothing's wrong,' the sonographer assured her immediately, putting a capable hand to one of Daisy's knees to gently force her legs and feet back into the instructed stance. 'Baby's just in an awkward position, and I just want to see if we can make them move around and say hi!'

Still numb with anxiety, Daisy did as she was told, lifting her hips from the bed and waggling them repeatedly from left to right.

'Okay, let's try again.' Once again the wand pressed in unrelentingly. 'That's a little better!' the sonographer said, brightening, before reaching out with the hand that wasn't holding the wand to push the screen on its bracket so that Daisy could see too.

It was exactly as she'd expected at first. A nondescript grey landscape, like the kind she'd seen a thousand times in movies, or on her Facebook newsfeed. The pale shape in the centre twitched and moved – moved! – and suddenly Daisy realised she could see an arm, could see the little slope of a nose.

'Okay, so this is the head,' the nurse confirmed, clicking a button and zooming in on the relevant part of the image. Daisy realised she was craning up on her elbows a little, desperate to see. 'And legs, and arms – see one of them is up by the side of the face?' Oh, yes, Daisy saw. 'That little black area in the middle there, that's baby's stomach. They'll already be swallowing and passing the amniotic fluid, so that's very good. And I'm just going to log the heartrate, but I can already tell it's about right.'

And Daisy started to cry: big, deep, unladylike, gasps – because there it was, the baby she hadn't even known had been growing inside of her for these long weeks, the true cause of her endless fatigue, her loss of appetite, the 'stomach flu' that had seen her off sick from work with her head down the toilet. And it was fine. Its little heart was right there, bright and flickering and strong and *fine*.

'Okay, so from the crown to rump length, I'm putting you at . . . 11 weeks and 6 days,' the sonographer confirmed with a smile. 'So that will put conception back around, ooh, September 20th or thereabouts.'

Daisy's eyes fluttered closed. Darren's birthday weekend. Well, they'd done the drunken duvet dance several times that night after dinner, so she guessed the odds were always going to have been that way inclined. Oh god. How was she ever going to look this child in the face whilst knowing that it was conceived during a stay at a self-advertised 'Sex Hotel' in Blackpool that had had a mirror stuck to the ceiling?

The sonographer chatted away happily, snapping pictures of the baby, zooming in and away and from different angles. Daisy drank it all in, ignoring the rub and burn as the lubricating gel ran thin and the ultrasound wand pressed across her, cry-laughing as she noticed how the baby squirmed away as if the pressure was bothering it. She couldn't believe how much it was moving – a bad dancer already, just like its mommy! – yet she couldn't feel the slightest thing. It was like a dream.

'Just a few more measurements now and we're all done. And you can go to the loo!' For all Daisy didn't want the appointment to end, this was welcome news: the appointment letter had been quite insistent that she come to the scan with a full bladder and she was more than a little uncomfortable at this point.

'Say, see you in two months, baby!' the sonographer trilled – before withdrawing the wand and leaving Daisy feeling oddly bereft – pulling the blue medical paper from the elastic of her underwear and swabbing up the smeared remnants of the gel on Daisy's stomach with it. Her skin still felt tacky and cold under all her winter layers as Daisy – stumbling and shell-shocked – exited the ultrasound suite. The slightly peaky-looking, I-need-the-toilet-jiggling woman sat in the waiting area outside shot her a conspiratorial smile. The husband or partner glanced up from his laminate-bound parenting tome to expectantly watch the suite doors, not-so-patiently awaiting his turn to greet his offspring.

Darren. She had to tell him. Daisy's palms suddenly felt very sweaty. She slipped the tiny square sonogram images the nurse had given to her into her planner to keep them safe. She pulled out her mobile phone. Shamefully, shamefully, she'd already deleted his number. She'd have to Facebook message him. Poke. Hey, remember me? Smiley face. Well, you certainly left me something to remember *you* by. . .

Well. Obviously her opening approach needed some careful crafting.

Heading in the direction of the toilets, hoping she had enough time left before her appointment for her blood tests, Daisy opened up her WhatsApp and tapped into Nora's Bridesmaids group for ease.

*Big news*, she typed out to her friends. *Immense, large-scale news. Immediate discussion mandatory. Dinner this week? xx*

# Chapter 33

*I was the maid of honour at a wedding where the bride and groom had written their own vows, and my mate gave them to me to look after until they were needed. Needless to say, beautiful empire-line bridesmaids' dresses do not have pockets, so I safely placed her beautifully written words of love into my cleavage whilst helping her with last minute touch-ups . . . Halfway through the ceremony it was time for the vows. My friend stared at me for a full minute before I remembered. So, right there at the front, next to a priest, I had to reach in-between my boobs, only to find the folded paper had slipped out of place and moved, making for an awkward, terribly silent few moments of me digging around.*

Becka, Bath

Bea inspected the Order of Service she'd just folded together with a critical eye. She was the better part of a glass of wine down and she suspected her accuracy might be suffering the effects. She tried to mitigate the wonky spine by lining up the corners a little more neatly. It was passable; she duly added it to the nearby pile.

Harry breezed through the front room, hairy shins and knees bravely bared to the December cold; Bea shivered in sympathy inside her cable corded knit and sipped gratefully at her glass of warming red.

'I won't be too long,' he promised Nora as he smoothed her hair back and kissed her jaw line. 'I'll just do the one set.'

'Still, your willpower puts me to shame,' Nora pointed out ruefully, inclining her own glass of wine towards him. Most brides hike up the weight loss efforts in the last few weeks but Nora, particularly with Christmas indulgences sat squarely between herself and the altar, seemed content to slide off the wagon (glass of red in hand). Still, she had definitely slimmed down over the months since her engagement; even just sat cross-legged in front of the sofa in leggings, fluffy socks and an over-sized jumper she seemed sharper, more gamine. Bea was put in mind of the teenaged Nora, that window of time between the melting away of pre-puberty puppy fat and the poor diet of the student years, where Nora had been a bit like this, all cheekbone.

'Well, can I pick up anything on the way back?' Harry offered, eyes twinkling. 'Something for dinner? Another bottle?'

Nora paused in her folding, clearly tempted. 'I shouldn't . . .'

'Are you sure? I'm literally walking back straight past Happy Dragon . . .'

'Oh, well then, it would be rude not to!' Bea laughed. 'Make mine sweet and sour chicken balls, please!'

Nora sighed dramatically. 'Well, I suppose it will be you

that has to deal with the melt-down if my dress doesn't button up on the day.'

Harry clapped his hands to his ears at the hint of bridal buttons and Nora laughed. He didn't want to know even the tiniest detail about the wedding dress.

'Okay then. How many calories can there even be in special fried rice? Don't answer that! Let me just see what I've got in the way of cash.' Nora unfolded her legs and hopped up to search out her eternally errant handbag, Harry trailing after her as he made a note of what to order later using an app on his phone. Knowing there would soon be greasy takeaway to soak up the alcohol and hopefully improve the straightness of her folding, Bea took another drink. She inspected Nora's own pile, which didn't seem all that much better than her own, and felt a little better.

Maybe she was just looking for the weight of tension, but would Harry normally go out to the gym when she was over? Had he met her eyes for a normal length of time when she'd asked for the chicken balls? For sure Cole had refused to speak to her since her return from France, had ignored every single phone call, every message left, pleading with him to let her explain.

*It's not like I meant for this to happen*, Bea had typed what felt like a hundred times over by now. *This isn't my fault*. Maybe if she typed it another hundred times, she'd start to feel like it was true.

At least her relationship with Nora didn't seem, on the face of it, to be too shaken. In fact, Nora never mentioned it, even going so far as to awkwardly try and change the subject if

Bea ever tentatively approached it. After being able to talk to Nora about anything and everything since, well, the moment Bea *could* talk, it felt slightly painful.

She'd contacted Sarah too, of course. She'd jacked in her job and bolted to her mother's house in Wales (she'd literally *fled the country*) and the horror and the guilt and the shame of it made Bea want to rip off her own skin with her fingernails. Bea remembered how she'd used to get so annoyed by how nicey nice Sarah was. Sarah was so nice, in fact, that she'd taken the time, somewhere in the midst of the demolition of her life and her marriage, to send Bea a short but polite message, saying that while it was Cole she blamed, not Bea, she'd appreciate it if Bea would stop calling, and leave her alone. And – after a brief paroxysm of indecision about whether or not agreeing to leave Sarah alone allowed for one more response confirming that she would indeed be doing that – Bea had decided to respect her erstwhile friend's wishes.

Bea had also heard very little from Daisy in the past few weeks. She wasn't ignoring her, not as such, more *avoiding* her. Bea had been desperate for some of her American friend's straight-talking sympathy, but after the third of fourth invitation somewhere for a bottle of something and a catch-up had been awkwardly swerved, Bea had gotten the message and stopped asking.

Weirdly, it was Cleo who was being the most normal around Bea. Maybe she was just taking her cue from Nora and refusing to get involved, but where Bea had expected only snide comments and recriminations from her best frenemy, Cleo had been kinder to her than she ever had been in the decade or so Bea had known her. So maybe that was something. . .

Harry called out his farewells from the flat door and Nora wandered back through to the front room, holding her handbag in one hand and her mobile phone in the other, idly checking her messages.

'I wonder what's so important,' she mused, her thumb working the touch screen. 'It's going to be a ballache finding somewhere for dinner short-notice in the city in December.'

She was referring to Daisy's enigmatic message of earlier that day, Bea realised. She'd messaged all four of them saying she had important news she needed to share.

'I think she's back with Darren,' Bea shrugged, folding another Order of Service as neatly as she could manage. 'It's that time of year, isn't it? Everyone wants someone to snuggle on the sofa with and watch Christmas films. Everybody wants somebody to kiss at midnight . . .' Her voice tailed off, remembering that this year, of course, when Big Ben chimed in another January, it would be signalling the end of her best friend's wedding day. Cole would be there, of course and so – as Nora had confirmed – would Sarah. Not having anyone to kiss at midnight would probably be the least of Bea's concerns.

Nora gracefully folded herself back down into her sitting position and grabbed up her glass of wine.

'Oh dear,' she laughed, surveying the unimpressive piles of completed Orders of Service. 'We're not being all that productive this evening, are we?'

'Oh, don't worry, Mel,' Bea assured her, trying to keep her voice light, folding up another and adding it to the pile. 'You've still got, oh, three weeks.'

# Chapter 34

Daisy made sure that she was fashionably late, glancing around the rammed gastro-pub as she arrived. Across the exposed kitchen bar, Nora looked up from her menu, meeting Daisy's eye contact and waving her over. Already there was a bottle of white wine ordered, opened and empty, four equal glasses poured out. Cleo and Bea were there already too, smiling expectantly. Sarah hadn't been able to make it over from where she was staying with her mom – December train fares were extortionate apparently (and, of course, Sarah currently had no income) – although Daisy did have to wonder if the negative RSVP had more to do with Sarah's unwillingness to be sat around a table with the woman who'd once boned her husband and kept it secret for two years . . . who knew.

Daisy nervously smoothed her dress over her stomach as she made her way across to her friends. She wasn't showing yet and probably wouldn't for a fair while, but still, it had become somewhat of a nervous habit over the past few weeks. She might not have a bump, per say, but already her jeggings and work chinos were feeling uncomfortably tight, forcing her into dresses. At least the festive season prevented her from looking suspiciously formal.

After a round of greetings – Daisy realised that this was the first time she was seeing her friends since they'd returned from Nora's hen weekend (she'd been a *little* distracted, after all . . .) – Daisy settled down into the chair left for her, concealing her smirk as Cleo pushed the fourth glass of wine towards her encouragingly.

'So, come on!' Bea demanded, characteristically unbothered with preamble. 'What's the big news?'

'Did you get that promotion?' Nora asked, all excitement.

'Oh, no. It's not that.' Daisy felt a little pang – she doubted the board would be considering her for that new managerial role once she informed them that she would be going on maternity leave in half a year's time. She rallied. 'It's more exciting than that!'

Bea and Nora exchanged a glance. 'Are you . . . seeing someone new?' Nora tried again, after a moment.

'Or, seeing someone *again*?' Bea bluntly clarified their drift. Oh. So they thought she'd gotten back together with Darren. Oh, the irony.

'Not really,' Daisy smiled. 'But you're getting warmer.'

Her three friends swapped baffled looks.

'So . . . this isn't anything to do with Darren?' Cleo asked, after a moment.

Daisy sighed. 'Well, actually, yes. It does have something to do with Darren I suppose. And that's why I need your help.'

'He's not bothering you, is he?' Bea's brows had snapped together threateningly.

Daisy laughed again. 'Oh, god, let me just tell you what's going on, before I get the poor guy in even more trouble.' Where to begin? 'Well, do you remember when I had that bad norovirus thing?' It took only that for ever-quick Cleo to join the dots; she pressed her lips together like she was stopping herself from reacting. 'And I'd just felt so shitty for weeks and weeks. And when we got back from Paris I thought, this is ridiculous, I'm going to ring the doctor. And when I was making the appointment, the receptionist was clicking through the booking calendar and said, super casual like, "you don't think you could be pregnant, do you?"'

The twin expressions of worry that Nora and Bea had been sporting melted away, as they realised what the truth of the matter was; Nora put her hands up to her mouth and pressed her fists against her wide smile.

'And I immediately went, oh no, no – but then I thought, actually, when was the last time I got my period?' Daisy continued, smiling. She was laughing about it now, but she'd remember that moment as one of the most defining – and horrifying – moments of her life. 'And so, I bought a test. And then another one. And another one.' She laughed. 'And after three positive results, it finally started to sink in.'

Nora could take no more; she leapt to her feet and threw her arms around the still sitting Daisy, squealing into her ear. 'Oh my god, oh my god!'

'Wait, wait, wait! I've got pictures.' Daisy fumbled in her bag for her scan pictures and spread them out across the table top. Her eyes felt hot and prickly with tears. She'd already told her mom and older sister over Skype, of course, but this was the first time she'd been able to feel the excitement, the hugs, the joy that news of her child's existence brought to the world. She crossed her arms in her lap, picturing that little bean, somewhere deep behind her pelvic bone, sensing its mother's heart racing and blood rushing and wondering what on earth was going on out there.

'What did Darren say?' Cleo asked, after a few minutes of passing the little square scan pictures around and indiscriminate cooing. 'Is he excited? Horrified? Both? Somewhere in between?'

'I don't know. I haven't told him yet. I don't suppose any of you guys have kept his phone number actually, have you?'

The girls exchanged a look as they shook their heads.

'I might have his email address still saved,' Nora offered.

Daisy laughed sharply. 'Well, I suppose that's marginally better than sending him a Facebook message.'

'Marginally, yes,' Cleo agreed, wide-eyed.

'Oh god, can you imagine? "Dear Darren, how are you? Please see attached. File name, 12-week-scan-dot-jpeg. Can we discuss. Best, Daisy Frankel."'

'Best?' Bea snorted. 'You're currently incubating his sperm into a person. You can stretch to "kind regards," I think.'

'I need to get his number,' Daisy groaned. 'You don't think Harry has it do you, or Cole?'

'I don't think so hun,' Nora said, apologetically. 'They weren't exactly bezzie mates or anything, were they?'

'I'll have to Facebook him and ask him to call me. At least I didn't get around to de-friending him. Having to send him a Friend Request first would just have been the pits.' Daisy eyed up the obviously untouched fourth glass of wine, feeling that despite her continued low-level nausea she quite possibly had never wanted a drink more in her life than she did in that moment, imagining her soon-to-be-had call with her ex-boyfriend turned unexpected baby-daddy.

'Okay, well just make sure that it's actually Darren who's calling you from an unknown number before you go blurting anything out,' Bea advised wisely, as she picked up her own glass. 'You don't need to be telling some telemarketer from an Indian call centre that you've gotten yourself up the duff.'

# Chapter 35

Cleo bustled herself through the revolving doors into the hotel lobby with more haste than class, shaking the smears of sleet from the shoulders of her dark coat and crossing her fingers that her hair wasn't too frizzy. It had only been a short dash from the nearest tube to the venue, but, still, she wished that she'd been able to cram her umbrella into her diddy clutch bag.

Removing her damp coat and throwing it over her arm, Cleo followed the signs for the Oaklands Christmas Party through the warren of a hotel, noting that she wasn't noticing any familiar faces. She'd been going for fashionably late, but maybe she'd veered into the offensively late bracket. She'd spent a little bit longer in the bath than she'd meant to, and far too much attention to her makeup (which, please god, had hopefully managed to stay put through the pressing fug of the tube journey and the spitting shower of sleet).

As she approached the atrium for the second-floor function area a blank-faced man in a dark suit appeared as if from nowhere and offered to take her coat and scarf to the cloakroom; Cleo gave up her damp, wintery burden gratefully. This place was even fancier than she'd anticipated. There had been talk that it would be. The headmaster's ancient PA had finally retired that last summer, and with her went the tradition of a limp three-course turkey dinner in the little reservable area near the toilets at the pub a couple of roads away from the school. The PA's replacement (who didn't look like she was long out of secondary school herself . . .) had absolutely no interest in the fusty local, nor a mandatory novelty jumper rule. Cleo smoothed her palms against her new cocktail dress nervously. A stupid expense (particularly this close to Christmas) – but when she'd seen it in the shop she knew she had to have it. It was a soft and shiny material in rose gold which slouched forward a tad daringly off of her shoulders and hung loose across her frame, allowing it to flow over her body, catching the sheen of the lights. It felt festive and decadent and sexy (Cleo hoped that she herself would accordingly follow suit).

The broad space of the function room was lit at low-level only, but the white, silver and blue colour theme served to brighten the area. It felt more like a wedding than an office Christmas party, each round, white-clothed table sporting huge centre-pieces – oversized martini glasses filled with prickly sprigs of holly and soft, fat plumes of white feathers. Glitter-dipped laser-cut snowflakes in shades of gleaming silver, snow white and ice blue hung from the high ceiling, like something out of *Frozen*. Bright strands of silver lametta draped from the branches of a distastefully large real Christmas tree taking up one entire corner of the room. The standard rust-coloured hard-wearing carpeting detracted from, but didn't ruin, the general effect.

Spying a work mate taking an artfully-angled photo of the tree, Cleo made a bee-line over to her.

'You look amazing,' Tia told her, approvingly, aiming an air-kiss in the vicinity of one cheek, then the other (events like this were weird, thought Cleo – it's not like they greeted one another in the staff room like that). 'Have you got a drink?'

'No, not yet. I'm going to pace myself. Don't want a repeat of last year and all that!' Cleo laughed self-depreciatingly.

Tia raised one expertly-threaded eyebrow. 'Well, don't wait too long. There's a budget behind that free bar, you know.'

Cleo double-took. 'Free bar?'

'Yup. The management board has put an undisclosed sum behind the bar as a little festive bonus. You know, in lieu of us getting paid actual festive bonuses? But when it's gone, it's gone,' Tia shrugged, taking a generous gulp from her generously-large glass of white wine.

Cleo glanced behind her – that definitely explained the popularity of the bar area, which was already thronged with people. 'Well, in that case,' she laughed. 'I wouldn't want to miss out on my bonus!'

Weighing up the merits between starting with and sticking with wine and mixing things up with a cheeky gin and tonic, Cleo approached the press of her glad-ragged colleagues, wondering ruefully if there was going to be anything left of the magical bar tab by the time she managed to get to the front and get served.

Then she saw him, at the front of the group, impeccable in a slim-fit navy suit with a silky-looking tie in a shade of lilac that a lesser man probably wouldn't have got away with.

Gray locked eyes with her. She saw him hesitate, a small exhale that hung over his lips, just for a moment. Then he rallied, gave her the international tipping hand to mouth motion that meant 'do you want a drink?' Cleo beamed back as she nodded and mouthed 'wine, please!'

Cleo hung back and watched as Gray's turn at the bar arrived, watched him turn his megawatt smile on the male bartender (he just couldn't stop himself from flirting, no matter who the recipient was, could he?). A minute or two later Gray pushed his way carefully through the queue and across to her, carrying a slender pint of Peroni in one hand and a large glass of wine in the other. Cleo took it gratefully.

'Lifesaver. Thank you.'

Gray glanced at her fully, taking her in from head to toe, sort of like he didn't want to, but also like he couldn't help himself. 'You look nice,' he announced; Cleo tried to convince herself she'd imagined the slight grudging edge to his tone.

'You're looking pretty sharp yourself there. Happy Christmas.' Gray accepted the proffered cheers, lightly clinking his glass against hers. Cleo took a drink, hoping it would serve to blunt the awkwardness. The wine was lovely, chilled and just the level of dryness that she liked best. (She hated that she hadn't even had to specify.)

'Not on the amaretto, then?' Gray asked her, after a minute.

'No, not this year.' God, was it really a year since the night she'd tossed the hot and alcoholic contents of her stomach across Gray's polyester jumper? And now they were come to this, an ill-advised crush and an iller-advised text message, and a year that had left her heart feeling a bit tossed, hot and alcoholic too.

'So, how much do you think they've actually coughed up and put behind the bar?' Gray asked conversationally, as his eyes continued to wander across Cleo, and she saw how he noticed her dark plum manicure, chosen to match well with her favourite winter-toned lipstick, the delicate style of the high heels she'd borrowed from Nora, impractical in this weather but gorgeous with the dress. That had always been one of her favourite things about Gray. She knew that he really *noticed* things, noticed *her*.

'Enough,' Cleo answered, vaguely. 'I'm on my best behaviour tonight.'

'Oh,' Gray said mildly, before raising his pint to his lips. 'Shame. You know how much I love Drunk Cleo.'

There it was – her opening. 'Well, I think I'm still recovering from Nora's hen do,' Cleo said in a jokey tone. 'Deathly hungover on the Eurostar – not my finest morning.'

Gray appraised her, hopefully expertly reading between the lines of the pseudo-conversation. 'Well, that's a bridesmaid's prerogative, I feel. Getting wasted, I mean. It's . . . fair enough.'

What? What was fair enough? That she had decided to call his flirty bullshit bluff? That she fancied him (she surely couldn't be the first secretly lovesick mate Gray had ever come across)? Or was it literally just fair enough she'd had a bit to drink on her best friend's hen night? Arghhh!

Deciding that to back away from the conversational mine-field was as dangerous as wading forward, Cleo persevered. 'Yeah. It was overdue.' She took a deep breath and chickened out. 'A big, blowout night like that, I mean.'

Gray continued to look at her a little more intently than she felt was strictly warranted. 'Should we get back in the queue for another drink before the bar tab is closed?' he asked, after a moment.

Cleo motioned with her wine glass, meaning to illustrate that she was fully stocked up and fine, but was a little startled to see that over half of her drink was already gone. Her resolution to avoid the twin temptations that were alcohol and Gray Somers wavered appallingly. As if he sensed it, Gray twisted back towards the bar area and offered his elbow to her, like something out of a period drama. Cleo looped her free hand through it and allowed him to escort her. She felt the heaviness of his suit jacket through the slippery material of her dress and against her hip, took a moment to appreciate the fluid rhythm that their two bodies found immediately. She tried to ignore how her heart felt huge and heavy in her chest.

'This room is massive,' Gray pointed out as they crossed it, shaking his head. 'It will never fill up.'

'Yeah, they must be used to much bigger functions than the Oakland Academy Chrimbo piss-up,' Cleo agreed. 'Classy, plus-one, corporate affairs.'

'Isn't that what this is?' teased Gray.

'God, can you imagine bringing a plus-one to a work thing?' Cleo shuddered dramatically.

'Well, you're my forever favourite plus-one when it comes to professional festive indulgence, don't forget.'

* * *

The recently divorced Head of English was having a whale of a time. Her dark lipstick had rubbed off on the rims of countless glasses of vodka tonics, leaving her with an odd, clown-like red ring around her mouth. Vodka in one hand, a slightly bedraggled sprig of mistletoe in the other, she danced from bloke to bloke demanding they plant one on her over-powdered cheek. Gray obliged politely when she targeted him, wishing her a Merry Christmas as he did so. Highly amused with herself, their sozzled colleague then proceeded to waggle the mistletoe above Cleo's head.

Cleo startled, wondering if the old dear was after a little I-kissed-a-girl-cherry-chapstick action, before jumping almost out of her skin when Gray, quicker on the uptake, stepped forward to kiss her. His lips were warm but dry, and he landed half on her lips and half on her chin, and it was all over before she really knew it was happening. Giggling away to herself, the squiffy department head trotted off to find further victims.

Cleo couldn't help but laugh. 'Wow. I think that was my first ever kiss under the mistletoe. Thanks.'

Gray immediately coloured. 'Happy to oblige,' he blustered. 'Did you know that, er, mistletoe, it's really interesting, the, er, history of it, I mean.'

Cleo smiled. She liked it when Gray got his history geek on. 'Go on then.'

'Well, the ancient druids thought it was a powerful fertility symbol. The Greeks too, they used it as an aphrodisiac. But then the Victorians started hanging it up at Christmas time and all the poor old maids used to hang around underneath it all night. If they got a kiss from someone then that meant that they were going to get married the following year.'

Cleo laughed again. 'Well, I guess I'm alright then,' she teased. 'Phew. Good to know. I'll just get Nora's out of the way and then I'll get right on with that wedding planning.' Gray coloured even further and there was a delicious little squirm of enjoyment in Cleo's tummy at the sight of it.

The uninterested looking DJ had been setting up his decks in the opposite corner to the Christmas tree for the last twenty minutes or so and finally began to announce the start of his set over the crackly speakers. Feeling decidedly more festive, Cleo tossed back what little was left of her drink. The opening bars of *Blurred Lines* boomed out into the room. Cleo wondered, as she always did in this scenario, if it was anti-feminist of her to immediately crash her way to the dance floor (she vehemently hated this song whilst sober – her feelings towards the song were a reasonably useful sort of drunk barometer, actually).

Her colleagues – all keyed up on festive (and free bar) euphoria – descended on the small parquet-tiled dance floor area en masse and immediately set about dad dancing, lots of vague shuffling rhythmically from one foot to the other accompanied by plenty of pointing at the ceiling. The Head of English twirled past, a few sheets of toilet paper trailing her like a wedding train, pierced in place by her kitten heel. The usually extremely stately Head of Admissions was wearing his tie around his forehead, Rambo-style; a few alarmingly thick puffs of chest hair curled out from the now-gaping neck of his shirt. Tia was swaying on the spot, completely out of time with the beat of the song, with her eyes closed and holding her wine glass aloft over her head like it was a lighter at a festival. Cleo let one of the guys who taught P.E. spin her around, feeling her dress swim and settle, feeling silly and light and free.

Gray grabbed her hands when the DJ started playing *Fairytale of New York*, his palms large and warm and dry, his grip assured but gentle. He bounced with her as everyone screamed out the words to the chorus, spinning her around to face him so that she could sing the Kirsty MacColl parts of the verses to him and he could respond with the Shane MacGowan lines in turn. And Cleo thought about how she was very much in love with him, almost abstractly, like she was thinking about the heart of somebody else entirely. The thought didn't thrill, and it didn't hurt – it just settled into her bones like marrow, and that was that. Gray brought her in close as the song wound to an end, all instrumental, bending their elbows until suddenly they were dancing with one another, as opposed to just next to one another. And, even though she knew so much better, Cleo let her eyes flutter closed, felt her face do the universally recognised 'kiss-me' tilt towards his, at last giving up the ghost of resistance after a long, painful year. Finally, Gray would kiss her. And then, in the immortal words of Taylor Swift, it was going to be forever, or it was going to go down in flames. But at least it would be *something*.

An enthusiastically Irish-dancing colleague Riverdanced past them, catching Gray's shoulder and jostling them; Cleo clung to the spell of the moment before, as if through sheer force of will she could prevent it from breaking. It didn't work; Gray stepped back; his hands disengaged from hers. The track changed to something thumping; the speaker system crackled in protest. Gray smiled at her, and there was something sad around the edges of it.

*I'll get us some drinks*, he mouthed over the boom and crash of the music, before making his quick getaway towards the bar area, now sadly cash only, leaving Cleo standing still in the middle of the dancefloor, like the eye in a storm of drunkenly dancing teaching staff. She felt the bubble of hope and excitement popping in her chest, the remnants fizzing against her skin. Heedless, Tia grabbed up the hands that Gray had just dropped, sweeping Cleo into a semi-waltz. Her laughter, as it always did, forced laughter from Cleo, and when Gray returned from the bar, large white wine in hand, she stepped back to allow him into their jokey box step, but she didn't tilt her head again.

# Chapter 36

'You know, December really is a legitimately busy month,' Eli was saying. Bea was, to be honest, more than halfway to sleep, the combination of the steady rush of the windscreen wipers and the drum of the rain against the roof of the car far too lulling. She hated driving in the rain. She hated driving full stop. She'd done the done thing and gotten her license at 17 like the rest of her peers, but years of living equidistant between two tube stops had spoiled her, and she hadn't owned a car or gotten behind the wheel of one for about a decade. She wasn't even 100% sure which was the clutch pedal anymore.

Luckily Eli had kept his driving skills up. He'd been the first of them to pass his test, actually, which was understandable seeing as his older brother was a driving instructor. He'd worked whatever shifts he could get at the Woolworths on the high street all through college and had gone off to university the proud owner of an early nineties Volkswagen Polo that was more rust than paint and with one buckled rear door that wouldn't open. Bea missed that old banger, for all she used to complain mercilessly about having to clamber across the back seat from the other side.

He'd remained brand loyal when he'd eventually upgraded to his brand new, part-financed Golf. Bea watched sleepily as Eli craned forward against the wheel in order to better read the overhanging motorway signs through the curtain of rain. The car had all the usual modern bells and whistles, including a built-in Sat-Nav that glided smoothly from inside the dashboard, but Eli refused to use it.

'Well, aside from the wedding, my dance card is pretty empty,' Bea admitted. 'They even held my work Christmas party in November, in order to save money.'

'Cheap bastards.'

'Yeah. I definitely felt cheap anyway. Something very wrong about wearing a paper hat and eating sprouts with your colleagues at the best of times, let alone when it's really closer to Bonfire Night. How much longer?'

'Not sure. We're still a few junctions away. I've never driven to this airport before. Nobody has.'

'Well some people must, or I can't imagine the airport would have stayed in business very long,' Bea pointed out reasonably. 'You know if we'd put it on the Sat-Nav then there'd be a really useful estimated time of arrival thing . . .' she teased.

Eli rolled his eyes. 'Look it up on your phone if you're that bothered.'

Bea didn't. She wasn't particularly worried about arriving at the airport at any actual speed.

'Use the wedding. You're going to be so busy being at Nora's beck and call. Isn't that a Maid of Honour's job description?' Bea decided not to point out that, technically, she wasn't the

Maid of Honour. 'Or maybe, you know, if it all gets way too much, text me and I'll throw an impromptu party,' Eli continued, grinning.

Bea buried her face in the crook of her elbows. 'Don't joke. She'd probably try to come, and think she might get to pull one of your mates. Oh god. If you were really my friend, you'd let her stay with you!' She was only sort of joking.

Eli shook his head empathically as he remained focused on the slick road ahead. 'Hey, you know I love you, girl, and much like Meatloaf, I would do anything for love, but I won't do that.'

Bea sighed dramatically as she repositioned herself against the slippery leather seat. 'Three weeks,' she moaned. 'I don't think I've ever spent three straight weeks in my mother's company . . .'

'I think biology dictates you spent at least nine straight months in her company . . .' Eli pointed out; Bea waved her hand impatiently.

'You know what I mean. Three weeks. She's just going to be there. In my flat. And the week after next Kirsty will be sodding off back up North for the Christmas break and it's just going to be me and her. Me and her.'

'Maybe it will be nice,' Eli reasoned. 'You can reconnect.'

'Reconnect?' Bea echoed. 'The only thing I wish my mother was 'connecting' to is an onward flight,' she grumbled.

'You'd better work on that,' Eli laughed, as he smoothly changed lanes to avoid the wheel-spray from the HGV in front. 'Two more junctions to go.'

'And she couldn't even fly into Heathrow, or Gatwick,' Bea

continued to complain. 'Instead she demands to get picked up from Luton. Bloody Luton. I didn't even realise there was an airport in Luton!' She gave Eli a sideways glance. 'Thanks again, by the way . . .'

Eli was focused on overtaking again so he didn't look over, but his jaw squared as he smiled. 'No problem.'

Hannah Milton still had a heart, or at least an under-standing of what was socially expected of a woman whose goddaughter was getting married. She'd RSVP'd promptly. Nora had called Bea up immediately upon receipt.

'So, apparently, your mother *is* coming to the wedding' she'd announced without preamble, the second Bea had answered the phone.

'Really?' Bea had been utterly unconvinced. 'I wouldn't hold your breath.'

'No, no, she's actually sent the little RSVP card back and everything. Filled out her meal choices. Put in a DJ request for us to play bloody Eternal, *Power of a Woman*.'

Bea had burst out laughing. 'Amazing. Looks like you'll have *two* embarrassing mothers at your wedding then, Mel.'

'Three if you count Harry's mum,' Nora had groaned. 'Do you know she asked me the other day if I thought that she should be getting one of those huge, ridiculous hats commis-sioned, you know, like those chavvy slapper types wear to the races on Ladies Day? Gah!'

'I hope you told her yes,' Bea had replied, mock-serious.

'I told her that it wasn't going to be a 'fancy hat' type of occasion . . .'

'I'll cancel my order,' Bea had told her, solemnly. 'But in

the meantime, don't worry about Hannah. She probably thinks she's coming now. But I'll believe it when I see it.'

Part way through November Bea had received an email. This was her mother's favourite method of communication. While reasonably infrequent, Hannah's emails were usually long and rambling, full of gossip and complaints about the ex-pat community of retirees that she lived amongst and inappropriate levels of detail concerning her sex life (depressingly far more active than Bea's own). She also insisted on always emailing through to Bea's work email, no matter how many times Bea had reminded her of her personal email address and warned her mother that her 'colourful language' was likely to be setting off alarms in the IT department.

Nestled amongst the usual fare of moaning about who hadn't paid their fair share of the service charge lately and a long diatribe about finding out that her latest boyfriend had a pregnant significant other when she'd bumped into them in a local shop, Hannah had mentioned the wedding, almost in passing. She'd booked her tickets, she'd confirmed, and as the wedding was on New Year's Eve she might as well make a Christmas of it. Bea could pick her up from Luton Airport on December 17th. Not for the first time in her life Bea wished with all of her heart that she'd had siblings, not just for the familial love and companionship, but people with which she could share the load that was their mother.

'It's this junction,' Eli announced, as he turned the indicator on and moved towards the slip road. 'Your nerves are rubbing off on me. I was looking forward to seeing Hannah again. She used to buy us our booze.'

Bea rolled her eyes. 'Yes but, a note for the future, that's not a quality you should be looking for in the future mother of your children.'

Eli bit back a laugh as they left the motorway. 'I'll keep that in mind.'

# Chapter 37

Daisy was ready. Well, as ready as she was ever going to be. She'd taken the afternoon off work in order to better emotionally prepare. She'd had a bath, preoccupying herself with her most extravagant beauty routine, almost as if she was headed to a hot date, instead of the absolute opposite. She listened to her most empowering Spotify playlist and slicked on her happiest lipstick, a bright orange-toned red that shouldn't work with her colouring but somehow did. She took an Uber to the bar rather than have to worry about struggling there on the tube, and timed it so that she was a perfectly acceptable six minutes late.

Darren was there and waiting – he'd always been quite punctual. The bar was low-ceilinged and even lower-lit, but still Daisy saw so clearly how his face brightened when he saw her arrive in the doorway. She felt her resolve hitch up, tighten somewhere behind her heart. She was about to smash apart his entire reality as he knew it. She'd picked the venue to be closer to his flat than hers, a place that had good memories, where they had spent many evenings sat, elbows on the table tops, faces close, twirling the others fingers against their own. Daisy remembered how – when they were first together – they'd spent hours on the little bistro tables outside on the patio, people watching, sharing a bottle of wine and feeling the residual summer heat from the pavements rising into the night.

She must have hesitated in the entrance a moment too long. Darren looked slightly concerned and waved awkwardly, like she might not have recognised him, gesturing at the table which already sported a large glass of wine in front of her empty chair. Daisy swallowed down the hitch and nervously smoothed her coat and dress over her abdomen. She was only thirteen weeks gone and the girls swore up and down she wasn't showing yet, and lord knows she'd had a bit of tummy padding to play with anyway, but she felt obvious and huge already nevertheless.

Darren stood up as she approached the little table-for-two, reaching out for her elbow and holding her as he kissed her cheek in a way that felt entirely un-Darren. He smelled like he'd recently shaved, and faintly of cloves, like he'd just recently brushed his teeth. He was as nervous as she was. Daisy smiled genuinely as she shrugged her heavy winter coat off over her shoulders and down her arms before slinging it over the back of the chair.

'It's so good to see you,' Darren said, simply, taking his seat and leaning across the table as if he needed to be even closer to her. 'How have you been? I've missed you. You look great!'

Daisy laughed at the mile-a-minute introduction to the conversation. 'Thank you. You look good too.' He'd definitely made an effort. By the end of their six-month courtship standards had slipped. Daisy remembered one specific example where he'd worn the same ratty tee with a hole in one armpit for three days running. Of course, her meticulous leg-shaving and matching underwear-wearing had also petered out around the same time, so she couldn't really point fingers. But tonight Darren was wearing a nice stiff-collared shirt, dark jeans and shoes that appeared to not be dirty Converses. With a jolt of guilt Daisy thought back to how carefully she'd applied her eyeliner that evening, how she'd agonised standing in front of her open wardrobe. It wasn't the same. She hadn't come here tonight hoping for a reconciliation. It had just seemed important to her that Darren thought she looked pretty, a little girl's power game that felt stupid now.

Not for the first time, Daisy wished there was an emotional switch inside of her that she could flick on. Or she wished she was the type of person who could be happy to settle. Darren was a perfectly great guy and now, poor thing, he was going to be the father of her child, tied to her forever and ever. How perfect if she could love him. She knew she never would.

'I suppose you're wondering why I asked you out for a drink,' she said hurriedly. She'd been intentionally vague in her Facebook message; she hadn't wanted to ring any alarm bells. Looking back now though, it was clear she may have accidentally given the impression that she might be open to rekindling their relationship – understandable, particularly with the holidays fast approaching.

Darren just smiled at her. 'It's just good to see you,' he repeated. His eyes flicked to her untouched glass of wine. 'Did

I get the right kind?' he asked, concerned.

Daisy felt panic start to crowd her throat. She forced herself to breathe through it. Ripping off a band-aid. She had made all these grand plans to ease into it, be super conversational: ask him how work was going, if his parents were doing fine, but she knew that if she didn't do it now, somehow it would be last orders and she still wouldn't have forced the words from her throat. She slid her hands down from the table, cupped them in her lap, pictured the little life the two of them had inadvertently created resting somewhere beyond, and gathered her strength. 'Darren, I'm pregnant.'

He didn't react right away. In fact, he even took a drink from his pint before responding, his Adam's apple bobbing deeply as he swallowed for long, silent moments.

Just when Daisy felt like she was about to scream 'say something!' Darren placed his pint back down on the table and looked at her searchingly.

'Is it mine?' he asked, voice oddly hoarse despite the fact that he'd just been drinking.

Daisy felt the indignation jolt and burn all the way down to the soles of her feet. 'Of course it's yours!' she snapped. 'For crying out loud!'

'Well, we broke up in October,' Darren blustered, moving to pick up his glass again but deciding at the last minute to leave it where it was.

'Yes. And I fell pregnant in September.'

Darren ran the heels of his hands over his temples and across his hair.

'And before you insult me further by asking, yes, you are

the only person I was sleeping with in September. I haven't slept with anyone since we broke up.' Daisy gestured wildly, palms open, feeling slightly hysterical already. 'Face it, it's yours.'

'Face it,' Darren echoed, incredulous. 'Give me a minute here. You've had weeks to take this in.' He paused. 'How many months pregnant are you then?'

'They measure it in weeks, rather than months,' Daisy informed him, snippily. 'I'm thirteen weeks.'

'You've known about this for thirteen weeks and you're just telling me now?'

Daisy felt the outrage bite again. 'No, I haven't known for thirteen weeks. I've only just found out. I'm still 'taking it in' myself, I assure you.'

'Sorry, I'm sorry, it's just.' Darren didn't so much tail off as just stop dead. 'Wow. This is insane. I – I don't know what to say. Is everything . . . okay?'

Daisy nodded. 'Everything's fine. I went for a scan as soon as I found out. Here, I've got the pictures.' She grabbed her handbag up from under the table and fished around inside her planner for the scan pictures, passing them across to Darren, feeling oddly shy. He studied them closely, angling each small square so as to catch the best light to see by. He went through the small stack three times before lowering his hands.

'It looks so human already,' he said quietly, his voice full of marvel. 'I can see the nose and the chin.'

Daisy nodded enthusiastically. 'I know. I know. And it was moving around so much during the scan. You could see fingers.

And feet.'

Darren swallowed, looking down at the monochrome photos still in his hand. 'Do you have another scan soon? I'd like to come. If that's okay.'

'Of course that's okay. It's more than okay. I don't have another scan until twenty weeks, but, you know, we can pay for a private one before that, if you'd like.'

Darren nodded slowly. 'I would like that. And can I get some copies of these? To, you know, show to my mum and stuff?'

'Of course. I'll send them across to you tomorrow.'

'This is mad. Mad.' Darren gave a throaty laugh. 'Do you know, I thought you might be meeting up because you wanted to get back together.' He looked up. 'I guess you don't . . .'

Daisy shook her head. 'No. But I do want to do this together, as far as we can . . .'

'Yeah. Thank you.'

Daisy shifted in her seat, uncomfortable. 'Don't thank me. This is your baby.'

'Our baby,' Darren corrected her. 'Wow. We're having a baby. Do you know, I wondered once or twice, if you were the one, if we'd end up having kids together.' There was still a slight bruising behind his eyes as he said the words. 'I mean, obviously, this isn't exactly how I planned it . . .' He laughed, but there was no real bitterness to it. 'But this is great, Daise. We might not have been meant to be, but – maybe this baby was?'

Daisy felt the emotion swell, warm and fulsome, and she was on her feet and hugging a still half-sitting Darren before she realised what she was doing.

'I think so too,' she murmured against his profile. 'I think so too.'

# Chapter 38

Sarah rested her forehead against the window, allowing her eyes to unfocus as the landscape sped by, the blurring beyond becoming more brown, more grey as they reached the suburbs. None of the windows in the train carriage were open – they weren't even capable of being opened – but still somehow the winter outside whistled in and forced itself down the neck of her jumper. She was wonderfully anonymous – just another wheelie suitcase toting stranger travelling into the capital for the New Year.

Across from her, sharing the table seat, was a harried mother and two red-cheeked children under five, off on a day trip to see the lights of Oxford Street. Sarah bit back the advice that the lights weren't worth the stress – the crush of the crowd and the press of the traffic – and wondered when she'd become such a magicless misery guts. She remembered dragging her ex Christmas shopping in the West End not long after they'd moved to London, back when she thought that was a thing that actual Londoners did, and how he had moaned, but also how the lights had hung in bright and heavy ropes over the heads of the crowd. She'd made a point of going back each

Christmas since, even though it was cheesy; it was part of her holiday routine, getting that warm little festive buzz each December. Who was she to bad-mouth it now?

The train began to slow, the view already nothing but dirty rail sidings and long-disused platforms, seeded over with clumps of crabgrass; they were approaching Paddington all too soon. Sarah checked her phone. She was right on time. She supposed First Great Western had to manage it on occasion, but still, how typical. Cole hadn't messaged her, which was surprising. Knowing him as she did, she'd assumed that he'd have been there super early, would have scoped out the quietest of the many cafes on the concourse, claimed an appropriate table and text her with the information. Maybe their marital strife had shaken his usual poise? Maybe she didn't know him as well as she thought.

Feeling the ache in her shoulder as she pulled her suitcase behind her along the platform, Sarah plucked at the seam of her tights through her dress; they were weirdly twisted – she'd have to nip into the station toilets and try and sort them out. Although she was loathed to pay 50p, one couldn't meet for crisis talks with one's estranged husband with wonky hosiery. That plan was quickly killed – Cole was waiting for her at the ticket gates.

She saw him long before he saw her – she still had the anonymity of the crowd spilling from the carriage doors, all moving in the same direction, lost in a tide of humanity. She slowed, giving herself a shade more time. Cole was an achingly familiar figure, tall and broad in the charcoal peacoat she'd bought for him at the onset of autumn, his hands in his

296

pockets and his elbows sticking out at 45 degrees either side, that same old confident stance. But maybe, maybe, Sarah thought as she neared, his jaw was a little sharper than before, his eyes a little more shadowed underneath. She knew the exact moment he recognised her in the crowd; he looked both delighted and sick, all in one instant.

Sarah fumbled with her ticket at the gates, the little slip of card bending and refusing to slide neatly into the appropriate slot; Sarah felt heat creeping over the back of her neck at the mortifying combination of holding up the press of people behind her and appearing to lose the better part of her motor skills upon coming into the presence of her husband for the first time in weeks.

When she finally made it through the gates, Cole reached for her immediately. Habit, auto-pilot, or embarrassment, she didn't exactly know why, but she stepped forward into the circle of his arm and turned her face to his in anticipation of a kiss hello. Cole pulled up short in surprise, before he rallied himself and kissed her softly on the cheek. Sarah suddenly realised, that moment too late, that he hadn't been going to kiss her – he'd been reaching to take her bag – and she felt like she'd quite like to curl up and die.

With one arm solidly but lightly along Sarah's back and the other occupied with manoeuvring the wheelie suitcase, Cole guided them out of the crush of the platform gate area and over to a quieter part of the huge concourse. Emboldened, perhaps, by the way she'd stepped so easily towards him, so normal and familiar, he left his arm curved around her.

'It's so good to see you,' he said, after a moment. 'How

have you been? You look great.' Sarah wondered if he was being disingenuous, or just polite. She looked no different, aside from looking a bit like someone with wonky tights who'd spent the last few hours on a cross-country train. She'd resisted the stereotypical urge to get a drastic makeover or haircut during this relationship hangover stage; if anything, a month or so of crippling sadness, her mother's home cooking and not much exercise had left her a little puffy and grey.

'Thank you,' she said, purposefully not complimenting him in return, even though he looked annoyingly good. 'Are we going to grab a coffee, or something?'

Cole looked as sad as she felt, their marriage boiled down to a quick drink in a train station Starbucks or Costa. 'Okay. When are you due at Cleo's?' he asked. Sarah had arranged to stay with Cleo for the few days leading up to the wedding, despite Cole making it clear that she was more than welcome to stay at their house, and if she couldn't bear his presence, even in the spare room, he'd find somewhere else to be. The idea of staying in the house, no matter how much she loved and missed it, hadn't appealed – Sarah knew she'd just get fixated on the empty corner where her Christmas tree should have been standing for the last few weeks, or how Cole hadn't been stacking the glasses or side plates correctly in the kitchen cupboards, and then she'd never leave again. So, the other half of Cleo's bed it was.

'We left it pretty open,' she answered, which was true– she'd had no idea how long this was likely to take. 'But we said we'd do dinner,' she said hurriedly.

'Okay.' Still managing her bag for her, Cole let her lead them into the quietest looking of the cafes nearby, meekly agreeing to share a pot of tea and sitting down opposite her, with a face like a man who anticipated a blow; Sarah realised she was loathed to be the one to deliver it. Cole had been the one to suggest this meeting. She methodically stirred milk and sweetener into her tea and waited for him to say what he wanted to say. She didn't have to wait too long.

'I'm not going to insult you by asking you to come back to me,' Cole began; he hadn't yet poured out his half of the tea. 'Although, obviously, that's all I want,' he added quickly, as if he couldn't help himself. 'But I do want you to come home.'

Sarah shifted awkwardly in the uncomfortable seat. 'Cole—'

'I'm the one who did wrong. And you've lost your home, and your job. It . . . it doesn't seem fair.'

'You know very well that you basically always paid the entire mortgage,' Sarah countered. 'It's your house.'

'It's our house,' Cole corrected her. 'It's your home. You love that house.' Sarah didn't bother denying it. 'So, I'm going to flat-sit for Harry and Nora while they're on honeymoon for the next fortnight, and I'm going to find some place to rent with a rolling monthly contract. And, when you're ready, if you'd like to, I'd like to see you for more cups of tea. Maybe a glass of wine, or a dinner. I miss you so much, Sar. I mean it. I feel like I'm missing . . .'

'An arm?' Sarah supplied, after Cole's awkward silence had gone on a whisper too long.

He looked at her sadly. 'My heart.'

Sarah swallowed heavily, studied her rapidly cooling cup

of tea. 'Well. I need to think about it.'

'Of course.'

'The moving back home. I don't know if I'm necessarily up for cosy dinner dates with you any time soon.'

'They don't have to be dates. I just can't imagine you not being in my life. I'm selfish like that.'

'You're selfish in a lot of ways, Cole.'

'I deserved that. But you know, back when, Bea and I, when we . . . did what we did. Back then, I didn't know how much I was going to love you. I know, I know: ignorance is no excuse, but it's the truth. When I realised you could actually find out what I did and dump me, I felt like I was going to be sick. It made me realise how much you meant to me, made me realise that I was crazy about you. I've spent the last few years terrified that you'd learn about what happened and I'd lose you. I'd lose our life and I'd lose our home and I'd lose our future kids. As horrendous as this is, it's almost a relief. I've hated keeping it from you. I just didn't know what to do.'

Sarah let Cole's fingers brush over her own for a heartbeat before sitting back in her chair, pulling her hands away from his, studiously avoiding looking at the patent misery on her husband's face.

'Let's just get through this wedding, okay?' she managed, after a moment. 'There's no need for what's going on between you and me to impact on Harry and Nora,' she insisted, feeling brave and stupid and weak. It was that same weakness that had caused her tears standing in the doorway of her empty nursery afflicting her again, except now it was the threshold of divorce she was paused upon, and all she wanted to do was to comfort her feckless, cheating husband, to go home with him – because to her, he was still home.

'I would never do anything to disrupt their day,' Cole was saying, all affront. 'And I know you never would too.'

'Okay then, so that's agreed.' Sarah nodded at the forgotten teapot, sat squatly between them like a little barrier. 'Drink up. I've got to get to Cleo's in a bit.'

# Chapter 39

For the first few days of her visit, Bea's mother, Hannah, had been mysteriously absent in the evenings, catching up with old London-based friends, probably propping up a few bars somewhere. In fact, Bea had only spent one actual stretch of time in the company of her mother – Christmas Day itself – and even that had been down the pub. But when Bea came home from work on the Thursday Hannah was in, sitting on the sofa in an unnecessarily elaborate and floaty kaftan-style top with gigantic gold rhinestones around the neck. She'd helped herself to a glass of red from somewhere. (Bea half-hoped she'd gotten her own supplies in rather than cracking open the bottle of Châteauneuf-du-Pape that Bea had been hoarding in the back of a cupboard for over six months, but she knew better than to expect that really.)

'There you are!' Hannah exclaimed crossly, like she was playing at a mother waiting up for an errant teenager twenty minutes after curfew (which was wonderfully ironic, as she had never bothered being that sort of mother before, even when Bea *was* an errant teen). 'God, you work late.'

Bea double-checked the time on the kitchen wall clock

before answering. 'It's only 6.45. This is a pretty normal time for people to get home from work, Mum.'

Hannah frowned. 'Is it? Well, I suppose people have different priorities on the continent.'

Bea allowed herself an eye-roll as she turned her back on her mother to throw her handbag onto the kitchen table. For someone who lived somewhere that was a sleepy fishing village in the winter and a Club 18-30 pissfest in the summer, Hannah was growing increasingly up herself with these imagined 'continental' habits and quirks.

'What are you up to tonight?' Bea decided to change the subject as she made her way back into the living area, collecting up the detritus of her Mother's Day: several mugs with milky, filmy puddles in the bottom; a Peperami wrapper; two empty packets of Wotsits (seriously, it was a wonder Bea hadn't developed scurvy as a child).

'We're having a girls' night,' Hannah announced airily; Bea almost dropped the collection of mugs she was holding precariously by their handles with her splayed fingers.

'Girls' night?' she echoed, alarmed.

'Yes, a girls' night,' Hannah repeated, her usual fractious tone already bleeding back into her voice. 'Don't you want to spend any time with your mother, for Christ's sake?' Bea dodged the question neatly by ferrying the washing up into the kitchen.

'Okay, fine, so what's the plan?' she asked, on returning to the living room. 'Are we going to watch *Dirty Dancing* and do a Ouija board?'

'Mainly I thought we'd just chat.'

'Okay. Chat. What do you want to chat about?'

'Well, I thought we could talk about you sleeping with Cole.'

Bea blinked. And blinked again. 'Me sleeping with Cole?'

'Yes, you sleeping with Cole.'

'Who told you about that?' Bea snapped, in a panic. (Damn. There goes the option of pretending it didn't happen.)

'Eileen told me,' Hannah admitted. Damn Nora and her bloody big Irish gossiping mouth.

'Oh. Right. Of course. In which case, I'd better get a drink.'

Feeling a little punch-drunk, Bea returned to the kitchen, ignoring the bottle of wine sat open on the counter (which *was* her bloody Châteauneuf-du-Pape) and making a bee-line straight to the fridge. She rummaged at the back and fished out a small individual sized bottle of Coke that had accompanied some ancient takeaway and then reached for Kirsty's emergency bottle of vodka from the bottom drawer of the freezer (sorry Kirsty, Bea mentally apologised to her flatmate, but this most certainly counts as an emergency). She didn't even get a glass right away: she just swigged first from one and then the other, standing in front of the fridge-freezer, the icy vodka causing her sensitive teeth to pang, the cheap sweetness of the cola making the inside of her cheeks feel furry, and neither making her feel particularly better about what was to come.

'Why do you want to talk about me sleeping with Cole?' Bea decided it was safer to lead the conversation rather than risk her mother dragging her through it. 'That was years ago. And, might I add, none of your bloody business.'

Giving her daughter a doleful look while she folded her legs up under her on the sofa, Hannah placed her glass of wine on the coffee table. 'What were you thinking?' she asked, but at least she sounded more curious than judgemental.

Bea sat heavily in the old armchair that filled one corner of the modest living space. 'I don't know. Not a lot, obviously.'

'Are you in love with him?'

'Cole? God, no!'

'*Were* you in love with him?'

'No. I've never been in love with Cole Norris. I was pissed off my face. I barely remember it. You'd think, the bloody trouble it's caused, it should've at least been the best shag of my life . . .'

'Did he come on to you, or did you start it?'

'I've already said, I can't remember,' Bea snapped. A scattershot of hazy memory: Bea dropping her keys at the front door; Bea almost falling off her stool at the bar, and the solidity of Cole's body against hers as he supported her; Bea staring at her mobile phone early that night, the harsh blue light from the screen hurting her eyes in the dimly-lit bar, feeling lonely like it was a physical thing, like something she'd eaten and not quite managed to digest; the words she couldn't remember, the ones that Cole had mouthed against her lips, her neck, her breasts; the way those first few kisses up against her front door had somehow tasted sad and desperate.

'He kissed me,' she assured Hannah, after a minute. 'But it was such a weird night, Mum; you can't really blame him.' *You can't really blame me*, was the unspoken echo.

'Bea. I just wish I knew how to help you,' Hannah said,

after a moment's thought. 'You're so self-destructive.'

Bea recoiled, both from the sting of the words themselves and the fact that they parroted Nora's immediate reaction, back in Paris. 'Well where do you think I get it from?' she spat. 'My brilliant role-model mum?'

Hannah looked surprised. 'Hey, don't take this out on me. I have a great life.'

'Oh yeah,' Bea scoffed. 'Bar-tending to pay the bills and shagging Portuguese supermarket bagging boys?'

'But I'm happy,' Hannah said, mildly. 'I love where I live. I love the lifestyle, and the sun. I wanted to take you to live abroad when you were tiny but before I knew it, you were at school, and it would have been too much of a disruption for you.' Hannah's eyes glazed over. 'You would have loved it. You should see the local kids. Brown as nuts, and in and out of the sea all year long! And I love my job, too,' she continued. 'You may not think that working in a bar is particularly impressive, Miss Hotshot-in-the-office, but it's social, it's flex-ible. It keeps me active. And I'm never lonely anymore.' That last word chimed against Bea's frustration; it was almost impossible to think of her draconian mother as feeling some-thing as familiar to Bea as loneliness.

'And I may not have ever gotten married. And I may not have exactly been lucky in my search for long-term love,' Hannah continued. 'But I do alright. And, most importantly,' she added, after a moment's pause, 'I have a wonderful daughter.'

Bea snorted derisively, even as the compliment warmed her. 'A wonderful daughter?' she echoed. 'I'm sorry, but isn't this entire conversation revolving around how fucked up I am?'

'You're not fucked up,' Hannah told her, firmly. 'You're just a little lost. Look, I know I was never the best mother. I never made roasts, like Eileen on a Sunday, or popped out little brothers and sisters for you to play with. I didn't have much money for nice things, and I worked shifts so I wasn't always home with you. I didn't know what to do with you really. I was young, and my mum wasn't around, but I loved you fiercely all the same and I always wanted what was best for you. But I know you grew up lonely, and – come on, let's face it - maybe too attached to the Dervans. I'm not surprised you panicked a little when you thought that Nora was growing away from you. Nora will always love you, honey, but she has her own life. It's time for you to have yours. Stop beating yourself up. Live a little. Take some risks.'

Bea rolled her eyes dramatically, even as she fought against a hot thickening in her throat. 'Okay, okay. That's enough clichés now. Point taken.'

Hannah watched her carefully. 'And you know, you could always come and live with me. It's never too late for you to get tanned and skinny-dip in the ocean. We could open a bar together. I could do the serving and you could do all the accounts and stuff.'

Bea laughed, feeing the knot inside her chest loosening. Funny, how it was such a balm simply being reminded that there was somebody in the world who loved you. 'Yeah, that sounds about right. You have all the fun, and I'll do all the work.'

Hannah smiled and sat back against the back of the sofa,

her bejewelled top glinting like something out of Arabian Nights. 'Well, it's just good to have a Plan B in life, isn't it? Even if it is just your old mum.' She reached forward again and picked up her wine from the coffee table. 'Do you actually have *Dirty Dancing* on DVD, by the way? I quite fancy that now you've said . . . Oh, and have you got any face masks?'

# Chapter 40

*It was a winter wedding, and the heavy, floor-length chiffon bridesmaids' dresses had seemed lovely and romantic in theory. The church was packed, the aisle laid with a burlap and lace runner, edged with flickering tea lights, scattered with white rose petals. The first bridesmaid down managed to take half the candles and flowers with her on the train of her dress. The second caught fire. . .*

Sarai, Cardiff

Daisy eyed her bridesmaid dress with more than a shade of concern. It had still done up fine two weeks ago at the final fitting, but, right then and there, the waistline looked impossibly small. The four silver frocks hung serenely from the living room curtain rail in Nora's flat, two each side of Nora's own gown, which was still cocooned inside its huge black dress bag for safely.

She'd been fretting about how Sarah would take it ('it' being her unexpected *delicate condition*). It did seem like the most awful sort of F-you. *Hey Sar, I know you've been struggling with infertility, and – oh – your marriage just somewhat imploded, but . . . guess what??* Sarah had been suitably excited and gracious over messages since hearing the news, but, still, Daisy feared there may be awkwardness there in person, and considering that there was already going to be awkwardness in spades between Sarah and Bea, she hadn't really wanted to exacerbate matters.

Bea had yet to arrive – she was having dinner with her mother before heading over to Bridal HQ apparently, which – knowing how much Bea disliked spending time with said mother – smacked of an excuse. Nora and Cleo clattered about in the kitchen – the blender hummed happily and reassuringly, Nora's bright laugh rising above it. She was marrying the love of her life – what use had she for nerves? Daisy had never seen a woman with feet so warm. The last time Daisy had been here listening to that blender churn, Nora had been making frozen margaritas for Harry's birthday. Tonight she was making nutritious vegetable smoothies so as to ensure they all had glowing skin come the morn.

'And the baby will LOVE IT,' Nora had declared, after she had finished waxing lyrical about the toxin-busting benefits of drinking the powdered juice of young green barley. (Daisy had the sense that baby would be happier with a Mars Bar, if she was being honest, but she'd go with the anti-oxidant flow.)

'You're so strong, Daisy.' Sarah picked up her silent phone before putting it straight back down for at least the third time since she'd arrived at the flat. 'You're having this baby on your own. I mean, I know you're not on your own, own – just you're not with Darren anymore. Your family is across the ocean. You know.'

'I know.' Daisy smiled and laced her hands across the curve of her stomach, an affectation in pregnant woman that had always irritated her, yet she had adopted almost immediately without even realising it. 'I'm going to be a single mom, yeah. But this child is going to be so loved. So loved. I mean, just look at how much its aunties are spoiling it already!' Daisy gestured over to her clutch of small gifts on the coffee table – each of her friends had turned up with 'something small' that they 'couldn't resist': soft, square muslins printed with silver moons and stars; a suitably unisex Babygro with a circus motif across the front; a tiny plush lamb doll with a sleeping face and preposterously white woollen fluff.

Sarah smiled. 'I know. Lucky tyke.'

'And Darren is, if anything, almost too involved.' Daisy rolled her eyes. 'I think he'd move in with me if I let him. You know, he's messaged me all week going all like, hey, what's up, what are you having for lunch? And I thought he was just making conversation, being nice. Then I realised he was monitoring my diet for sufficient intake of leafy green veg.'

Sarah giggled. 'He'll be thrilled with what you're about to get given to drink then.'

'I know. I don't want to tell him about it, to be honest. I don't want to set a precedent.'

'You're not tempted then? Having him move in, at least for a little while?'

'God no. Me and Belly are just fine on our own,' Daisy assured her; her middle wasn't yet distinguished enough for her to truly get away with 'Bump', so she'd settled on Belly for now.

'I just suck at being alone,' Sarah confided. 'I was sat there opposite Cole yesterday, and it was all I could do not to just take him back. Eurgh. I never thought I'd be that girl. Nobody wants to be that girl.'

'What girl?' Daisy probed gently. 'The girl who misses her husband, who she loves? You know I love Cole – granted it was a shitty, shithead thing of him to do – but I've always been a great believer in not throwing the baby out with the bathwater.'

Sarah smiled. 'And is my marriage the baby or the bathwater in this brilliant and topical metaphor?'

Daisy laughed. 'Does it matter? I just mean, if you miss the man, spend some time with him. Let him beg on his knees for forgiveness. It might be the best way for you both to heal, even if ultimately you don't end up staying together. I think it's a stronger sort of woman who knuckles down and saves what's worth saving – you know?'

Sarah was saved from responding – the flat's buzzer made her jump.

'Can somebody let Bea in please?' Nora called from the kitchen. Daisy immediately made a move to unfold her legs out from underneath her. Sarah hopped to her feet.

'Don't worry. I'll go.'

Bea was rosy-nosed from the cold, a thick bobble hat pulled down low over her brows and an oversized chunky-knit scarf wound round and round her neck. She obviously hadn't been expecting Sarah to be the one to open the door to her; her smile froze on her face.

'Hey.' Sarah stepped back to let Bea in to the warm. 'You're just in time. I think we're about to get some sort of juiced up tree to drink.'

'And here I thought we'd be drinking champagne.' Bea cautiously moved around Sarah, tentative, like you would edge past an animal you thought might be inclined to bite you. She shed her coat, started to unwind her long scarf. 'How are— have you been— okay?' she asked, stilted.

'I'm good. I've been looking forward to this weekend.' Sarah hesitated for a moment. 'I wouldn't want my – personal problems – to impact on Nora's big day at all.' Let's let the awkwardness belong to another weekend.

Bea smiled ruefully, obviously reading her loud and clear. 'If we're talking impact, I've got a bit of a confession.' She walked on into the living space.

'Mel!' Nora, her hair slathered in conditioning mask and wrapped tightly in a microfiber turban, half hugged and half palmed off a pint glass full of concerningly thick, dark green liquid to Bea. 'Bridesmaids, assembled!' she bellowed, like she was referring to a troupe of superheroes. She took a deep gulp from her own glass of veggie concoction and – to her very great credit – didn't allow her reaction to show too much on her face.

'Okay, now I've brought wedding flicks!' Cleo was pulling plastic DVD boxes out from an Asda carrier bag. '*Confetti. Bridesmaids. The Proposal. Four Weddings and a Funeral. Muriel's Wedding. 27 Dresses. Father of the Bride* – parts 1 and 2, naturally.'

'Woah, easy there Blockbusters!' Nora laughed, seeing that the plastic bag of films was hardly depleted. 'We haven't got all week.'

'Stick on *The Proposal*,' Daisy demanded, from where she still lounged on the sofa. 'Ryan Reynolds is *always* a good idea.'

'Seconded,' Sarah agreed, politely sipping from her own smoothie.

'Okay, hang on. First, I've got a confession to make,' Bea winced. The room froze.

'What is it?' Nora asked, dubiously. (Bea heard 'what now?')

'So I've been reconnecting with my mum.'

'That's great!' Nora beamed.

Bea smiled back through gritted teeth. 'Don't think that too soon. Anyway, we had a bit of a girlie evening. She decided to . . . do my hair.'

Nora's eyes flicked up; Bea was still wearing her bobble hat.

'Oh, god. Just tell me that you still HAVE hair,' she begged.

'I've been trying to wash it out all day,' Bea promised, as she reached up and removed her headgear. Her usual sharply shaped long bob fell free to her collar bones, but gone was the usual glossy brunette. Instead Bea had been left with a strong pinkish rinse that left her looking like she'd soaked her head in Ribena for a week straight.

The other four girls fell about laughing, veggie smoothies only barely escaping relations with Nora's cream carpets.

'SHE SAID IT WOULD BE WARMING,' Bea yelled over the hysterics. 'WARMING WINTER LOW-LIGHTS. FUCK.'

'And this is it after you've been washing it out?' Cleo asked through her giggles.

'Yes, and I've even tried to put permanent brown dye over

the top of it. It's just too, too . . .'

'BRIGHT!' Daisy supplied with a delighted squeal, before falling about laughing all over again.

'Oh, Mel, you look like a Myspace profile picture,' Nora sniggered.

'To be fair, your mum's not wrong. It's a lovely, warm shade. It's just maybe a little . . . vibrant. Particularly considering it's by accident.' Sarah grabbed up her handbag. 'Okay, Nora, where's the nearest food shop?'

'We've got food in, Sar,' Nora blinked, obviously confused by the abrupt change in topic.

'We need lemons to strip out the dye,' Sarah declared matter-of-factly. She glanced at Bea's pink barnet again. 'Lots of lemons.'

'Right!' Nora grabbed up her keys and coat. 'Five minutes' walk back towards the tube. I'll show you. Get the film on,' she instructed Cleo and Daisy. 'And, Jesus, you'd better open a bottle of wine as well. We can drink it *as well as* the smoothie.'

'Your hair.' Bea gestured weakly at the towel-turban, but Nora pished-pished it.

'Who cares!' she cried. 'I'M GETTING MARRIED TOMORROW. And my bridesmaid looks like a cartoon character.' She darted away as Bea reached out to smack her arm. 'Come on, look alive, if we get moving we can be back before the scenes where Ryan takes his shirt off. TO THE TESCO METRO!'

# Chapter 41

B ea knew before she cracked her eyelids open that she was the only one awake. The flat felt thickly silent. Her cheek and ear were damp with sweat from where they'd spent all night pressed up against the cream leather of Nora's sofa and there was a bruisy ache in the small of her back from hours of inappropriate lumbar support. Still, it could be worse. Below her, taking up pretty much the entirety of the living room's floor space, Cleo and Sarah lay sharing a blow-up double mattress. Cleo looked small and cute in a stereotypical foetus position, her curled hands up by her curled hair. Sarah lay sprawled on her back, hips splayed wide and mouth lolled open. (Of course, Daisy's sharing of Nora's bed hadn't been contested.)

Bea wondered if anyone had thought to turn the heating down before they'd all crashed out. The room was impossibly warm, a combination of central heating and body warmth, and it smelt like skin, clashing perfumes and something that Bea could only assume was coming from the five glasses of only-partially drunk vegetable juice. Bea peeled herself up to a sitting position. The room was lit all in a twilight grey; she knew outside it was the morning of New Year's Eve, but it could be anywhere from 5am to 10am, for all she knew. Knowing that they had the travel into the countryside to the venue ahead of them before any real bridal prep could begin, Bea sincerely hoped that it was closer to 5am.

Not wanting to disturb Cleo and Sarah, Bea swung around and clambered off the sofa over the arm, rubbing out the kink in the back of her neck with the flat of her hand as she padded towards the bathroom, double-taking as she passed the open kitchen door. Nora sat alone, silent, her elbows on the Formica table top, her cupped hands wrapped around a large mug of black coffee.

'Hey Mel,' Bea greeted, in a hushed tone, pulling out the other chair from the table. She reached forward to grasp her best friend's chin lightly in her hand. 'Looking good and clear there.' After watching *My Big Fat Greek Wedding* last night, Nora had become convinced that she'd wake up with an unsightly constellation of zits stretched across her jawline.

'I should be drinking coconut water or something, just to make sure I'm glowing later.' Nora didn't bother stifling a wide yawn, just raised her hands and the coffee mug up to cover her open mouth. 'But I didn't really sleep. I needed the caffeine.'

'Last minute nerves?'

'No, not nerves. Just anticipation. And paranoia. Like, I kept picturing myself walking down the aisle with my dress tucked into my knickers, or something.'

Bea snorted. 'The size of the skirt on that thing, could never happen.'

Nora cracked a smile. 'I know, I'm just being silly . . .'

'Your boob could always pop out the front though,' Bea pointed out, thoughtfully. 'I'd be more worried about that if I were you.'

Nora's smile stretched into a grin. 'Well, I think boob-watching is part of the bridesmaid job-description. At the first hint of a nipple-slip from me I fully expect you to divert attention by stripping full on naked.'

Bea nodded, faux-serious. 'Noted. I'm going to get in on that,' she nodded at the coffee, the smell of which was driving her to distraction, before moving over to Nora's coffee machine and selecting a pod from the basket nearby.

'I wish my dad was here.' Nora spoke in a small voice, the minute that Bea's attention was turned. Bea abandoned her attempts to slot the pod into the machine's feeder and returned to the table to hug her friend. John Dervan had died when they were both so young, that all Bea could really remember of the man was the boom of loud laughter, the spicy fug of his brand of cigarettes, how he'd insisted the entire family dress up on Sundays. Bea had never known her father, and Nora's had always been terrifying and thrilling to her in equal measure. It seemed like a million years ago, but now suddenly they were at the day where Eileen would walk her first child down the aisle in the place of her long-dead husband.

'He'll be watching on,' Bea comforted.

Nora leaned into the hug. 'You don't believe in Heaven,' she pointed out.

'No. But he did.' Bea smoothed her god-sister's hair down over her ears and her heart filled up with all the Noras she had known and loved across her life: the child; the teen; the woman; the friend; the sister. Nora the bride smiled.

'Better think about rousing the troops. There are a lot of us to get showered, and the cars will be here at nine.'

'Do you want to get in the shower first?' Bea asked. 'So you don't feel rushed?'

Nora shook her head. 'Why don't you go first. Then if your hair still looks pink when it's dry you can go again,' she teased.

'Bugger off,' Bea shot back, reaching for Nora's coffee in lieu of her own and taking a fortifying gulp.

# Chapter 42

*I was at a wedding where somebody got absolutely plas-
tered and spilled red wine on the flower girl in the white
dress – just before the photos. And then they hid and tried
to pretend they didn't do it. Okay, it was me. . .*

Michelle, Ipswich

The Hall in winter was exactly as Cleo had imagined it
would be. As the first of the hired Bentleys swept through
the gates and along in front of the old building, the pebbled
drive popping and crackling under the tyres, Cleo's immediate
thought was that it had snowed when she hadn't been paying
attention. After a beat, she realised that it was just frost
crisping the lawn and the sloping roof tiles, silver and shining.
Already there was the bustle of activity, big white supplier
vans with their doors flung open, industrious looking
members of staff ferrying boxes, thick pillar candles and fussy,
frothy bouquets of flowers through the stately entrance doors.

Beside her on the back seat, Cleo felt Nora craning to look
around as the car glided smoothly to a stop. Cleo felt herself

leaning forward a little too; the control freak in her wanted to leap from the car and begin coordinating, and it was hell to know that she couldn't, that she had to leave it all to the events' manager and her team. The groom's party were due to arrive before too long, and Nora had to be closeted away in the honeymoon suite long before then. Nora might be an independent, modern, Destiny's Child-bellowing female, but she was proving oddly traditional when it came to certain aspects of her wedding day, with her big, white dress and her something blue, and with Harry banned from laying eyes on her until she arrived aisle-side.

As Cleo exited the car she saw Bea doing the same from the second Bentley, staggering a little under the weight of Nora's dress bag, Nora's mother Eileen following at her heels, her hair already tightly in rollers. Nora's teenaged sister Finola slunk from the back seats, her earbuds defiantly in place, trailing shocking pink wires from each side of her face and down into her phone, on which she was fixated, flicking at the touch screen lazily with one thumb. Daisy unfurled herself from the front seat of the first car, stretching her hands up towards the cold winter sky, and for a moment Cleo fancied she could see the new curves that were being laid down over her friend's bones.

Nora approached her mother, tentative. 'What do you think, Mammy?'

Eileen glanced around at the stately home, looking impressed despite herself. 'Very grand,' she allowed. 'It will do very well.'

The wedding coordinator met them at the doors, looking

reassuringly corporate in a black dress suit and crisp white blouse, so on the ball that she must have been watching out for them. At an almost imperceptible signal from her, identically dressed minions appeared as if from nowhere to whisk the dress bag away from Bea's clutches and begin to empty the hire cars' boots of the girls' own dresses, overnight bags and general luggage, spiriting everything up to the honeymoon suite. Feeling slightly redundant, Cleo went through the motions of 'supervising'.

She remembered her trip out here back in the spring, how Gray had stepped up to offer up his Saturday and his driving services, how the trees on the estate had been fat with blossom and how the year ahead had felt unbelievably long and full of possibility, stretching out in front of them. Back when her growing crush on Gray had nested in only a small part of her heart, back before too many things had been unsaid.

Sarah wondered why Nora had even bothered to get dressed just to sit in a car from the doorway of her block of flats to the doorway of the wedding venue. Within three minutes of being ensconced in the honeymoon suite, she had whipped off her jeans and jumper and dived into a white fluffy dressing gown, the word 'bride' proudly picked out across the back in curling, baby-blue script. The staff glided in with mirrored silver trays loaded with glazed breakfast pastries, bottles of champagne and carafes of orange juice. A film-perfect fire crackled merrily in the grate inside an ancient-looking stone fireplace

It was all a far cry from Sarah's registry office and gastropub jobbie a few years earlier, but, still, she looked at Nora's colourless cheeks and nervous fingers moving against the slender stem of her champagne flute and recognised much of herself on her own wedding morning. She remembered how it had all been over in a flash – her mother had had to reassure her that, yes, all the legal formalities had been dealt with – they'd said 'I do' at all the right moments and signed their signatures in the right place. She'd watched Cole's profile instead of eating her roast lunch afterwards, too sick with happiness to contemplate a single bite. *Cole Norris, her husband. My husband. Sarah Norris' husband.*

Nora was largely ignoring her glass of Buck's Fizz, peering out of the windows at the expanse of grey skies beyond. 'It's saying it's due to rain between four and six,' she said again, after consulting the weather app on her mobile phone. 'But four and six isn't too bad, because that's when we'll all be inside eating the wedding breakfast anyway, right?'

'Honey, stop driving yourself mad with that thing.' Daisy deftly confiscated the bride's phone. 'Not even you can stop it from raining.'

'My mammy said that rain on a wedding day symbolises the number of tears the bride will shed during the marriage,' Eileen droned from across the room. Nora glanced miserably out of the window again, before grabbing a pastry and commencing comfort-eating.

The unmistakeable crackle of tyres on the drive heralded the arrival of the menfolk.

'Stay back,' Bea ordered from the window, holding her arm out as if she would very literally hold Nora at arm's length. 'It's Harry's cars.'

'Does he look worried about the rain too?' Nora enquired,

urgently. Bea, who had no idea what sort of expression someone who was worried about the rain might display, didn't respond. (She also decided not to mention the – quite frankly alarming – amount of Carlsberg Export that seemed to be being unloaded from one of the boots.)

'Come here and check over the presents then,' Cleo urged Nora, with the teacher's super-senses for the need for distraction. 'Is everything here?' Nora and Harry had decided to exchange bags of small but sentimental gifts – and Nora had spent the last two weeks agonising about what to write in the card. Although she'd checked them twice the previous night, Nora removed each neatly wrapped parcel from the bag, counting them, checking that the sticky tape was still lying flat and fixed, holding each close to her heart for a moment.

'Are you okay to deliver these?' Nora asked Bea. Bea had already been informed that the bride/groom present swap was going to be one of her morning duties and had accepted with pleasure.

'Sure. I'll let Eli know it's time to head to *the drop point*,' Bea teased, grabbing up her phone and shoving her feet into a nearby pair of fluffy slippers.

* * *

One of the things that Nora had most loved about Withysteeple was the beautiful staircase, which wound down from a wide, airy mezzanine to the great hall below, and would – no doubt – serve as a sufficiently dramatic entrance for any bride. Bea ran her fingertips lightly over the dark, oiled wood of the banister as she made her way and, not for the first time that morning, thought on how Nora (damnit) had definitely made the right venue choice.

Eli was waiting at the far end of the big landing, his elbows on the balustrade and face unreadable as he stared out across the open space, so clearly in a world of his own. Bea slowed as she approached him. He'd obviously been part way through getting dressed when the call to present-courier had arrived. He was still wearing his jeans, twist-style, loose on his hips and comfortable-looking, and his feet were bare, the toes peeking out oddly intimate. On top he wore a crisp white dress shirt, hurriedly fastened, still open at the neck, navel and cuffs. Bea felt her pulse in odd points of her body. It was inappropriately sexy. She felt the recent cruel-to-be-kind words of Nora and her mother scraping over the surface of her bones.

She'd been dating one of the more loserish entries in her parade of loser ex-boyfriends around the time her best friends returned home from their undergraduate adventures. He'd had a pimped-up car and called Bea 'baby', and at twenty-one it had been an odd tightrope between feeling pleasingly adult and horribly cringey. Back then, non-student Bea was of course the only one of them not living with the parentals, so they'd spent an awful lot of time crammed into her studio flat, a space so meagre one corner of the kitchen worktop worked as both coffee table and bedside table, depending on the need.

Bea had been complaining, as was standard. 'He's driving me mad,' she confessed, as she handed Eli a beer. She remembered, he'd been sitting on her kitchen side, denim-ed legs trailing down the front of the cabinets, towering over her and making her feel agreeably dainty.

'You don't need him now we're back,' Nora had laughed, before turning back to the others and leaving Eli and Bea on their own.

'True.' With her little day bed/sofa already full, Bea had leaned up next to Eli; he'd clinked the necks of their bottles together.

'To new chapters,' was all he'd said.

'For you guys, maybe,' Bea had said ruefully. 'I imagine my life will go on much as it was before. But what's next for you? Job Centre on Monday?' Her entire class had just graduated into the worst of the recession and a non-existent job market, the only thing that made Bea feel like not going to university had been the better decision.

Eli had shaken his head. 'Meeting at the bank. I'm going to try and get that Career Development Loan.' Bea stood up straighter. Eli had been mentioning on and off that he'd like to do a Masters, train as an architect.

'Wow, big stuff! So, back to Cardiff?' He'd been the furthest away the last three years, and Bea had felt a surprisingly strong pang at the thought of him leaving again.

Eli had shrugged. 'A lot of places offer good Architecture courses. I'm keeping my options open.'

'Oh! So you could stay round London?' Bea had been delighted.

'Look, are you going to actually break up with this guy?' Eli had suddenly and wildly changed the subject.

'Um. I dunno? What's it to you?'

'What's it to me?' Eli had echoed, in disbelief. 'Oh, I don't know. Maybe, Bea, it matters to me because we've been friends forever, and I'd like you to be happy? Is that so mad?'

'No.' Bea had felt that burning flush of discomfort she always felt whenever anyone was overly-nice to her.

'How about this one then. How about: it matters to me because I've been thinking lately that we would be good together. You and I,' he had clarified, finally, as if Bea would somehow mistake what he meant by 'we'.

They'd been skirting around this for years. There had been awkward teenaged crushes – but never at the same time; there had been unfinished sentences and over-long looks. But Bea had never actually thought they'd tip over that knife-edge. The silence stretched out between them, a judgmental observer to the conversation they weren't having, urging her to say something, *say something*. She needed time to think. She needed for Nora and Cole and Harry to not be mere feet away. And, as was always her way, Bea just groped for the status quo.

'Don't be daft.' She had said it firmly but not unkindly. 'You're like my best mate.'

And Eli, bless him, had given it just one more try.

'Okay, so, to be clear here, you're friend-zoning me?' He'd mirrored her tone, faux-normal, but his eyes were dark. Bea had felt the panic pinching harder.

'Let's not do this,' she'd ground out.

And, somehow, without perceptively moving at all, Eli had turned away from her.

'Okay,' he'd said, still with that harshly pleasant inflection. 'We won't do this.'

Bea still remembered the sickly, hoppy smell from the necks of their beer bottles, and on their breath, and how Eli had been wearing a white-and-navy raglan tee. She'd rehashed that almost-conversation at least a hundred times over the past decade or so, during idle moments, insomniac in the dead of night, or when she was feeling particularly low and lonely – but less often as the years went past. But she was reminded of it now. Maybe she and Eli could have been that 'we', had their own wedding day with their own grand staircase. She shook her head, amused and despairing at the same time; the motion caught Eli's attention finally. His blank face stretched into a wide smile.

Bea stepped forward and gave her old friend a spontaneous hug, pulling him so close that she saw his pulse jumping in his throat.

'What was that for?' he smiled as they parted.

Bea shrugged. 'I'm just feeling sentimental today.'

# Chapter 43

'It's a, nice day for a, white wedding,' Daisy growled into the hairbrush she was holding as she surveyed her reflection in the full-length mirror. She still had hair and makeup to do, and it wasn't as if she'd been the most trim-and-toned of the bridesmaid contingent even before she'd gotten knocked up, but she was pretty pleased with what she saw. The soft silver fabric skimmed away and pulled in in all the right places.

'You look fab,' Nora called from where she was sat in the corner having her hair seen to by an enthusiastic professional. 'Remind me to ask you to be bridesmaid at all my future weddings.'

'Plus in future it will be a buy-one-get-one-free deal,' Daisy teased, patting her stomach. 'Bridesmaid plus matching flower girl or page boy.'

'At this rate your kid will be *way* too old to be a flower girl or page boy at my wedding,' Bea grumbled, as she vacated the makeup artist's stool and tagged Daisy in for her cosmetic attentions, moving over to join Cleo near the fire. Cleo was tethered to the wall by her mobile phone's charging cable, an overly tormented expression across her face. Bea had never been able to fathom why the girl always let her emotions show so clearly. She poured them both fresh glasses of Buck's Fizz as she checked the time on the carriage clock standing on the mantelpiece. Less than an hour until show-time.

'Gray?' she asked, without preamble, handing Cleo the champagne flute. Cleo startled, guilt reddening her face under the already expertly-applied powder.

'Yeah. He was just asking me to wish Nora luck for today.' Cleo pointedly put her phone down.

'You're going to have to explain it to me again. Why don't you just go out with the guy?'

Cleo's blush darkened, but to her credit she didn't try and wiggle away. Instead, she just sighed, light and final. 'He hasn't asked me.'

Bea could barely contain her eye-roll. 'You know it's not the fifties, yeah? Why don't you just ask *him* out?'

'I wouldn't be able to stand him saying no. I'm not strong like you.'

Slightly disarmed by the unexpected compliment, Bea immediately back-tracked. 'Why do you even think he'd say no? He's so into you. And why wouldn't he be? You're smart, you're gorgeous.'

Probably as painfully aware as Bea was that this was the nicest they'd ever been to one another in the long decade of their close acquaintance, Cleo met her eyes squarely. 'Thanks.'

'So? Are you going to go for it?' Bea urged.

'Go for it?' Cleo echoed, with a laugh. 'Go for what?'

'Grab life by the balls. Hell, grab *him* by the balls,' Bea added impatiently. 'The next time you see him.'

Cleo sighed again. 'The thing is, I think Gray and his Tinder-finger are a bit one-weekend-wonder. I don't want to just be a fun few days to him. Don't get me wrong, it certainly would be . . . *fun* . . .' Cleo grinned, a little wickedly. 'But that's not what I want.'

'What is it that you want then?'

'Oh, I want the fun. But I want it forever,' Cleo answered simply. 'Nothing else seems worth it.'

And Bea remembered that lost moment in that pokey studio flat, Eli in the raglan tee, her pulse banging sharp and painful, her brave friend offering her his heart, her being too unsure of the sincerity – hers, his – to take it. She understood Cleo better than she knew.

'Next time you see him,' Bea repeated softly, 'just remember. If you're crazy in love with him anyway, your friendship is already screwed.'

'Okay, the registrar will be up in a minute. It's dress time!' the hairdresser announced, punctuating the statement with an incredibly liberal mist of hairspray, having already used enough that morning across the bridal party to cause new concerns about the ozone. Nora leapt to her feet like she'd been unleashed.

'Oh! I'm getting in my wedding dress! *I'm getting married!*' she hollered, putting her hands up to her face to tug at her earlobes, a quirk of hers when she was nervous or excited; Bea saw both the makeup artist and the hairdresser wince a little.

Cleo moved across to her friend and firmly placed her hands on top of hers, bringing them down and holding them loosely between them. 'Yes my love, you are!'

Bea hung back for a moment, watching the two, waiting to feel that ugly whirl of jealousy as usual, but she was pleased that when it came it was more a butterfly flapping than a tornado storming. You don't get to pick your family, but at least you get to pick your friends; it was a maxim that Bea had often repeated. The trouble was, of course, you don't get to pick your friend's friends. So, actually, she guessed she was lucky that Cleo Adkins - that wholly irritating student lounging on Nora's bed all those years ago - had turned out to be such a good egg after all. Daisy and Sarah crowded round Nora too, Sarah already carrying the bridal veil reverently, eagerly awaiting its application as the piece de resistance. They were pretty damn good eggs too.

Nora glanced across at where Bea still lingered by the fire. She freed one of her hands from Cleo's hold and held it out in a wordless invite. Equally wordlessly, Bea went to her and joined the loose silver-clad circle, four bridesmaids ringing their lovely friend for those last few minutes.

# Chapter 44

*We got married at the beautiful old Scottish church where his grandparents had. It had been raining non-stop for a week, but when we came out into the grounds for our photographs, the clouds parted and the sun shone down. The wedding party all posed on a grassy embankment, but while the photographer was trying to arrange us, the Best Man trod heavily on my dress. I tried to balance myself, but I was too precarious in heels on the wet grass, and toppled arse over tit all the way down the hill, coming to a rest on a medieval grave. A muddy medieval grave.*

Adele, York

The little white faux-fur stoles that Nora had sourced were absolutely charming, but they were doing bugger all against the winter chill.

'Okay, ladies, just dip those shoulders just a little more. A little more.' The photographer had been calling out ridiculous instructions at them for the last quarter of an hour. Sarah felt officially chilled to the bone. If it wasn't for the warm and solid presence of Barlow to her front and Cole to her back, she might literally freeze. Still, obediently, she dipped her shoulder and shot her toothy smiles at the camera lens. The problem with being a bridesmaid, whilst obviously a great honour, is that it means that you spend much of the first part of the day off posing like a prat in a field/on a beach/up some stairs while the rest of the wedding guests get to see off the free drinks. . .

Nora – seemingly unaffected by the biting cold aside from the fetching pinkness it had raised in her cheeks and on the tip of her nose – kept staring up at Harry like she expected him to have changed from minute to minute. He too was heavily preoccupied with his new wife, dropping little kisses on her hair, the small of her neck, that shoulder she was being instructed to dip. How was it only two years since her own wedding day? It felt a lifetime ago. As if sensing the run of her thoughts, her estranged husband shifted behind her, angling himself differently, blocking out a little more of the icy air.

Finally they were released from posing oppression, albeit warned not to stray too far away in case they were needed for some more shots after the family ones were completed. Sarah gratefully accepted a glass of Winter Pimms from a hovering waiter and carefully picked her way across the crispy lawns to the sturdier pathway. She felt a steadying presence at her elbow, the weight of someone's morning jacket on her shoulders, already warm with body heat. She turned, expecting Cole, but it was Barlow smiling at her in his shirtsleeves.

'How have you been? I haven't wanted to bother you, but I've been thinking about you a lot.'

Sarah had felt the same. She and Barlow had always been close – working long hours keeping *The Hand in Hand* in business for that first year or so had forged their friendship in fire. But he'd been Cole's friend long before a bedraggled Sarah had ever appeared at his bar and ordered that fateful glass of wine, and she'd felt too awkward to get in touch with him over the last few weeks.

'I've been better,' she admitted.

'Is your mum driving you mad?'

Sarah laughed. 'Literally insane. What's worse is that I think she wants me gone as much as I want to be gone. I need to get another job, be in back in Wales or up in London or – who knows – somewhere new and wonderful. How's work?' she asked after a beat. She'd never moved on from a vested interest in *The Hand in Hand*. She knew things must be going well, as Barlow was in the middle of buying his first house, and the pub was always heaving every time Sarah dropped in.

Barlow's beam confirmed her guess. 'Really, really good. In fact, I'm buying another pub. In Chiswick. We're expanding, baby!'

'Barlow, that's amazing!'

'It is. But it's also presented me with a problem. It's actually another reason I've been meaning to get in contact with you.'

'Oh?'

'See, I can't be owner/manager of two different establishments really.'

'If anyone can handle it, it'd be you.'

'I'd be pulling out my beard with stress after one week,' Barlow laughed. 'No, I need to get a good team in place in Wimbledon so I can really concentrate on making the new branch a success.'

Sarah felt a pang at the thought of *The Hand in Hand* left without Barlow's good-natured but sharp supervision. The junior bar and kitchen staff turnover was pretty high, pretty usual in the service industry, but, still, it would take a dedicated manager to keep morale and standards up.

'Are you going to promote Angie then?' The current assistant-manager had originally started as a bartender when Sarah had been there. She liked her fine, but she was a bit workshy, and – not that Sarah had ever dobbed her in to Barlow – had always had a habit of calling in sick to work and then checking in as out for drinks with her mates on Facebook that same evening (so, both a skiver and a little bit thick).

Barlow laughed. 'God no, not Angie.'

'Ah, recruiting then? Seen anyone for interview yet?'

'Not yet. I was going to offer you first refusal.'

It took a beat or two for Barlow's words to sink in. 'Me?'

'You,' Barlow confirmed, with a grin.

'Me? Manager of *The Hand*?'

'Can't think of anyone better.'

'I've never managed anything in my life!'

'Come off it. You were basically doing it for me when I was only paying you a part-time bar staff wage and you had a whole other job during the day,' Barlow scoffed.

'You're not just saying this because I'm jobless and homeless, are you?'

'Not at all. I was already gearing up to talk to you about it before you and Cole – before you, ah, left London.'

Sarah stupidly felt like she could cry at the sheer weight of the blessing that had just fallen into her lap. A job – and not just any job, one she could really care about. Combined with Cole's promise that he'd move out of their house to give her space, all of a sudden her life felt like it could be hers again. She blinked back the heat that had massed at her lashes.

'Are you sure?'

'I am one hundred percent sure, Sar.'

'And do you promise you'll fire me immediately if I turn out to be absolute crap?'

Barlow laugh was loud and fond. 'I promise.'

'Then okay.' Sarah threw herself into her friend's arms and he squeezed her thoroughly.

'Do you not even want to talk about the logistics? Salary?' Barlow laughed.

'We can get to that. My answer will still be yes!' Sarah was oddly breathless. 'Thank you, Barlow. You have no idea what this means to me.'

'Hey, it's not a favour, remember,' he reminded her gently. 'If anything I'm taking complete advantage of your amazing-ness.'

'Okay. I'll do my best to be amazing for you.'

'Can I have the bridesmaids back, please?' the photographer called impatiently from the middle of the lawns. 'I just want some shots with the sisters of the bride.'

Sarah got halfway back across the grass before she remembered she was still wearing Barlow's jacket, and had to tumble back over to return it to him. As she stood in the line and posed and dipped and beamed on cue, she hoped very much that she wouldn't look as daftly over-excited as she felt in the final photos, but at least she knew that all the smiles were utterly genuine.

\* \* \*

Bea's cheeks ached from all the enforced smiling. She resisted the urge to rub them and helped herself to a flute of champagne instead. Nora and Harry had been pulled away to take cringingly romantic, staring-into-one-another's-eyes couple photos in the rich late-afternoon light before the wedding breakfast was served, and so, for the bridesmaids, a brief reprieve in duties.

Just as she had made up her mind that she probably had enough time to nip upstairs to her room, check on her hair and slip off her heels for a bit, a familiar voice carried to her ears.

Claire, in the middle of informing a stricken waiter carrying a tray of canapes all about her current dietary requirements, had apparently decided to throw a middle finger up at December and was wearing a peacock print maxi dress and open-toe sandals; she looked fabulous, albeit more at home on a fancy resort holiday. Bea had clocked her sat near the front during the ceremony; they hadn't spoken since that night in Paris. With a last lingering thought for her aching feet, Bea grabbed another glass of champagne from the stash kept behind for the wedding party and approached her old friend.

'The best peace offering may be diamonds,' Bea said conversationally as she handed over the glass, 'but champagne has got to be up there too, right?'

Claire accepted the drink with a quick shrug of her shoulders. 'Thanks. For all I should really be taking it easy. It turns out I become a complete gobby bitch when I've had too much to drink.'

'That's nothing.' Bea sighed dramatically. 'I shag completely inappropriate blokes when *I've* had too much to drink.'

'That's not true,' Claire protested. 'You do that sober sometimes too.'

The tease startled a laugh out of Bea. 'Fair. And you're a mouthy cow pretty much 24/7 too.'

'Well, I'm glad we got that straightened out,' Claire nodded, saluting Bea with her glass before taking a drink. 'I really am sorry. Sorry I was jealous,' she added, after a beat. 'And for what I did in Paris.'

'And I'm sorry for what I was saying about you. And that I slept with Cole in the first place.' Bea looked forward to the day where she wouldn't feel quite so genuinely awful about a night she could barely remember. 'We're terrible people.'

Claire surveyed her over the rim of her champagne flute, eyes uncharacteristically shrewd. 'I think we're just people.' After a moment, she reached out and touched the material of the bridesmaid dress gathered at Bea's shoulder. 'I like these,' she said softly. 'They're beautiful. The colour wouldn't have done much for me though.'

'I think you would have looked great.' Bea threw her free arm around the bare, winter-impervious shoulders of her friend and gave her a quick squeeze. Maybe Claire would never quite get over the sting of not getting to be one of Nora's bridesmaids, but at least she was proving mature enough not to let it affect her friendships.

'I'm so happy for Nora. And Harry,' Claire said, as if on cue. 'Their happy ever after. It's like a fairy tale.'

Bea, who had had a front row seat to all of Nora and Harry's previous relationships, the disasters and the almost-could-have-been-somethings and everything in between; the handful of times Nora had been adamant that getting together with Harry had been a huge mistake, the once or twice they'd even broken up, however temporary: if it was a fairy tale, it was a very *modern* sort of fairy tale, Bea thought with a wry smile.

'You know, you, mine and Nora's friendship has already lasted way longer than the average marriage,' Bea pointed out.

'Here's to the successes.' Claire offered her glass for Bea to chink against, and Bea did: whether Claire meant friendships, marriages or people, it didn't really matter.

# Chapter 45

The ballroom went into uproar to welcome the new Mr and Mrs Clarke to their wedding breakfast. Nora was so in love with her bridal gown that she'd refused to contemplate having a smaller 'evening' dress, but she had changed to flats and lost the intricate veil for the sit-down meal. The head table was dedicated to immediate family (Nora's vastly outnumbering that of Harry) whilst the groomsmen and bridesmaids shared a large table nearby. Cleo had to appreciate the careful rejigging that had clearly gone in to the table plan, with Sarah, Cole and Bea unsubtly equidistant from one another, but it might not have been necessary: the atmosphere was relaxed and festive, the wine and jokes flowing free.

Despite knowing there was going to be a four-course meal, Cleo had bolted down probably more than her fair share of the canapes. Eli hadn't been so prepared.

'I'm absolutely starving,' he complained, having beasted down his starter before the fourth table on the round had even been served theirs. Bea, sat to his left, had approached her parfait and melba toast with a little more decorum.

'Stop complaining. Eat another bread roll,' she nodded her

head towards the basket in the centre of the table. Eli reached for one while using his butter knife to pilfer a corner of Bea's parfait. She stabbed at his knuckles with her fork, only half-kidding.

'Remind me to do some sort of a buffet thing when I get married,' Eli asked Bea as he liberally spread parfait onto the roll. Bea didn't respond – she just bit off a piece of her melba toast with a snap.

Eventually the dessert plates were cleared away, with another member of staff following behind to dispense new champagne into waiting flutes for the speeches. Eileen was up first, in lieu of the Father of the Bride. Nora hadn't been sure if it was a good idea, but Eileen had been oddly insistent.

Right on cue, as the last glasses of fizz were being poured, the Master of Ceremonies went to stand behind the head table and called out across the room: 'Ladies and gentlemen, please charge your glasses for the Mother of the Bride.'

Eileen got to her feet; she had no notes, and no preamble. 'My wedding to Nora's father was nothing like this,' she began. Cleo sought Nora's face; her jaw was slightly tight – she'd confessed her concerns that Eileen would use her speech to start soapboxing on the fact that Nora hadn't gotten married in a church, and it seemed she may have been right to worry. 'We were young,' Eileen continued; Nora's jaw worked itself a little tighter. 'Strangers to each other, really. Strangers to ourselves. But it was exciting. Not to know what life had in store. Would we be staying on in the village, or going over to London, or Liverpool? Would there be babies? I had a lot of younger brothers and sisters, and I fancied myself for a good mother. I could picture them, even picture the grandchildren, and me and Shaun there happy and old.

'We talked about it a lot – Shaun was never too emotional now, of course, not like me. But when I told him we were expecting he couldn't do enough for me, and when he came to see us in the hospital, I swear the man had tears in his eyes. He picked Nora up and went to hold her by the window, so he could look at her in the light. She was screaming murder, hitting his chest with her little fists – Lord, red as a tomato she was. And he was so proud. My little boxer, he called her. And they were thick as thieves from then on. She was his little shadow.

'So when he died, it was Nora I was worried for, more than the others. She was older – I knew she'd remember him more, and I didn't know if that was more of a blessing or a curse, if I'm honest.

'And I worried it would change her. That she wouldn't be that little fighter anymore. But she became even more so. She was so fierce and lovely as she grew, and I knew Shaun would have been even prouder of her than I was.'

Eileen had been speaking slightly fast, as if she was in a rush to get the words out before any unseemly emotion choked her voice. She paused there; the room hung with her. Nora was openly crying, dabbing underneath her lower lashes with her white linen napkin in a brave attempt to save her makeup; Harry had closed his fingers around her fist.

'He liked young Henry,' Eileen continued after a moment, even now sticking firmly with her new son-in-law's full Christian name. 'Thought he had spunk.' Cleo just about managed to swallow her inappropriate giggle re the unfortunate word choice (others around her were not so circumspect). 'He would be very happy today. All the other men he probably would have chased off with a brick!' Eileen laughed. 'But Henry, now: Shaun would have thrown his arm around his shoulders. He would have said, 'here now, son, welcome to the family properly.' He would have known that you'd look after our girl. And that she'd look after you.

'Anyway, now, it's not me you're here to listen to, not really.' Bluster back in her voice, Eileen reached down for her glass. 'I just wanted to make sure it was like Shaun could be saying a few words. Although, of course, it wouldn't have been just 'a few', not with that man; he'd be gabbing all night!' Laughing along with her audience, Eileen raised her arm straight, her champagne high. 'So, Henry, welcome properly to a family that already loves you. And Nora. If your daddy was here, he could talk non-stop for ten years and still not get across how much we love you, how proud we are of the girl you were and the woman you've become. And so, for the first toast, please charge your glasses. To family.'

'To family,' the tables echoed, shining flutes of champagne catching the candlelight from the centrepieces.

\* \* \*

After Cole had delivered the final speech as the Best Man, the waiting staff circled around once more, clearing away empty flutes and pouring teas and coffees in their place. Despite the winter outside the ballroom was warm and fuggy with candle-smoke, jackets and wraps thrown over the backs of chairs, ties loosened, seats pushed back, the rigidity of the earlier table plan already forgotten.

'Great speech, mate,' Harry's best work friend Adam called across to Cole from the next table as he returned to his seat. 'Great day,' he continued. 'Weddings get me all romantic!' He grinned wickedly at his girlfriend, Harriet.

'Christ, no,' Harriet groaned in response, shifting her alarmingly pregnant frame on the delicate looking dining chair while gestured at her huge bump with the folded seat card she'd been listlessly fanning herself with. 'Look at where your last bout of romance got me.'

The speeches had overrun, of course, but only lightly. But still – the DJ was impatiently waiting with his decks and speakers, and the evening guests were massing and corralled in the lobby. The guests were all lethargic and disinclined to move after all the good food and long speeches, no matter how unsubtle the staff were with their hints that they needed to clear and move the tables aside for the dancing. Sarah knew as a bridesmaid she should probably be chivvying people– or at the very least leading by example – but she felt warm and happy and comfortable right where she was. She even smiled at Cole as he approached her, sitting down next to her in the chair that Eli had recently vacated.

'Was that okay?' he asked her as he sat, his face a little over-worried. He'd delivered a pitch-perfect Best Man speech from behind his usual 'lad' persona, but Sarah knew her husband, and he was forever worried he hadn't done enough to meet people's expectations. It's what had pushed him to become so successful professionally, but Sarah knew that the thought he could let down Harry and Nora would have been eating him up over the last few days. She reached out and touched the back of his hand.

'It was great,' she assured him.

Cole quickly grabbed up her hand before she could retract it, squeezing it gratefully. Sarah remembered their wedding day again – she guessed it made sense to be haunted by it today, of all days – particularly how she and Cole had retired to their hotel room after the festivities, how Cole had stood behind her, his big hands clumsy against her back as he picked apart the laced-up eyelets of her simple gown, asking her over and over was she okay, was she happy?

'Barlow has offered me a job,' Sarah said, keeping her tone light. Surprise registered only briefly on Cole's face, although he did send quite a hard look towards the back of his friend's head; he'd always made comments that were only half-jokes about Barlow being in love with Sarah.

'At the pub?'

'Yes. Manager.'

'Good. You'll be amazing,' Cole said, with easy confidence. 'It's a no-brainer, really.' His quick mind jumped ahead before she had the chance to continue. 'I've got a few flats to view next week. Don't worry, I won't be in the house. It's yours.' A smile twitched at the corner of his mouth, for all he hadn't been able to completely mask the sadness in his voice. 'You can even get rid of the chair, if you want to.' He had finally let go of her hand; she could feel the reluctance as he did so in every finger.

Sarah groaned. Cole's grim old recliner had been a constant source of squabbles in their house. He'd insisted on keeping it – for all it was ancient, with cracked, hard leather, and completely clashed with the rest of the interior design she'd slaved over. By rights she should be jumping for joy at the permission to chuck the damn thing, but Sarah realised after a moment that she was thinking of the old thing almost fondly, about how nice it would be to get home to her own space and curl up on it, tucking her feet under her bottom and draping a throw over her knees like she had on countless evenings before. After all, just because something wasn't perfect, it didn't mean it needed to be thrown away.

Sarah took up the hand that had just released hers.

'So,' she said, conversationally, calmly. 'You said you wanted to take me on a date?'

# Chapter 46

*One time I was a bit too enthusiastic on the old wedding dancefloor during a particularly 'banging' tune near the end of the evening. Suddenly a friend of mine leapt on my back and proceeded to whisper urgently in my ear something about my bridesmaid dress. Turns out I'd been 'banging' so hard that I'd managed to rip it along the zip. We backed away from the dancefloor towards a convenient wall where I commandeered someone's suit jacket and sat there on a chair for the rest of the night.*

Hayley, Frankfurt

Gray wasn't in the first flow of evening guests released into the ballroom. He'd hung back, sharing what looked like a companionable drink with Darren, who of course he'd met a few times before. Cleo was pleased they'd each found someone – the evening guests were a veritable tide, all coiffed and hyper, with a lot more energy remaining than the slightly-jaded day guests – and any port in a storm. Darren, by lieu of being Daisy's baby-daddy, had been bumped back up to

353

invitee at pretty much the last minute, but he'd taken it with good grace and was looking very smart in his jacket-tie-chinos combination.

Gray had gone for the more traditional three-piece, his charcoal grey waistcoat fitting well across his chest. Cleo allowed herself to watch him for a moment or two, feeling sufficiently anonymous in the crowd, but his eyes found her faster than she anticipated they would; they both smiled at one another across the expanse of room. She continued to stand guard in front of the small curtained alcove where Nora and Bea were currently crammed, the latter attempting to get the veil back on the head of the former, who had decided at the last second she wanted it on for the first dance and cake-cutting photographs.

Father Michaels, the Dervan family priest, had been first in the door – Nora had eventually relented just far enough to let her mother have him as an evening guest. He'd made an immediate beeline to where Eileen was holding court on one of the tables moved into the corner, holding her hand briefly, lightly, reverently as if she was the Queen, or as if he was just about to bring it to his lips. Cleo had met the old man several times, at family functions Nora had invited her to over the years, and she was struck once again, as she watched him with Eileen, how much his aquiline nose and the run of his jawline reminded her of Nora's sister Fin when she was caught in profile. But before her mind could run away with its fantasies about the tragic young widow and the handsome Catholic priest, Nora emerged from the alcove, re-veiled and ready for action. Cleo preoccupied herself with signalling for Harry; an observant Daisy cued the DJ.

After months and months of back and forth, Harry and Nora had ended up returning to the first track they'd considered for their first dance. Cleo couldn't suppress her smile as the opening chords of Aqualung's *Brighter Than Sunshine* filled the huge room. Neither Nora nor Harry would ever claim to be much of a dancer, but – to be honest – the dress did most of the work, fanning and flying around their feet as they side- and back-stepped their way around the space, beaming stupidly at one another, completely unheeding of the multitude of camera phones that ringed them, flashing away.

*Love will remain a mystery, but give me your hand and you will see, your heart is keeping time with me.*

Gray, abandoned by Darren who'd sought out Daisy, had circled as close to Cleo as his manners would allow. He could never be anonymous in a crowd, not to her – he stood out easily amongst all of his fellow be-suited guests watching the newlyweds twirl one another around, his eyes and expression soft; Cleo felt a matching softness in her belly. He looked at Harry and Nora like she herself sometimes caught herself doing – like they had something he envied.

Harry's enthusiastic dipping of Nora obviously caught her off-guard as the song ended. She giggled as she reached up to steady her veil where it was now only loosely clipped through her hair, and Harry kissed her laughing mouth thoroughly. Cleo joined in with the assembly's delighted applause; the DJ neatly dovetailed into a nineties power ballad and impatient guests flooded the dance floor, surrounding and swallowing the still-kissing newlyweds in an instant.

Cleo looked back towards Gray; he was already waiting

for her eye contact. He smiled and tipped his hand to his mouth in the universal mime for 'do you want a drink?' Cleo shook her head, her smile widening as Gray began to make his way over to her through the crowd.

'Okay, who are you and what have you done with the real Cleo Adkins?' was his opening gag, his head bent right down into the space between her cheek and her shoulder so she could hear him over the music; it was an old joke between them, worn and comfortable.

'Hey, remember I'm on duty,' Cleo admonished him in return, nodding in the direction of the bride and groom. 'Poised for action. Prepared for anything!'

'Surely you don't expect there to be any more bridesmaids secretly having slept with groomsman revelations?'

'One can only hope.'

'Well, they're married now. Surely the bulk of the job is done? Do you want to dance?'

Cleo shook her head, smiling. 'I'm not drunk enough to dance.'

'Then you really do need to let me get you a drink,' Gray insisted, grinning.

\* \* \*

It seemed like Bea had blinked and the day was almost over, the pressure of time ticking away only sharpened by the fact it was New Year's Eve. The guests with young children, or with far to travel, had already made their excuses, while the swirling crowd on the dance floor thickened as people grew more inebriated, more relaxed. Bea had been among them until her feet began to hurt past bearing, and she'd gone to rest at a table with Daisy and Claire. Daisy had since been hauled back up to dance, and Claire had gone to queue at the bar, but Bea found she didn't mind the momentary solitude. It only lasted a minute or too before Eli crashed down into the chair beside her.

'Hey,' he greeted her, his grin the loose and easy one he wore when he'd seen the bottom of a few pint glasses. 'Cheer up. You're at your best friend's wedding.'

'Indeed. And I'm much like Julia Roberts at the end of that terrible film.'

'Okay, I've never seen it, so I don't get the reference, unfortunately,' Eli confessed.

Bea gestured expansively. 'The bitter, bitchy bitch in the bridesmaid's dress. Alone aside from her gay best friend.'

Eli laughed. 'Okay, you might be bitter, but I'm not gay, thank you very much.'

Bea shrugged. 'Same difference.'

Eli sighed, impatient. 'Don't do that.'

'Do what?'

'You know.' Eli glared at her. 'You just want a reaction from me. You want me to tell you that you're a great person and puff you up again. Like I've done for years and years. Not tonight, please.'

Bea bristled even as she recognised the truth in his words, the fact that she was constantly craving all his little validations. 'What are you on about? You don't "puff me up".'

'Are you kidding?' Eli sat forward in his chair. 'That's all I bloody do.'

'Well. *Clearly* I've needed a lot of puffing,' Bea retorted mulishly. 'But it's not my fault I'm so damn unlovable.'

'It's not your fault?' Eli echoed.

'Well, okay, maybe it is a little,' Bea consented, staring down at her dirty bare feet against the shiny parquet flooring of the ballroom. 'I suck at putting on liquid eyeliner and I never get birthday presents right. I can never keep my shoes on when I'm drinking. I get involved with inappropriate men and I piss off my friends. I probably don't recycle as much as I should. So, I'm a shit, shitty person.' She tipped back in her chair a little and stared at the ceiling. 'But I would like someone to love me, all the same.'

Eli took a deep breath. 'Bea. I love you, I really do, but you need to snap out of this.'

'Snap out of what?'

'Your bullshit!'

Bea was momentarily lost for words; Eli wasn't normally so forceful with her. 'How is it bullshit? I'm sorry, but I must have somehow missed the queue of men beating down my door over the last decade or so.'

'For once, you need to actually listen to me. *I love you.* I've been saying it for years. I said it thirty seconds ago for Christ's sake.'

For the first time in her life, Bea fell completely silent. Her overthinking brain faltered and fell quiet; she could have sworn that even her heart skipped a few knocks.

'You love me?' she got out, after a moment, hating how she couldn't strip the sarcasm out of her voice, even then.

Eli gave her a hard glare, not looking remotely like somebody who was confessing to a secret love.

'Yes, you idiot,' he snapped, his tone defensive and sharp. 'I loved you when we were ten years old, and you played Pokémon cards with me even though you didn't understand the rules. I loved you when we were fifteen, and I'd sign in and out of MSN Messenger all bloody night long, hoping to get your attention. I loved you when we were twenty and I invited you to visit me in Cardiff so I could tell you how I felt about you, but you got drunk and pulled my housemate before I could. And I love you now, tonight, right down to your dirty feet. I'll probably love you for always. More bloody fool me.'

Bea felt heat rush to her face, to her hands, to her eyes. 'Oh,' she managed, weakly.

Eli waved a hand dismissively, looking faintly disgusted, although Bea wasn't sure if the disgust was aimed at her or at himself. 'Forget about it. God knows I've tried.' Suddenly he lurched to his feet. Without another word he pushed himself back through the crowd of dancing guests.

Bea was standing only a half-second behind him, pausing stupidly to hook her high heels out from underneath the table and stuff her feet back into them.

'Wait, wait,' she called after Eli, her voice useless against the loud music. She caught up with him in the very centre of the dance floor, at the point where the two sides of disco lights met in a criss-cross of colour, the point where, just hours before, Harry and Nora had shared their first dance. She grabbed at him, not bothering to be gentle when she used his arm to pull him around to face her. She felt her heart cracking a little at the way he looked at her – like he was scared of her. Still, he bent his ear to her mouth to let her speak.

The DJ was playing *Livin' On A Prayer*. 'I've always hated this song,' Bea thought, distractedly; 'at least, if this goes badly, it won't ruin a song I like.'

'I'm sorry,' she blurted, 'it's just . . . Well, I know why I would be in love with someone like you, but why would you be in love with someone like me?'

Eli looked at her, half-thrilled at her words, half-cautious. 'I just do,' he answered, simply.

Bea's body flooded with something unknowable, her mouth dried up. 'I do,' she whispered. 'I do too.' Eli pressed closer to her, trying to hear her over the crash of Jon Bon Jovi, trying to read her lips, her eyes, her face. She lunged closer, already on her tiptoes in the heels, desperate to be heard. 'I do too.'

She felt him stiffen; he grabbed her by her upper arms and pulled her back away from him. Bea felt sick. But instead of moving away, Eli just searched her face.

'Don't just say it,' he said, voice strange.

'I'm not,' she swore. 'I'm really not.'

'Okay.' He exhaled, laughing slightly. Bea laughed too.

'Okay? And you don't care that I slept with Cole?'

Eli made a face. 'No. Not that I'd like you to make a habit of it or anything.'

'Don't worry about that.' He was still holding her by her upper arms; Bea slid her hands up along his, a willing mirror.

'So now what?' he asked.

'Well. I guess we've got two options. You kiss me now, in front of everyone, and we totally steal a load of thunder from Nora and Harry's big day.' Eli screwed up his face, obviously as torn about that as she was. 'Or we just keep dancing. And we revisit this when we can talk properly. And be alone.' A smile twitched at her lips. 'Next year.'

Eli exhaled, running his fingers down her arms, taking up her hands in his. 'Well. I've waited twenty years, I suppose. I can wait a little longer. Let's dance.'

And so, Bea kicked off her high heels, and danced.

# Chapter 47

*I went to a wedding where the bride got so hammered that she started picking up glasses on random tables, throwing up into them, and then setting them back down and wandering off. . .*

Briana, Nottingham

It was coming close to midnight, but the DJ was ramping up rather than down. Cleo was aware that she was severely neglecting her bridesmaid duties, but Nora seemed more than fine, slow-dancing to a fast song with her new husband. The bar would be calling last orders soon, causing a rush of people eager to charge their glasses to welcome in the new year, but for now Cleo was content, faux-drunk on the carnival atmosphere, not to mention her dance partner.

I need air, she mimed at Gray, flapping her hands to her face. They bypassed the table where they'd left their layers to collect them en route out of the ballroom, Gray shaking his head at the slip of a stole Cleo went to wrap around her shoulders and dropping his heavy winter coat in place there instead. Away past the bottom of the grand staircase, and through the lobby with its cheerful, crackling fire and out into a midnight diamond-bright with stars, heavy with the permissiveness of New Year's Eve. In a companionable silence, they leaned over a granite balustrade, looking out over the silent grounds of the estate, the noise from the party behind them muffled and soft even at this short distance.

'I know your game,' Gray said, after a moment, as easy and confident as ever. 'Getting me alone for midnight . . . You're after a New Year's kiss!' he teased.

Cleo turned back to face the Hall, pressing her back into the stone banister, feeling small but scrappy in the oversized sleeves of Gray's coat. 'So what if I am?' she answered baldly, smiling as Gray visibly startled, feeling an agreeable surge of control at being the one to put him on the back foot, for a change.

'Cleo. You know very well I'd be very happy to give you a New Year's kiss,' he said quietly, after a moment.

'But what about just a standard Sunday afternoon kiss? Cleo asked, softly. 'Or a Thursday morning? A birthday, a Valentine's Day?'

Gray turned away from the vista to stare at her. 'I didn't know you had any interest in me kissing you on Thursday mornings,' he said, carefully. 'I feel like we've wasted a lot of Thursday mornings, if that's the case.'

'I didn't think you'd wasted many mornings. A new Tinder date every week.'

Gray turned fully to face her. 'And you don't think I've not been absolutely hamming all that up all year trying to get a reaction out of you?' He shook his head. 'There may have been a lot of dates, but there haven't been any, er, Thursday morning kisses; trust me.'

The noise floating across to them from the Hall changed somehow; the air took on a new expectancy. Gray pushed his sleeve up to check his watch. 'Almost midnight,' he confirmed.

'Are you ready for a brand new year?' Cleo asked. She turned her body so that it was angled towards his, a wordless invitation, grabbing life by the balls. Gray didn't need any further solicitation; he immediately came closer. The buzz from the ballroom shifted again, now unmistakably a count-down.

'Oh, I'm ready,' he answered. 'How about you?'

Cleo smiled. 'I have a feeling it's going to be an interesting year.'

Cheers and applause broke like a wave, the stroke of midnight. And with no misgivings, Cleo turned to kiss her colleague. But instead of pressing his lips to hers, Gray softly drew the pad of his thumb across her smile, a maddening pause.

'What are you waiting for?' Cleo asked, almost breathless.

'Nothing. I've been wanting to kiss you for so damn long,' Gray admitted, almost with a groan. 'It's just that this kiss will change everything.'

'Good,' Cleo said. 'It's about bloody time.' And she pushed herself up on her tiptoes, and kissed him.

# Chapter 48

*The most memorable moment at my wedding isn't the vows, or the kiss, or the dance. It was the moment when my new husband and I were driving away from the venue, in an old Morris Minor, tin cans on ribbon rattling behind – and we ran over the foot of a kid watching at the road-side, breaking three of his toes.*

Emma, Runcorn

'I can't believe it's all over!' Harry groaned.

Nora shot him a look. 'It's not "all over",' she rebuked him gently. 'Okay, the wedding day is, but *the marriage*, that's just begun.'

Harry shot her a grin, racing round the corner of the four-poster bed to take his wife up in his arms. 'I know, I know,' he murmured into her neck, her collarbones. Her hair, previously so carefully coiffed, had long-since fallen in limp strands around her face. She could feel where the little paper hearts they'd used as confetti were stuck to her sweaty skin under her dress. The train of her expensive, beloved gown, even though she'd tried hard to keep it pinned up and away from the floor, was greyed with dirt and dust. She wondered if there would be another moment where she'd ever feel as happy as she did in this one.

After what felt like an hour spent saying thank you and farewell to guests – long, long after the music had stopped and the lights had come up – Nora had said goodnight to her four bridesmaids standing on the mezzanine above the sweeping staircase, each about to head off to their separate bedrooms. Cleo's mouth had been dark from kissing.

'I'll give you all the goss when you get back from your honeymoon!' she'd fobbed Nora off, laughing. 'Plus, give us two weeks and there might actually be some gossip worth talking about,' she'd added, mischievously.

Bea had been much more tight-lipped, but even through the immense distraction of her own wedding reception Nora had noticed her with Eli, somehow different, suddenly charged, their eyes and hands hungry on one another. Nora wondered if they'd hear footsteps across the mezzanine later, after the Hall had fallen quiet: someone slipping from one bedroom to another. She wondered very much what her god-sister might have to catch her up with after a fortnight had passed. . .

Harry's hands busied themselves with the row of little buttons holding Nora's dress together. Nora leaned forward, arching her back to make it easier for him, starting to pull out some of the multitude of hidden pins from her hair. And she thought about happenstance and mistakes. How her mother and Hannah had become friends back in the 80s, bringing Bea inextricably into her life. How it was mouthy, confident Bea who'd ensured they'd become friends with Cole and Harry, now her husband, his deft fingers still working at her back. The ex-boyfriend she thought that one day she'd marry. The ex-girlfriend of Harry's she'd inexplicably hated, years before she'd grown to realise that she loved him.

She thought about the night Sarah had walked into Barlow's bar and walked out with the job that, little did she know, would come with a husband. She thought about the random-ness of university room allocations that had put her in the same hall as Cleo, picturing the admin assistant who would have dealt with residence applications opening first her form, and then Cleo's, placing them together in a pile. She thought about the night that she'd shared an earbud with the scary American girl, and about how she might never have seen Daisy again were it not for her work transferring her to London years later. She thought about the 'accident' that was the conception of Darren and Daisy's child, and about how it might just be the most wonderful of all of the mistakes any of them had ever made.

Finally free from the wedding dress, Nora stepped away from the fall of tulle and lace. Little pieces of confetti twirled free from her body. Harry caught her up again, bringing her body to his.

'We've got good friends, haven't we?' Nora smiled, winding her arms around her husband's neck.

'We do,' Harry agreed, 'but let's not talk about them tonight.'

Printed by RR Donnelley at Glasgow, UK